"So let me make sure I understand what the deal would be."

Juni held up the index finger on her right hand as she reviewed the pertinent information. "First, I need a solid reason to avoid rushing home to help my cousin. You're providing that by offering me a contract to do design work for your committee that will have a provision that requires I remain in Dunbar until the work is completed."

When Ryder nodded, she held up a second finger. "In return, I will be your fake plus-one on what could be multiple occasions to help convince your family that your engagement to Jasmine is truly over. Once they have accepted the truth of the situation, you and I will have our own amicable 'break up,' leaving both of us free to move on."

He leaned back in his chair, trying to look more relaxed than he really was. "Got it on the first try. What do you think?"

"I think I'll be making a trip into Seattle to buy a dress."

Dear Reader,

I am really pleased to be bringing you another story in my Heroes of Dunbar Mountain series.

This one features Ryder Davis, who was very briefly introduced in *Second Chance Deputy* (January 2024) and played a bigger role in *The Unexpected Family Man* (March 2025). All we really learned about him was that he helps out at the local animal shelter and serves as a volunteer firefighter.

Not even Ryder's closest friends know much about his life before he moved to Dunbar, and he likes it that way. That all begins to change when graphic artist Juni Voss, another newcomer to the area, moves in next door. Their lives become entangled when he needs a pretend girlfriend and she needs a pretend client. The only problem comes when their fake relationship suddenly starts feeling a little too real.

I hope you enjoy their story as much as I enjoyed writing it.

Happy reading!

Alexis

THE FIREFIGHTER
NEXT DOOR

ALEXIS MORGAN

HEARTWARMING

Harlequin®
HEARTWARMING™

ISBN-13: 978-1-335-05152-3

The Firefighter Next Door

Copyright © 2025 by Patricia L. Pritchard

Recycling programs for this product may not exist in your area.

Harlequin Enterprises ULC
22 Adelaide St. West, 41st Floor
Toronto, Ontario M5H 4E3, Canada
www.Harlequin.com

Printed in Lithuania

MIX
Paper | Supporting responsible forestry
FSC® C021394

USA TODAY bestselling author **Alexis Morgan** has always loved reading and now spends her days creating worlds filled with strong heroes and gutsy heroines. She is the author of over fifty novels, novellas and short stories that span a wide variety of genres: American West historicals; paranormal and fantasy romances; cozy mysteries; and contemporary romances. More information about her books can be found on her website, alexismorgan.com.

I would like to dedicate this story to all of those caring people who work so hard to find forever homes for animals of all kinds. Esther, our wonderful granddog, was a stray who found her way into our hearts and lives through the efforts of a whole bunch of kind people. We will always be grateful for their efforts.

CHAPTER ONE

JUNI VOSS CROSSED her fingers and prayed for patience. She couldn't afford to offend the woman on the other end of the line, but it would really be nice if Sabrina Luberti would make up her mind. When Sabrina finally ran out of steam, Juni jumped back into the conversation, doing her best to summarize the latest set of changes Sabrina wanted in the artwork that Juni had sent her.

"Okay, let me make sure I've got everything. The faces should be rounder, the ears more prominent and the brown more realistic."

Juni wasn't sure what that last part meant, but Sabrina had been quite emphatic about it. Relieved there were no more suggestions forthcoming, she hastened to end the conversation. "I'll work on all of this and send the updated artwork to you by the end of the week. I really appreciate your getting back to me so quickly with your helpful input."

That wasn't exactly true, but it was best to

err on the side of caution. Sabrina Luberti was a best-selling children's author, and her endorsement could help further Juni's career as an illustrator.

After disconnecting the call, Juni closed her eyes and tried to center herself, but that didn't work. Maybe a breath of fresh air would help soothe away the rough edges so she could get back to work. Grabbing her keys and the pack that held her sketch pad and pencils, she headed out the front door of the small A-frame cabin she'd leased for the next six months.

Once outside, it struck her again how different morning felt on the western slopes of the Cascade Mountains. Back home, on the other side of Washington state, the weather would already be noticeably warmer and drier even this early in the spring.

But here the air was cool, slightly damp and heavy with the rich scent from the enormous Douglas firs and cedars that surrounded the cabin. A little closer to the mountain pass over the Cascades toward the east, there were still patches of snow tucked away in the corners and crevices that the sunshine never quite reached. She'd been living just outside the small town of Dunbar for the past week and was quickly coming to love the area. She'd only crossed paths with a few people in town so far, but they'd all been incredibly welcoming.

In fact, an anonymous neighbor had left a large "Welcome to the Neighborhood" gift on her front porch the morning she was due to move in. The basket contained all kinds of goodies—coffee, tea, chocolate and various munchies. It was much appreciated, especially the gift certificate to have a pizza delivered, so she hadn't had to cook that first night. She really wanted to thank her benefactor, but so far she hadn't figured out who was behind the kind gesture. However, there was only one other house that shared the same small private road where her rental was located. Figuring whoever lived in it was the most likely candidate, she'd stopped by twice but had yet to find anyone at home.

For now, Juni was too antsy to remain still, so she left the porch behind to follow the trail she'd discovered shortly after moving into the cabin. The narrow path wound its way through the woods and down to a small river where she could sit on the rocky bank and work on her sketches. Hopefully, that would help clear her head enough to process the design changes she needed to make in her artwork.

The trail skirted the boundary between her place and her mysterious neighbor. For the first time she could hear a man's voice coming from somewhere off to her left. Judging by the heavy dose of frustration in his voice, Juni thought this might not be the best time to introduce herself, so she continued forward with caution. From what she could make out, he was talking to someone; although so far the conversation had been completely one-sided. She crept closer to get a better idea of what was going on.

"I mean it. Come down here. Right now."

A few seconds later, that order was followed by, "Darn it. I don't have time for this."

Juni continued her cautious approach as the trees thinned out enough for her to catch her first glimpse of what was going on. That sight only left her with more questions than answers. Was that guy perched high up on a tree branch her neighbor? Who was he talking to? And finally, why was he dressed as a firefighter when there was no sign of a fire truck or anyone else in the immediate vicinity?

Before she could figure any of that out, he made a quick grab at something above his head. When his hand came up empty, he grumbled in frustration as he continued to glare at someone or maybe some *thing* farther up the tree. Juni doubted he found any humor in the situation, but it all struck her as really funny. She immediately covered her mouth in an attempt to smother a laugh. Unfortunately, her effort failed miserably, because the man immediately turned his attention in her direction. He stared down at her for several seconds, a confused look on his face. Finally, he blinked twice and shook his head as if to clear it.

"Look, if you're going to laugh at me, you could at least come over and give me a hand."

Juni debated the wisdom of taking orders from a total stranger, even a handsome one with sky blue eyes, but her curiosity won out over caution. She slowly approached the tree and asked, "So, what's going on up there?"

That earned her an eye roll and the tiniest hint of snark. "What does it look like I'm doing?"

She studied both his attire and his location. "Actually, I'm not sure."

"What most firefighters up a tree would be doing—I'm trying to catch a feral kitten."

He looked a little exasperated with the entire situation as he pointed in the general direction of the branch over his head. "I've already caught one, but this one managed to get past me to scoot up the tree."

Juni edged closer and finally spied a tiny kitten tucked in close to the trunk. "How can I help?"

"I'm going to make another attempt to catch her. If I'm successful, I'll put her in this bag and lower it to you to hold on to until I climb back down to the ground."

She wasn't sure that would be a good idea. "Won't that scare the poor little thing?"

He let out an impatient sigh. "Lady, she's already scared. Once I put her in the crate with her brother, she'll do fine. Trust me, I do this sort of thing all the time."

Really? He made a habit of shinnying up trees to trap kittens? "What will you do with them?"

"I'll take them to a local no-kill shelter. After the vet there checks them over, they'll be farmed out to one of their volunteers who fosters feral kittens. The hope is they can be tamed enough to be adopted." He glanced down at Juni. "Either way, they're too young to survive out here on their own."

Okay, that made sense. She had one more question. "Where's their mother?"

His expression turned grim as he looked back up at the kitten. "I've been leaving food out for her on my deck, but she hasn't shown up the last few days. I'd just gotten back from a twenty-four-hour shift at the fire station when I spotted the kittens wandering around on their own, crying like they're lost and hungry."

Then, in another sudden move, his hand shot out toward the kitten. Success! It was quite the balancing act as he tried to hold on to the wriggly little ball of fur while he opened the cloth bag. Her breath caught in her throat when he wobbled enough that she feared that both he and the kitten would come tumbling to the ground.

At the last second, he caught his balance and slowly crouched down on the branch. When he lowered the bag to where Juni stood waiting, they ran into an unexpected glitch. If she'd been a few inches taller, the plan would have worked. But at only five foot two, even standing on tip-toe left a sizable distance between her hands and the bottom of the bag. She watched as he looped the drawstring over his arm and held on to the branch above his head so he could yank off his belt. After threading it through the drawstring, he dangled the bag over Juni's head.

The additional length was more than enough to close the gap, and Juni smiled up at the man above her. "I've got it now."

Retreating to a safe distance to give him room to maneuver down out of the tree, she held the bag close and murmured soft reassurances to the mewling kitten. Once he was on the ground, she tried to hand back the bag.

"Hold on to it while I get the crate. I left it over by those bushes."

He started to walk away, but then stopped to add, "Sorry, I should have said *please* hold on to it. I appreciate your help and don't mean to keep barking orders at you."

She followed along behind him. "No problem. You have a lot going on."

He crouched beside the crate and unlatched the wire-mesh door without actually opening it. "I'll take the bag now."

He loosened the drawstring and slowly lowered his hand inside. A second later, he gently lifted the kitten out of the bag. Rather than immediately shoving it into the crate, he took a second to stroke its small head with the tip of his finger, jerking it back out of reach when the kitten tried to take a bite out of him. Instead of complaining, he chuckled. "You're a feisty one, that's for sure. Someone is going to have their hands full with you, little lady."

Juni couldn't resist the temptation to pet the kitten herself. She eased closer, not wanting to startle the already terrified animal or the man who was now snuggling it next to his chest. "She's a pretty little thing. Is the other one a calico, too?"

"No, her brother is an orange tabby."

After giving Juni a chance to stroke the kitten's soft fur, he slipped the kitten inside the crate with her brother. Once it was securely latched, he picked it up. "Thanks for your help."

He started to walk away, but immediately

turned back in her direction. "By the way, I'm Ryder Davis. I live just past those trees. I'm guessing you're my new neighbor."

His introduction came across as a bit gruff. "You guessed right. I'm Juni Voss."

After acknowledging her response with a jerk of his head, he continued on his way. "Sorry I can't stick around to chat, but I really need to get these kittens to the shelter."

"No problem. I hope they find good homes."

"Me, too."

Before he disappeared into the trees, she thought to call after him. "By any chance are you the one who left that wonderful gift basket on my porch when I moved in? If so, I wanted to thank you."

He kept walking—only raising his hand to acknowledge he'd heard her. Juni watched until Ryder disappeared from sight. What an interesting man. Her first impression was that he didn't seem all that friendly, but it was clear he was tired. For now, she'd cut him some slack, especially considering she didn't know what kind of night he'd had while on duty at the fire department.

Besides, a man who gave total strangers gift baskets and also risked life and limb to rescue feral kittens couldn't be all bad. It also didn't hurt that he was handsome enough to grace the pages of one of those calendars that featured firefighters. The combination of his stunningly blue eyes and those broad shoulders would be a sure hit, especially if it was a shot of him standing on a tree limb cuddling a kitten.

Too bad she hadn't snapped a picture of him while she had the chance. However, as an artist, she had another option. Excited by the prospect, she resumed her trip down to the river. Once there, she sat on the ground and leaned back against a log. After getting settled, she closed her eyes and soaked up some sunshine for a few minutes. Then she got busy and sketched her new neighbor and the kittens while the images were still fresh in her mind.

BY THE TIME Ryder finally made it back to his cabin after delivering the kittens to the shelter, he was so tired that it hurt to breathe. All he wanted to do was crawl into bed and crash for a good ten to twelve hours. Before that, though, he needed to scrape up enough energy to shower and fix something to eat. Too bad he hadn't thought far enough ahead to order breakfast from the café in town. He could've used something more substantial than the protein shakes he kept in the fridge for just such occasions. It had been a long night of constant callouts at the fire station: two car accidents, a kitchen fire, a medical emergency and a kid who had somehow gotten his head stuck between two metal spindles in the staircase inside the family home.

The last thing Ryder had needed when he finally dragged himself home from the station was to spot that pair of kittens. He'd been searching for them ever since their mother quit showing up for breakfast. Although it was a relief to find them, the timing hadn't been ideal. He'd briefly considered putting off trying to capture them until after he'd gotten some sleep, but his conscience wouldn't let him do that. Even if he'd tried to get some shut-eye, he wouldn't have been able to sleep knowing they were at risk from any one of the predators that prowled the area.

It had been a stroke of luck that his new neighbor had shown up when she did, even if the unexpected appearance of the petite blonde in his woods had momentarily frozen his brain. Afterward, he'd written off the visceral response to his near exhaustion. Still, he wouldn't be forgetting those pretty eyes and that teasing smile anytime soon. It had been a long time since he'd met such an attractive woman, but it was never a good idea to get involved with someone who lived right next door. Besides, he was still gunshy after his last relationship had fallen apart in spectacular fashion.

That didn't mean he wasn't grateful that she

had shown up when she did. He might have figured out a way to get down out of the tree without hurting either himself or his tiny captive, but having someone there to take charge of the bag had definitely simplified the procedure. He was pretty sure he'd thanked her but may not have been particularly gracious about it. Being both short on sleep and hungry meant his memory of their brief conversation was on the fuzzy side.

He'd have to find some way to make amends. Not that he wanted to get all that chummy with… What was her name? Joanie? Jean? No, something more unusual that that. It took him a few more tries before he finally remembered it— Juni. Despite his difficulty recalling her name, her image had remained all too clear in his mind: petite, with honey blond hair, a bright smile and such huge eyes. He wasn't sure what color they were, but there was no mistaking the intelligence and humor in them as she watched him.

Regardless, he wasn't looking to be her new best friend. After all, he'd chosen to live out in the woods because he valued his privacy. Maybe he could drop off a slice of pie from Titus's diner or else a couple of pastries from Bea's bakery/ coffee shop in town. Either would make an acceptable token of appreciation, and he could leave them on her porch along with a note when she wasn't at home.

Yeah, that was the ticket. A show of manners with no further commitment.

He parked the van next to his A-frame, a bigger version of the one Juni rented next door. Not that she knew he was her landlord. He owned several rentals in the area, but paid someone else to handle the day-to-day details. Deciding against unloading his gear until later, he made sure all the doors on the van were locked and then dragged his weary carcass around to the front of the house. Even his sleep-deprived brain quickly realized that someone had been there during the time it had taken him to drive to the shelter and back. Whoever it was, they'd left a large piece of paper taped to his door.

After looking around the clearing to make sure they were long gone, he took a hesitant step up onto the porch and gently tugged the paper off the door. Turning it over, he couldn't help but grin. Someone—undoubtedly his new neighbor—had drawn an uncannily accurate caricature of him perched on that tree limb holding a wide-eyed kitten. The people at the shelter would love it. So would his friends at the fire station. Heck, maybe he'd even have it framed to hang on his living room wall.

Feeling loads better than he had only seconds before, he headed inside. All things considered, maybe Juni Voss deserved an entire pie.

CHAPTER TWO

RYDER'S DECISION TO keep his distance from his neighbor succeeded for almost a full week. He'd caught a glimpse of Juni walking through the woods down to the river a couple of times, but she didn't seem to be aware of his scrutiny. That worried him a little. She was in no danger from him, but she really should be more careful. There were black bears and the occasional cougar in the area.

That was a discussion for another day. Right now he found himself in a pretty desperate situation, and Juni was his best shot for getting the help he needed. Crossing his fingers that she'd step up to bat for him, he hustled through the woods, taking the most direct route from his place to hers. It was tempting to break into a run, but he didn't want to jostle the basket he was carrying.

"Please, please, please let her be home."

Because if she wasn't, he didn't know what he was going to do. He was already late in responding to the emergency call from the fire station. Even if he could afford the time to make another stop along the way, he had no idea who else might be available on such short notice.

He didn't draw a full breath until he spotted Juni's car parked next to the A-frame. As soon as he cleared the trees, he picked up the pace, charging up onto her porch to ring the doorbell several times in quick succession. A few seconds later, she cautiously peeked out of the window next to the door before finally opening it.

After giving the stuff he was carrying a suspicious look, she asked, "Mr. Davis, what can I do for you?"

Ryder set a bag with supplies on her porch but held on to the basket. "Look, I know we don't know each other at all, but I'm in a real bind right now and could use your help."

She didn't immediately leap to agree, but at least she hadn't slammed the door in his face. He pulled back the corner of the towel he'd put over the basket to reveal its contents. "These kittens lost their mother last night and were dropped off at the shelter earlier this morning. At three weeks, they are pretty much helpless and will need to be bottle-fed every few hours around the clock."

After replacing the cover, he continued explaining the situation. "I don't normally foster kittens for the shelter, but the regular person is out of town until tomorrow. I wasn't supposed to be on duty today, so I said I'd take them just this once. However, I've been called in to help fight a worsening grass fire out on the highway. I most likely won't be back home until tomorrow, which means I can't take care of them myself."

He realized there was something he hadn't even considered. "You aren't allergic to cats, are you?"

She shook her head, but still made no move to take the basket from him. "No, but I don't know anything about taking care of kittens."

"I promise it's not hard. The instructions, formula and everything else you need are all in the bag. I fed them about an hour ago, and they'll let you know when they're hungry again. Penning them up in a big box with a blanket in the bottom will help you keep track of them. That's what I do. My number is on the back of the instructions in case you have questions. To be honest, I might not be in a position to answer right away, but I promise I'll call you back as soon as I can."

Before Juni could respond, he held out the basket again. She shook her head and took a step back. Ryder wasn't normally given to begging for help, but right now he had no choice. "I know I'm asking a lot, Juni, but I need your help. No, *they* need your help. I'll owe you big-time."

She stared up at him for several seconds, looking exasperated. "Don't you know anyone else to ask?"

"Not on such short notice. I'm already late responding to the emergency call."

When she finally reached out for the basket, he surrendered it and stepped back. "Thanks, Juni. I wish I could stay long enough to help you get them settled, but I'm already overdue at the fire station. Like I said, call if you need me."

Then he took off running.

JUNI HAD NEVER seen a man disappear from sight so fast in her entire life. On the verge of panic, she considered changing her mind, but it was too late now. Besides, he couldn't babysit two kittens and fight a fire at the same time.

She'd do her best to take good care of her tiny charges, but that didn't mean she was happy about the situation. One reason she'd moved to Dunbar was to put some distance between herself and people who thought she should drop everything at a moment's notice to do their bidding. If she was no longer willing to do that for her family, she sure as heck didn't want to do it for a man she barely knew.

The muffled sound of the kittens crying under the towel drew her attention. It was a reminder they were the innocents here, and she wouldn't let them suffer. It was time to meet her house-guests and do what she could to make them comfortable. Rather than risk them escaping outside, she grabbed the bag of supplies Ryder had left for her and carried everything inside the cabin and firmly closed the door. It had been tempting to slam it shut to help work off her frustration, but she didn't want to scare the kittens.

Setting the basket on the coffee table, Juni fetched her cup of tea from the desk where she'd been working and sat down on the sofa to ponder her options. Well, not that Ryder had left her with many.

Rather than dwell on things she couldn't change, she contemplated what to do next. The kittens definitely needed some place larger to stay other than the basket. She was pretty sure there was a good-size box up in the loft from when she moved in that would do for such a short stay. At the sound of another soft meow, she leaned forward and quietly lifted the edge of the towel to peek inside the basket. Two small furry faces looked up at her, eyes blinking sleepily. One kitten was black with white paws and a splash of white on its chest. The other was solid black except for a small spot of white on its forehead and another on the tip of its tail. So cute.

As she gently stroked the tops of their heads, she realized she was fighting a losing battle to stay mad at Ryder. She found herself flashing back to their first encounter when he'd been up a tree trying to save that little calico kitten. He'd also been the one who'd left her the welcome basket, a thoughtful gesture on his part.

Besides, it wasn't as if he was blowing off his responsibility on a whim. Instead, he was going to put his life on the line to fight a wildfire, a real problem in the state. It wasn't just the damage a big blaze could cause to forests and towns. The detrimental effects of the smoke on people with certain health problems were just as bad. One of her friends from high school had asthma that was always much worse when fires raged in the area. If this one got out of control, lives and property would be at risk.

She met the curious gaze of her unexpected guests. "I'll still be having a talk with Ryder about this situation. Until then, though, I guess the three of us will be able to muddle along okay for one night."

Reaching out slowly, she picked up one kitten and then its sibling. Snuggling them in close to her chest, she murmured quiet reassurances until they started purring softly. After a few minutes, she settled them back into their basket to sleep. While they dozed, she read through the instructions Ryder had left her. It all seemed simple enough. She could even mix some of the kitten formula in advance, so it would be ready to go when she needed it.

In fact, now would be a good time to do that. She'd also get the box and dig up something soft to pad the bottom for them. For now, she'd leave them sleeping in the basket rather than risk waking them up while moving them into the box.

Fifteen minutes later, the bottles were filled and in the fridge, and she'd lined the box with a towel. With all of that finished, she fixed herself a sandwich and watched a video on caring for kittens while she waited for her young charges to wake up from their nap. There were a few aspects of the process that were unexpected, but none of it looked all that difficult. She added two small stuffed animals to the box that Ryder had included for the kittens to cuddle. For sure, she'd never heard of a warming disc for kittens, but heating it up in the microwave was easy enough.

With everything in place, she worked on a few tweaks on the latest drawing she'd done for Sabrina. It had taken some serious back-and-forth emailing to finally settle on the right shade of brown for the bears in the book. The ears had been an easy fix, as had the shape of the face. The next issue was the kind of furniture a family of bears would have in their cave. Rather than spend a lot of time fully developing her first idea in case Sabrina had other thoughts, Juni did some simpler sketches of several different designs. There would be plenty of time to fill in the details on whichever one Sabrina chose.

It didn't take long for Juni to do a deep dive into her artwork. Often when that happened, she lost track of time and her surroundings as the lines and colors flowed onto the page straight out of her imagination. Two hours passed before the kittens' soft cries finally dragged her back into the real world. She jumped up from her drawing table to check on them.

Keeping her voice to a low croon, she did her best to reassure them. "Okay, little ones. I'll warm up your bottles right now. After you're fed, I'm pretty sure you'll go right back to sleep, and I can get back to work."

She crossed her fingers that was true, because she'd promised Sabrina she'd have the preliminary sketches for the next set of pages done and ready to send to her by tomorrow evening. Three of the ideas were pretty much ready to go, but the other two needed more work.

After warming the bottles, Juni made her first attempt at feeding the kittens. The first one fussed a little but then settled right in and made quick work of filling his tummy. However, his sister wasn't nearly as cooperative. Almost an hour passed before Juni was able to coax her into taking the whole process seriously. No matter how cute the little rascal was, it was hard not to get frustrated. By the time Juni finally got them settled into the box, she needed a nap herself.

As she stretched out on the couch, she couldn't help but hope they'd just gotten off to a bit of a rough start due to her lack of experience. Now that she had a better idea of what was involved, the next time would no doubt go more smoothly. Crossing her fingers that was true, she drifted off to sleep.

IT HAD BEEN a long night, but the battle between fire and man had been won. The blaze was mostly out with the county fire department mopping up the last few hotspots. After returning to the station to put the equipment away, Ryder finally dragged himself back home around eight the next morning. More than anything he wanted to crawl into bed and pass out for a few hours, but that wasn't going to happen. He'd gotten a text from the manager of the shelter that the volunteer who usually fostered really young kittens was back and would be stopping by the shelter to pick up the kittens around noon. He didn't know about Juni, but he'd really be glad to pass the baton to someone who knew what they were doing.

With that in mind, he took a quick shower, changed into clothes that didn't reek of smoke and sweat, and drove the short distance to Juni's place. He hadn't lied yesterday when he'd told her he would owe her big-time for helping him out with no notice and no real chance to refuse the job. He could only hope that she'd had an easier night of it than he and the rest of the crew had had.

It took all the energy he could muster to ring her doorbell, which was met with nothing but silence. Before trying again, he leaned in close to the window next to the door to check out the situation inside. The lights were all off, but that could simply be because it was daylight. The bedroom was up in the loft, which he couldn't see from where he was standing. That was probably just as well. Juni wasn't likely to appreciate him intruding on her privacy like that.

Her car was in the driveway, but maybe she had gone on one of her walks. Under the circumstances, though, that didn't seem likely. He'd try the doorbell again. If that failed to get any response, he'd figure out what to do next. Too bad he hadn't gotten her phone number when he'd dropped the kittens off yesterday. He'd been halfway back to his place before he'd thought of it, but there had been no way he'd go back and risk giving her another chance to refuse to help him out.

This time he pressed the button twice in quick

order while still looking through the window. A movement over to the left drew his attention in the direction of the couch. The back of it faced the door, so he couldn't be sure if he'd actually seen anything or if his mind was playing tricks on him. Only one way to know for sure. He jabbed the doorbell three times while focusing on the area where he thought he'd seen something or someone moving.

Juni's head finally popped into view. She squinted in the direction of the door, her hair a halo of tangles around her pretty face. He winced and waved at her through the narrow pane of glass. So much for hoping that she hadn't had a tough time with the kittens. The experience had taken its toll, leaving her with dark circles under her eyes and confusion in her gaze.

When Juni finally stood up, she wobbled a bit before regaining her balance. Still dressed in pajamas, she slowly started in his direction, glaring at him every inch of the way.

He stepped back as she unlocked the door, not wanting to crowd her. As soon as the door was open far enough for her to look out, she snarled, "Ryder Davis, I hate you. Really, really hate you."

She left the door open and walked away, calling back over her shoulder, "I just thought you should know."

It was hard not to laugh, but right now he figured the last thing she would want to hear was how cute she was. He followed her across the room toward a box on the floor. She stopped to point at its contents. "You said they were kittens, but that was a lie. Those are definitely night owls. They napped peacefully all afternoon, lulling me into a false sense of complacency."

She shot him another dirty look. "But as soon as the sun went down, they refused to sleep more than half an hour at a stretch. I fed them, took care of their other bodily functions, petted them and cradled them in my arms. I even sang lullabies to them until I was hoarse. Nothing worked."

When she didn't continue berating him, he thought maybe she was waiting for him to contribute something to the conversation. "I'm sorry."

"Well, you should be."

She poked him in the chest with her finger. "Did it even occur to you to ask if I had any experience caring for baby animals? Or animals of any kind? For future reference, I don't."

Okay, that shocked him. "None? You never had a pet?"

"No, my cousin had allergies and couldn't have animals around. Since I lived with her and her parents, that meant I couldn't have any pets, either. I used to think I missed out on something special. After last night, I think I got off lucky."

What could he say to that? Considering his own brain was running on empty, he settled for repeating himself. "I'm sorry, Juni. It won't happen again."

"Yeah, right," she scoffed as she threw her hands up in the air. "Like I believe that. I've lived here less than two weeks, and you've already gotten me to help you with kittens twice. At least the first time, I wasn't the one up in a tree. Heaven knows what kind of misadventures you'll drag me into next."

She walked away. "I need coffee. Lots and lots of coffee."

Would it push her over the edge if he mentioned he'd give anything for some dark roast himself? Maybe he'd wait to ask until she finished off her first cup. While she banged around in the small kitchen off the living room, he sat down on the floor next to the box to check on the kittens. Right now they were both dozing peacefully, breathing softly, and occasionally twitching in their sleep. They were so cute curled up together next to a pair of stuffed animals, one an alligator and the other a small brontosaurus. Ryder got out his phone to snap a couple of pictures to forward to his friends at the shelter.

They were always looking for cute photos for their website and other social media.

The smell of coffee gradually wafted his way from the kitchen. He took a deep breath in the futile hope there was enough caffeine in the scent to clear out some of the cobwebs in his own sleep-deprived head. He was surprised a few seconds later when a mug appeared right in front of his face. Before reaching for it, he looked around to make sure Juni was actually offering it to him.

She showed him the matching mug in her other hand. "You look like you need this as much as I do. It's black, but there's sugar and cream in the kitchen if you want some."

"Black is perfect." He risked a small sip even though it was probably too hot to drink. It tasted like ambrosia. "Bless you, woman."

Juni dropped down on the floor next to him. The two of them sipped their drinks and watched the kittens, who were starting to stir. Finally, the one with white paws pushed herself up to her feet and took several awkward steps around the box. Her brother soon joined her in exploring their surroundings.

Juni leaned in closer to watch them. "I'll tell you two pesky creatures the same thing I said last night. You're just lucky you're cute."

When one of them meowed in what sounded

like a protest to her comment, Ryder leaned in closer to nudge Juni with his shoulder. "I apologize again. I seriously didn't know what else to do. They really did need all of our volunteer firefighters last night."

She studied him for a few seconds before nodding. "Did you manage to put out the fire?"

"Not all by myself, but yeah."

"That's good news."

"Some other good news—the regular volunteer is going to pick these two up at the shelter around noon."

Juni looked horrified. "You mean someone does this kind of stuff all the time? Because I've got to tell you, I only had them for about twenty hours and almost didn't survive the experience."

He figured that was a bit of an exaggeration, but he wisely kept that opinion to himself. "The shelter doesn't get orphaned kittens that are this young all that often, but thank goodness someone is willing to take on the job. At least once they get to four or five weeks old, they're eating some solid food and using a litter box."

He finished his coffee. "When did they last eat?"

Juni checked the time. "About three hours ago. Do you want to feed them again before taking them back to the shelter?"

"That's probably a good idea. I can take care

of that if you want to go get dressed. I'd like to take you to the café in town for a late breakfast after we drop them off at the shelter." He offered her a small smile. "I know that's not nearly enough to make up for what I asked of you. Maybe consider it a down payment."

She didn't immediately leap to accept his invitation. "I've never been to the café yet, but I've been meaning to try it. Is the food good?"

Ryder didn't hesitate to endorse the place. "My friend Titus Kondrat owns it. After culinary school, he trained in some five-star restaurants before moving to Dunbar to buy the café. I can say without hesitation that I've never had a bad meal there. Everything is made fresh, including the enormous cinnamon rolls, and his pies are to die for. I also love his omelets, his hamburgers and the Thursday special, which is chicken and dumplings."

Showing more energy than she had when he first arrived, she stood up. "You had me at cinnamon rolls. I'll go get ready to face the day. The kitten formula is already mixed up on the top shelf in the fridge. See you in a few minutes."

Before she started up the stairs to the loft, Juni grinned at him. "Just be warned, I'm starving. I'll probably have an omelet and a cinnamon roll. I might even order a piece of his pie to go. It will depend on what kind he has on the menu today."

He shrugged. "By all means, order whatever you want. I won't even complain if you decide to tack on something for dinner tonight if you don't feel like cooking today."

She blinked in surprise but then nodded. "You know, I might just do that. I have some work I'm behind on and not having to mess with cooking would help."

Ryder headed for the refrigerator to get the kitten formula. "Titus always has a variety of pies available. Besides the full-size slices, he makes them in a mini-size so you can order more than one flavor if you have trouble making up your mind."

Juni rubbed her hands together with greedy glee. "I think I'm going to really like Titus. He sounds like my kind of café owner."

Then she gave him a wink. "I can't wait to meet him."

That last comment rubbed Ryder the wrong way for some reason, but he did his best to sound calmer than he felt when he answered. "Just a heads-up, his wife carries a gun."

Instead of getting mad, Juni laughed. "Thanks for the warning."

CHAPTER THREE

EVEN WHEN OUT on a date, Juni never felt comfortable having to wait for someone else to open doors for her. That said, she knew Aunt Ruby would have approved of the way Ryder hustled ahead to open the door so that Juni could sail past him into the café. The problem was, this wasn't actually a date. In fact, she wasn't sure exactly what it was. They weren't business associates or even two friends simply getting together to catch up on things.

Instead, Ryder was an almost total stranger paying her back for losing a night's sleep to babysit a pair of kittens that didn't even belong to him. She knew he was a volunteer firefighter and helped out at an animal shelter. There'd been no mention of a wife or girlfriend, so she assumed he was single. Probably, anyway. She also had no idea if he had a job that actually paid a salary. Volunteering for worthy causes was great, but it didn't help pay the bills.

The bottom line was that she knew very little about the man.

In fairness, he didn't know all that much about her, either. Just that she'd only recently moved into the cabin on the same road as his, that she worked from home and had never owned a pet. Not much in the grand scheme of things. If he hadn't had two kitten crises in such a short period of time, they might not have even crossed paths.

As her mind continued to spin on an internal hamster wheel of disconnected thoughts, a tall man sporting a whole lot of tattoos and a boatload of attitude approached her and Ryder. His expression softened slightly when he met her gaze before turning his attention to her companion. "I'm surprised to see you out and about. I figured you'd be down for the count until dinnertime at least. From what Shay Barnaby told me, you guys were out on the front lines most of the night."

"That we were." Ryder gave a tired sigh before continuing. "I had a few things to take care of this morning, so getting some shut-eye will have to wait for a while."

When he stopped there, the other man jerked his head in her direction while giving Ryder a questioning look. Ryder looked chagrined. "Sorry, I'm running on empty and evidently forgot my manners. Titus Kondrat, this is my new neighbor, Juni Voss. She did me a solid last night when she offered to foster some kittens that had to be bottle-fed around the clock. I thought I'd buy her breakfast to express my gratitude."

"Nice to meet you, Juni."

Before she could respond, he turned back toward Ryder, looking a bit puzzled. "You don't usually foster kittens. Did something happen to Mrs. Trumble?"

"No, she's fine. She was just out of town for some family thing when the kittens were brought into the shelter. I wasn't supposed to be on call for the fire department, so I said I could take the kittens for one night. When the county fire department did an all-call for extra help last night, Juni generously volunteered to pick up the slack. We dropped the kittens back off at the shelter on the way here. Mrs. Trumble is supposed to pick them up around noon."

Juni learned one more thing about Ryder from his explanation—he had a talent for twisting the truth. She hadn't exactly volunteered. No, he'd semiguilted her into taking over for him. Now wasn't the time for that conversation.

"Well, let's get you two fed. If you'll come this way."

Titus picked up menus and led the way to a table set for two next to the window at the front of the café. As she followed him, she caught a strong whiff of cinnamon. She could almost taste the yeasty goodness of one of Titus's cinnamon rolls. Her tummy rumbled in response, an unsubtle reminder that she was starving. Hopefully the chatter of other customers and the clinking of dishes coming from the kitchen muffled her stomach's demand for food.

When she and Ryder were seated, Titus handed each of them a menu. "I'll start you off with a couple of the cinnamon rolls that just came out of the oven. They should tide you over while you figure out what else you want to order."

The man was a saint. "Thank you, Mr. Kondrat. That would be lovely."

"Call me Titus. And anyone brave enough to take on feeding kittens deserves a treat or two."

When he disappeared into the kitchen and presumably out of hearing, Juni dropped her voice to whisper to Ryder, "He's an interesting man. Kind of scary-looking, but I'm thinking that's just a facade."

Ryder laughed at that, his blue eyes glinting with good humor. "Not really. Titus can be truly scary when the occasion calls for it. Having said that, there's nothing he loves more than feeding people. You probably guessed that he also helps out at the shelter. That's how I first met him."

"He mentioned someone else when we came

in. I think his name was Shay something. Is he another friend?"

"Yeah, Shay Barnaby owns the tavern on the edge of town. He's another volunteer firefighter although he hasn't been able to help out as much since he recently took custody of a six-year-old kid. The boy's parents died in an accident, and they'd named Shay as Luca's guardian."

The situation he described hit pretty close to home for Juni. "That was nice of him. Not everyone would be willing to take on raising someone else's kid."

"According to Shay, neither the guy nor his wife had any family, but he and Shay were really close after serving together in the Marine Corps. It's been a heck of an adjustment for both Shay and the boy, but they're figuring things out. Shay also got married recently, so he went from being single to having a family in a matter of months. He's disgustingly happy these days."

That was great to hear. Not everyone got a storybook ending like that. Regardless, her heart hurt for the small boy. She'd lost her own parents when she hadn't been much older than he was. Luckily, her mom's older sister and her husband had taken custody of her. As far as Juni knew, they were the only ones on either side of her extended family who had been willing to do so.

Ryder leaned in closer from across the table.

"Juni, what's wrong? Did I say something to upset you?"

She wasn't ready to share her life story, so she lied. "No, I'm just tired."

He studied her for several seconds as if not sure he was buying what she was selling. Finally he nodded toward the menu. "We'd better decide what we want to order. Titus is on his way back with the cinnamon rolls."

After scanning the offerings, she grinned. "It all looks so good, it's hard to choose. I suppose it would be a bit over the top to order one of everything."

"A little, but feel free if you're that hungry. Otherwise, I'd suggest going with what sounds the best, and then we can order seconds if we're still hungry after we finish the first round."

Titus appeared by the table holding the two pastries he'd promised. When he set one down in front of her, Juni's eyes almost popped out of her head. "Those are enormous—not that I'm complaining. They look delicious."

Her comment seemed to please their host a great deal. "Glad you think so. It's my own recipe, and people seem to like them."

"I can see why."

He took out an old-fashioned order pad. "So what else can I get you?"

Ryder nodded for her to go first. She hadn't

been exaggerating. It was hard to choose, but she already knew this wasn't the only time she'd be eating at the café during her stay in Dunbar. "I'll have the spinach and Swiss cheese omelet with avocado. Fruit instead of hash browns and a glass of iced tea."

After handing his menu back to Titus, Ryder ordered the breakfast special of French toast, fried eggs and fresh fruit. Then he smiled at Juni. "The lady and I will be ordering some pie and dinner to go when we're done with our breakfasts. Neither of us is in the mood to cook today after last night."

"I'll check to see what will be ready to go this early, but we're sure to have something that will reheat well. The pies are all ready, so dessert won't be any problem."

"Thanks, Titus."

Before walking away, Titus pointed toward the cinnamon rolls. "Dig in, you two. Those are better eaten warm."

Neither of them had to be told twice. Juni really was hungry, but devouring her cinnamon roll also helped her avoid any further conversation for the moment. Normally she didn't have trouble talking to people, even total strangers. However, right now she was struggling to come up with a topic of conversation. It had been a long time since she'd sat across the table from a man as handsome as Ryder Davis, and she was out of practice.

Some people had a compulsion to fill any silence with meaningless chatter, but she wasn't normally one of them. Right now, though, the gap in their conversation seemed to be stretching out to the point of becoming awkward. By the time she was halfway done with her cinnamon roll, she was feeling a bit desperate.

Thinking back to what she didn't know about her companion, she blurted out, "So what do you do for a living?"

"That's a question we all keep asking him, but so far he's never answered it."

Titus's deep voice startled her into dropping her fork, barely catching it before it tumbled to the floor. How had she not noticed his approach? It wasn't as if he were the kind of person who faded into the background, but somehow he'd appeared out of nowhere carrying two plates piled high with their breakfasts.

She glared up at him. For such a big man, he sure was stealthy. "Do you always sneak up on customers like that?"

He wasn't actually smiling, but the twinkle in his eyes made it clear that he was enjoying himself. "Not deliberately."

She moved the small plate with what was left of her cinnamon roll to the side to make room for the second round of her breakfast. "Maybe consider wearing a bell."

His deep laugh rang out across the café. It sounded surprisingly rusty, but then Titus's normal speaking voice was pretty gravelly, too. She glanced toward Ryder, who clearly found the entire conversation entertaining. Then he winked at her and deflected Titus's attention back in his direction. "I'll talk about my job about the same time you talk about your life before culinary school."

That set off another round of chuckles from their host. "Fair enough, Ryder. I guess we'll both keep our secrets."

He looked as if he was going to say more when a commotion near the door caught his attention. A couple with a young boy had just walked in followed by a second woman in a police uniform. As soon as they spotted Ryder, they waved. Titus patted Juni on the shoulder. "Sorry, but I suspect you two are about to get some company."

Juni watched as the foursome made their way across the café. The cop stopped briefly to talk to someone, but then she hurried to catch up with the others. Meanwhile, Titus pushed the tables on either side of the one Juni and Ryder occupied closer. Next, he raised a drop leaf on each one to fill in the remaining space. Ryder's friends arrived just as Titus had everything arranged to his satisfaction.

To Juni's surprise the cop immediately wrapped her arms around Titus and kissed him. So that's what Ryder meant about Titus's wife carrying a gun. Juni also suspected she was about to meet Shay Barnaby and his new family. Feeling a bit like an intruder, she remained silent as Ryder greeted everyone. The little boy seemed really excited to see him, because he immediately launched into a detailed description about the new tricks he'd taught Beau and Bruno. Since the tricks involved throwing sticks really high for them to catch before the sticks hit the ground, she could only assume that Beau and Bruno were dogs and not people.

Ryder ruffled the boy's hair. "I can't wait to see them do that."

Then he turned in her direction. "Juni Voss, I'd like you to meet my friend Luca. He adopted two dogs from the shelter, and he's turned out to be a really great pet owner."

"Nice to meet you, Luca. That trick sounds amazing."

The boy turned a little shy, but still he said, "Nice to meet you, Ms. Juni."

Meanwhile, Ryder continued the introductions. "The lady wearing the uniform is Titus's wife, Moira. Carli and Shay belong to Luca."

She nodded to each one in turn to cement the names with the faces while Ryder kept talking. "Luca, Juni recently moved into the A-frame down from mine. This is her first visit to Titus's café."

Shay, his wife, and son took the table on the left while Moira sat on Juni's right. "I knew someone had moved into the cabin and have been meaning to stop by to introduce myself when I patrol that area. Are you planning on staying long?"

"I signed a six-month lease, but I may want to renew it depending on how long my current project takes to finish."

"What kind of project are you working on?"

"I'm a graphic artist, and I'm working on the illustrations for a children's book. The author thought it would be easier to collaborate on this first project if I lived closer to her. My family lives on the east side of the state."

Moira immediately glanced at Ryder and then back to Juni. "Oh, I bet you're the one who drew that great caricature of Ryder and a kitten up in that tree. We all loved it!"

That drew even more attention in Juni's direction. "Yeah, that was me. That's how we met."

When she finished telling the story, Shay crossed his arms over his broad chest and leaned back in his chair. "I really wish I could have seen that in real time, but the picture you drew was funny enough. You've got real talent."

By that point, Juni was pretty sure her cheeks were flushed pink. The nature of her job meant she spent most of her time working alone and only got feedback in emails, text messages or phone calls. "Thank you. I'm glad you think so."

Shay's wife, Carli, leaned in closer. "Did Ryder tell you he had the drawing matted and framed? He said he was going to hang it in his living room."

That was unexpected. "No, he didn't. It was just a rough sketch."

Ryder had been listening to Luca talk more about his dogs, but he must have noticed his name was being bandied about. "What did I do this time?"

Carli winced a bit. "I was telling Juni that you liked her drawing enough to have it framed to hang in your living room."

He shrugged. "I like it. I still smile each time I see it."

That might just be the best compliment Juni had ever received. "I'm glad."

Moira nudged her. "By the way, you'd better start eating that omelet. Titus doesn't take it well when people let his food go cold. If that happens, he threatens to ban them from the only café in town."

"I wouldn't want that to happen."

She dutifully picked up her fork and took a bite. It was every bit as good as it looked. Ryder dug into his French toast and just in the nick of time. Titus was back to take orders from the new arrivals. Juni concentrated on her breakfast as she listened to the flow of conversation around the group. She was feeling a bit overwhelmed at the moment, but that was mainly because she was pretty much running on empty.

"You doing okay over there?"

Juni managed a small smile for Ryder. "I'm fine. Just really tired."

"As soon as you're finished with your omelet, we can leave. I'll tell Titus to bring me the check and see if our dinners are ready to go."

"You shouldn't have to rush off because of me. I'm fine."

"You're not the only one who is dragging. Besides, they'll understand."

"If you're sure."

She'd been aware of Moira listening in and decided to explain. "It's been really nice meeting all of you, and we don't mean to rush off. But while Ryder was out fighting fires all night, I babysat a pair of kittens that had to be fed every few hours around the clock. Neither of us got any sleep."

"Not a problem. Besides, I can't stay much

longer myself. I'm on duty today." The other woman offered Juni a sympathetic smile. "I've had more than a few nights like that. Next time we decide to descend on the café en masse, we'll give you a call if you'd like. It happens pretty often, and we figure the more the merrier."

"That would be really nice."

Ryder finished off the last bite of his breakfast. "Before I hunt down Titus, what flavor pie do you like?"

"Blueberry if you're talking fruit pies. Banana or coconut if you're talking cream pies. But honestly, I don't think there's such a thing as a bad pie."

He was up and moving toward the kitchen, pausing only long enough to glance back at her one more time. As he turned away again, he muttered something that Juni suspected he didn't mean for her to hear. "A woman after my own heart."

Juni was pretty sure that he was only kidding, but for now she was too tired to figure out why he sounded so grim when he said it.

CHAPTER FOUR

"WOULD YOU AT least ask her?"

Ryder closed his eyes and prayed for patience. "No, I've imposed on Juni enough. I can't show up on her front porch again asking for another favor."

Granted, he wouldn't be asking for himself this time, and on some level he wouldn't mind having a legitimate excuse to drop by to visit Juni Voss. He hadn't seen her since he'd dropped her back at her place after leaving the café three days ago. That didn't mean he'd been able to stop thinking about her, and that was the problem. Heck, yesterday he'd even considered hanging out in the woods between their cabins in case he might accidentally run into her on one of her walks down to the river. He was pretty sure that would be skirting too close to stalking the woman.

Besides, he still wasn't looking to get involved with her—or anyone else right now, for that matter. It had taken him long enough to start rebuilding his life here in Dunbar. He didn't need any complications—and Juni would definitely be that. It wasn't as if she'd given him any indication that she was interested in striking up some type of friendship. After all, people who rented a remote cabin a mile outside a tiny town tended to value their privacy.

Although one thing about her puzzled him. Juni had mentioned she'd moved to Dunbar to be closer to the author of a book she was illustrating, but that didn't make a lot of sense to him. He'd dealt with graphic artists in his previous life, and they'd done everything over the internet. If she and the author needed to meet in person, an occasional overnight trip from the other side of the state would have sufficed. There had to be more to the move than that.

Max Volkov reached across the table to snap his fingers in front of Ryder's face. Ryder glared at the other man and shoved his hand to the side. "Hey, what's up with that?"

"I was trying to get your attention." Max relaxed back in his chair with the definite hint of a smirk in his gaze. "Seriously, Ryder, I don't know where you went right now, but you sure weren't here at the table with us. It also didn't look as if it was your happy place. Regardless, I'd really like to get this meeting over with so I can get back home."

Ryder hadn't gotten to know Max well until recently, but it was clear the man had found his own happy place right there in Dunbar. The lucky jerk had moved to town to write a book about his great-grandfather but had quickly ended up married to Rikki, the owner of a local bed-and-breakfast. He was now in the process of adopting her son. Weirdly, Max wasn't the only one in town who had fallen victim to Cupid's arrow. It seemed every guy Ryder knew was getting married these days.

Meanwhile, Max continued nagging at him. "Seriously, I need to go home and work. I'd really like to finish my daily quota of pages before dinner and then relax with my wife and son afterward. So, I'll ask you one last time— would you at least ask this Juni person if she'd be willing to do some pro bono artwork for our committee? You know her better than anyone else in town."

Resistance was futile, but Ryder wasn't ready to give up quite yet. "That's because I've imposed on her enough already. If I show up at her door again, she's likely to slam it in my face rather than jump at a chance to draw a bunch of pictures for people she doesn't even know, especially when she wouldn't get paid for it."

He had personal experience with people constantly approaching him and acting all friendly-like. Early on, he'd been flattered by the attention, but it hadn't taken long to figure out they weren't really interested in Ryder Davis, the man. Instead, one way or the other, they all wanted his time, his money or his connections. Well, no more. Now he chose his friends more carefully and supported causes he personally cared about. That's why he'd joined the local volunteer fire department and helped out at the animal shelter.

Meanwhile, he realized the other people seated at the table were staring at him. When the silence dragged on, Shelby Peters sighed. "Fine, Ryder. I'll talk to her. I've at least spoken with her a couple of times when she came into the post office. I'll drive out there later today after I get off work."

It was no surprise that Shelby had met Juni. You could count on the fingers of one hand the number of people in the area Shelby didn't know at least by sight. Not only had she grown up in Dunbar, she now ran the combination post office/ library/museum in town and had recently married the chief of police. She would no doubt handle the request with more finesse than Ryder himself might.

Each of the other people at the table had willingly volunteered to be on the committee to organize the annual celebration of the founding of Dunbar. They'd stepped in to save the day when several of the original volunteers had bowed out for various reasons. But that had been their choice, not Juni's. She had work to do and deadlines to meet.

He glanced around the table. All eyes were on him, and he finally nodded and held up his hands, surrendering to the inevitable. "Fine. I will ask her today. But if she says no, that's it. We won't try to pressure her into it."

Shelby, who had been elected to head up the committee, met his gaze directly. "Agreed."

"If we're done here, I'll be going."

Shelby reviewed the itinerary in front of her. "I think we should meet again in three days to see where we are on things. Does anyone have any questions about your assignments?"

Ryder held his breath, hoping against hope that no one would need any further explanations. Sadly, he should've known better. Otto Klaus's hand immediately shot up in the air. He was the former mayor of Dunbar and was married to Ilse, the current holder of said office. "I want to make sure I understand what Ilse needs to do. She can be pretty nitpicky when it comes to knowing all of the details."

No one denied the truth of that. It was also the reason that Ilse had taken over as mayor when her beloved husband had proven to be ineffectual after he'd beaten her in the election. He'd been a one-issue candidate, determined to prevent his wife from using tax dollars to turn the town's official van into an homage of the VW hippie van the couple had driven back in the day. Once Otto succeeded in that, he'd been at a complete loss as to what it took to govern.

Everyone had been relieved the town council had voted to allow Otto to resign and let his wife take over as mayor. Apart from Ilse's love of flower power–themed vans, she really was better suited for the job. In fact, the only reason Otto had attended today's meeting was that Ilse had needed to be somewhere else.

Ryder sighed and prepared to listen to Shelby patiently explain Ilse's assignment to Otto. Instead, she smiled at the older man. "Actually, I wrote everything out for her. I've also enclosed a more detailed copy of our agenda for this meeting. That should give her a pretty clear idea of everything we've discussed today."

She paused to slide an envelope across the table to Otto. "If you'll give this to Ilse for me, I would really appreciate it. She can call me with any questions after she's read it. I'll be at the post office until closing, but she can also call me at home tonight if that works better for her."

It was hard not to chuckle at the look of relief on Otto's face. No doubt the poor guy had been dreading facing his wife if he'd failed to take good notes on the meeting. Having met the woman on several occasions, Ryder figured Otto had good reason to be concerned. He knew a fair number of people who found the volatile relationship between the older couple both entertaining and confusing. That said, the pair had been married for around fifty years and were still going strong.

Shelby scanned her to-do list one last time. "So, Max will finish up the final promotion and press releases for the celebration. I'm going to be working with the decoration committee to make sure they have everything they need. Bea will finalize the list of those participating in the parade, and Ryder will ask Ms. Voss if she'd be willing to design some simple artwork for our advertising materials. I think that's everything."

When no one had anything to add, she smiled. "Okay, I'll see everyone at the next meeting."

Ryder bolted for the door, determined to get away before they came up with anything else for him to do. Yeah, he probably did have more free time than several of the other members of the committee. That didn't mean he wanted to spend every extra minute he had on the project. He was already committed to driving the town's newest fire truck in the parade as well as running the animal shelter's booth at the affair. They planned to have several cats and dogs available for adoption, and there was a lot of work involved in transporting them to and from the shelter.

Max made his escape from the meeting room right on Ryder's heels. "Sorry that I strong-armed you into talking to your neighbor. If she says no, maybe we can find someone else. Besides, if worse comes to worst, I guess we can always use the same artwork they've used for the past ten years."

Darn the man, anyway. One of the few things the entire committee had agreed on from the start was that everything about the Dunbar Days Festival had become seriously outdated and could really use a facelift. "I'll ask her, but I'm not making any promises. Juni's only been here a short time, and I can't promise she'll be interested in volunteering. She's barely had time to unpack."

That last part probably wasn't true. Her cabin had been neat and tidy the one time he'd been inside it. He rented the place furnished, but she'd definitely added her own touches to the decor.

"I know you volunteered to use your professional writer skills for the committee, but I'm guessing you and Rikki plan to live in Dunbar long-term. It makes sense for you to get involved in the town's affairs. That's true for me as well, but Juni only took out a six-month lease on the cabin. She also chose to live beyond the city limits even though there were available rentals in town. All of that suggests she's not here for the long term."

Max wasn't buying it. "Not necessarily. After all, you live next door to her, and you're involved in the town."

The last thing Ryder wanted was to stand out on the sidewalk debating the issue. "Like I said, I'll ask her. If she says no, I'll make some calls."

"Thanks, Ryder. Let me know if you need any help. Otherwise, I'll see you at the next meeting."

"Sounds good."

Max turned in the direction of the bed-and-breakfast where he lived while Ryder started down the street to his van. As he passed by Bea's bakery, he slowed to a halt. What if he picked up some pastries and two cups of coffee before heading to Juni's place? That would give him an excuse to stop by to check on her and maybe soften her up a bit before making his pitch. Even if it didn't work, he never turned down the chance to indulge his sweet tooth with one of Bea's fritters.

Right before he walked into the shop, his phone buzzed. He stopped and leaned against the front of the building. "Hi, Mom. What's up?"

Within seconds he regretted asking the question. Too bad he had a shift at the firehouse scheduled for later, because it was going to take something far stronger than a good cup of coffee to wash away the bad taste her news had left in his mouth.

JUNI HESITATED SEVERAL seconds before answering the phone. She normally wouldn't think of ignoring her aunt, but she had the strangest feeling she would regret taking this particular call. That was weird since Aunt Ruby no longer made a habit of interrupting Juni's workday and limited her calls to weekends or evenings. The fact that she was calling in the middle of the day could mean there was something wrong.

Or it could simply be that Aunt Ruby had come up with something else to worry about. She hadn't taken it well when Juni had announced her decision to move two hundred miles away from the rest of their family. Despite that now being a done deal, she continued to come up with reasons why Juni should pack up and hustle right back home. On her last call, Ruby had warned her about how dangerous the mountain passes were in the winter even though it was now spring and the chance of snow was almost past. Then there had been the whole lecture on the dangers of a woman living alone in the woods. The list of possible threats, both real and imagined, was apparently endless.

Sighing, Juni saved her work on the computer and answered the summons. "Hi, Aunt Ruby, what's up?"

To her surprise, it wasn't Ruby's face that appeared on the screen. Instead, it was cousin Erin, Ruby's daughter. "Well, it sure took you long enough to answer."

Juni wished time travel was a real thing. She would gladly rewind the past minute and let the call go to voicemail. "Sorry, but I was working."

Erin's answering sniff made her opinion on that subject all too clear. "You mean you were coloring pictures."

It was an old joke, one Juni had long grown tired of. She prayed for patience as she set her cell on its stand to free up her hands. "Yes, Erin, I'm coloring pictures. That's what I get paid to do."

Juni tried to hurry the conversation along. "So why did you call? And why are you using your mom's phone?"

"Because I was pretty sure you wouldn't answer if you saw my number instead of hers."

She wasn't wrong about that. Erin could be incredibly generous, but she sometimes forgot other people had busy lives, especially if she needed a favor or rescuing when she got caught up in a situation she couldn't handle on her own. That was how Juni had ended up getting drafted into spending hours decorating their high school gym for the prom when Erin had gotten in way over her head. As she waited for Erin to explain the reason for the call, Juni really wished that memory of the prom hadn't picked that moment to flash through her mind. It felt like a foreshadowing of yet another monumental imposition on Juni's time.

After a brief silence, her cousin pasted a bright smile on her face and then held her hand up and waggled her fingers. The sparkle on her left ring finger hadn't been there the last time she and Juni had been together. Evidently Erin's longtime boyfriend had finally popped the question. Hopefully her cousin was only calling to share the big news.

"Congratulations, Erin. I'm so happy for you and Phillip. When is the big day?"

Erin's smile faded slightly. "That's why I'm calling. For starters, I want you to be my maid of honor. Having you standing at my side on the most important day of my life would mean the world to me."

Juni didn't even hesitate. "Of course, Erin. I'd be honored."

"That's great. Mom will be happy to hear that." She drew a deep breath, then started speaking as if she couldn't get the words out fast enough. "We're getting married in seven months. We've already reserved the church. It's everything else I need your help with."

Juni did a spit take with her coffee, spewing a fine spray of caffeine all over her desktop.

Grabbing a tissue, she began mopping up the small mess. Had it even crossed Erin's mind that Juni might be busy or that it would be an incredible imposition given that Juni was living on the other side of the state from Crestville, their hometown?

Evidently not, because she immediately launched into a long and detailed list of everything that needed to be purchased, planned or arranged before the big day. "I want to have the reception somewhere classy, not just the basement of the church. For one thing, they won't let us serve alcohol there. We'll need to make trips to Spokane to find my dress. It has to be perfect. After that we'll have to go again to find the right bridesmaids' dresses."

Juni let her ramble on, knowing she wouldn't get a word in edgewise until Erin ran out of steam. With every word she spoke, the sick feeling in Juni's stomach grew worse. What was she going to do about this?

That's when she noticed that she had unexpected company standing out on the porch—

Ryder Davis. She'd left the front door open because it was such a pleasant day outside. Since she hadn't heard a car pulling into her driveway, he must have walked over from his place. When Ryder realized she'd spotted him, he held up a cardboard tray holding two cups of what was probably coffee and a bag that she really hoped had something sugary inside. After getting hit with her cousin's outrageous demands, she could use some guilty-pleasure food in her life.

She waved for Ryder to come inside, hoping to use his arrival as a legitimate excuse to get off the phone. He approached her desk, frowning as he listened to whatever Erin was prattling on about now.

"Erin, I hate to interrupt, but I'm going to have to hang up now. Someone has just come into my office, and I have to see what he needs. You can tell me more about your big plans when I call your mom on Sunday."

Before she could disconnect the call, Erin jumped right back into the conversation. "I'm sorry, Juni, but we're going to be talking every day. It would mean so much to me to have you help plan my wedding. We grew up like sisters, and you're the one person I know who will help make sure my special day will be perfect."

Hoping she sounded calmer than she felt, Juni aimed for a polite refusal. "I want your day to be perfect, too, but I don't see how I can be of much help from this distance."

Erin leaned in closer to the phone, filling the screen with her face. "I realize it will be harder from where you are. Too bad you can't move back home sooner than you planned."

Then she smiled as if she hadn't just hinted Juni should break her lease, abandon the chance to regularly meet with Sabrina Luberti in person and come running back home.

"I'm sorry, but I can't do that, Erin. I signed a lease that I can't break without paying significant financial penalties. I also have professional commitments here that are important to me. I can't simply walk away them from without damaging both my reputation and my career. But that said, I'll help pick out the dresses for the bridesmaids to wear."

Crossing her fingers that that would be enough to satisfy her cousin, she offered an alternative way for Erin to get the help she needed. "I'm sure there are great wedding organizers there in Crestville who can handle everything. They would have the right connections when it comes to booking the best vendors. Like you said, you'll need a florist, a caterer, a DJ, someone to do the music for the service itself. Honestly, the list is endless."

That was true. Hiring a professional was the

only reasonable solution to the problem. Unfortunately Juni knew it was never easy to convince Erin to change direction once she'd settled on a course of action. Her cousin's next words proved her right. "Sorry, Juni, but I don't want some stranger organizing my wedding. You already know my tastes while they'd be starting from scratch. I was thinking you could come home on the weekends."

At a loss for words, all Juni could do was stare as her cousin rattled on and on. In a surprise move, Ryder set down the tray and the bag and picked up the phone to stare at Erin. By the time he spoke, his expression had turned stern and frigidly cold, to the point Juni wasn't sure she would have recognized him. "Excuse me, who are you exactly?"

After a brief silence, Erin sputtered, "I'm Juni's cousin."

"Well, cousin, I am Ms. Voss's newest client. I have an ironclad contract with her, and we have a business meeting scheduled for now. As she said, I'm sure she'll be glad to hear all about your— was it a party of some kind? Well, not that it matters. She and I are operating on a short time line and need to get right to work."

Then he disconnected the call and immediately turned off the phone, no doubt figuring Erin would try calling back. He wasn't mistaken.

Knowing her cousin, she'd keep dialing until Juni was foolish enough to finally answer. When that happened, Juni would no doubt get an earful from both Erin and her aunt about Ryder's bad behavior, but right now all she wanted to do was hug the man for what he'd just done.

CHAPTER FIVE

AFTER PLACING JUNI'S phone back on its stand, Ryder pulled up a handy chair and sat down to give Juni a few seconds to collect herself. When he'd first walked into the cabin, she'd been staring down at her phone with her mouth gaping like a guppy's with no sound coming out as her cousin prattled on and on. He had every faith that Juni would have eventually regained her ability to speak, but he'd made the executive decision to put her out of her misery. If she wasn't happy about it, so be it.

"Sorry if I overstepped, but you looked like you were stuck. If I should apologize to your cousin, I will."

While he waited for her to respond, he set Juni's coffee down and then laid one of the doughnuts on a napkin within easy reach. It had been disappointing that Bea had been all out of apple fritters, but her bacon-maple bars ran a close second in his list of all-time favorites in her shop. The huge rectangular doughnut was slathered with a thick layer of maple icing and then topped with a crisp strip of hickory-smoked bacon. He'd never heard of such a concoction before moving to Dunbar, but it had taken only one bite to sell him on the deliciousness of the unusual combination of flavors. So, so good.

If Juni didn't find it to her liking, so much the better. He'd cheerfully take the maple bar off her hands. He was already on the fourth bite of his own before she finally snapped back into focus.

"Ryder, you hung up on my cousin!"

He couldn't quite tell if Juni was shocked or angry and was unsure how to proceed. It didn't help that he also felt guilty because her cousin wasn't the only one about to ask Juni for a huge favor. He settled on a partial truth. "I was afraid to let her ramble on about everything she thought you should do for her. If that kept up, you might have already been dragging out boxes and packing by now."

Juni's shoulders sagged a little. "I wish I could honestly say you were wrong about that, but some habits are hard to break. I love my cousin, and I hate to disappoint her."

Her smile was a bit rueful when she added, "But there's a reason I jumped at the chance to move to the other side of the state."

Juni paused to take a bite of her maple bar,

her eyes immediately flaring wide in delight. As soon as she swallowed, she asked, "Please tell me you bought this in town. Otherwise I'll be making a lot of road trips to buy more."

Ryder grinned at her. "Honestly, I'm actually sorry to hear you like it so much. I was sort of hoping you'd decide maple icing and bacon don't go together. That way I could be all noble and offer to eat yours and let you have the other doughnuts I bought."

She set the maple bar back down to sip her coffee, but he noted that she made sure it was out of his reach. "A better person would hand over the maple bar out of gratitude for your help dealing with Erin. To be honest, I'm not at all interested in heading back home to organize her entire wedding. For the record, I did agree to help pick out the bridesmaids' dresses, but that's it."

Juni gave her maple bar a pointed look. "I also don't feel the least bit bad about eating the doughnut you voluntarily gave me."

That was disappointing, but he didn't blame her. "Fine."

"I am, however, grateful that you bought it for me." She narrowed her eyes and held up her coffee cup before continuing. "But I am curious as to why you showed up with what I suspect were bribes in hand."

"Hey, maybe it's because I hadn't seen you in a while and wanted to make sure you were doing okay."

"Nope, not buying it." Juni made a show of looking around the room. "At least you didn't come armed with kittens this time. That's a definite improvement."

He wasn't so sure about that. To buy himself a few seconds to consider how to approach the situation, he offered Juni her choice of the cake doughnut with chocolate icing or the vanilla one with sprinkles. As she considered her options, it dawned on him that they both had similar family-based problems and could possibly help each other out.

After choosing the one with sprinkles, she glanced up at him and frowned big-time. He'd been trying to maintain an innocent facade, but clearly he'd missed the mark. Juni set the doughnut down and crossed her arms over her chest. "I feel safe in assuming that I won't like whatever you're about to say."

That wasn't exactly a question, but he answered it anyway. "No, probably not. However, I was thinking we might be able to help each other."

"How so?"

"Your cousin thinks you should drop everything and come running. You obviously don't want to do that."

"True."

"Well, you're not the only one who has family making unwelcome demands today. My mother announced she's planning a dinner party and insists that I attend even though she knows I hate such things."

By that point, Juni looked a little confused. "So what are you thinking?"

"You probably aren't aware that every year the town puts on a parade and festival to honor the founding of Dunbar. For various reasons, I ended up on the committee that is organizing it this time. The biggest problem we have is that prior committees have kept right on using the same old formats for everything. That includes the graphics for advertising. Believe me when I say that it's all become a bit stale."

He took the time to eat a bite of his doughnut to let her absorb that much before he got to the tricky part. "It was suggested—and not by me, just so you know—that you might be willing to design some new artwork we could use to advertise the event. Several of the people on the committee have seen the caricature you did of me in the tree and really admired your talent."

He paused to see if she wanted to comment, but she waved her hand in a circle signaling that he should just keep going. "They were hoping you would be willing to donate your time and talent. However, I've found someone who will pay the going rate for your services with the provision that his donation remain secret, as in not even the committee can know you're being paid. He's concerned that they would try to get him to fork over big bucks for other projects if they knew about the arrangement. The thing is this guy prefers to pick and choose what he wants to spend his money on rather than being bombarded all the time with requests."

Juni slowly nodded. "I can understand that. You hear about stuff like that happening whenever someone wins the lottery."

"Exactly. But anyway, if you actually had that ironclad contract I mentioned to your cousin, it would definitely include a requirement that you need to stay in the area until the work is completed. If your family has questions, I will be the public face for the deal and would be happy to verify the terms of the contract."

"And beyond the artwork, what else would you need me to do in return?"

Juni looked skeptical, but at least she hadn't immediately said no. Crossing his fingers, he moved on to the other half of the deal. "In return, I'd like you to be my plus-one at my mother's dinner party later this month. It would also be really nice if you could pretend that it wasn't our first date."

For sure she was having some serious doubts

now. "Why do you want your family to think you're seeing someone even though you aren't?"

Smart woman. He should've known she would guess there was more to it than that. "See, the real problem is that my mother mentioned she'd invited my fiancée, too."

Juni lurched to her feet, her hands clenched in fists. "You're engaged but still want to take a date? Sorry, but I'm not about to play the 'other woman' in your family drama. What kind of person do you think I am?"

He motioned time-out with his hands. "Sorry, sorry. I'm not making myself clear. Jasmine is actually my ex-fiancée. We broke up almost two years ago. Well, technically, I broke up with her, but I assure you it was the right thing to do for both of us. The problem is that my mother thinks I'm not really over Jazz. I swear I have absolutely no desire to pick up where we left off, but no one believes me. Not her and definitely not my parents."

"Why not?"

Feeling pretty defensive by then, he made himself meet her gaze head-on. "Mainly because I haven't dated anyone since the breakup."

Juni looked honestly shocked by that. "No one at all? Really?"

Why did that seem to upset her so much? He hated having to talk about all of this, but he couldn't expect Juni to walk into what could be a tense situation without knowing all the players in the game. "Really. For starters, the dating pool here in Dunbar is pretty limited. But the main reason is that breaking up with Jazz wasn't the only major change I made in my life. Without going into detail, I'll just simply say I've been dealing with a lot."

It occurred to him that he had no idea if Juni had left someone waiting for her back in her hometown. He should probably have found that out before asking her to be his pretend girlfriend. There was no time like the present.

Clearing his throat, he asked, "On that subject, is there someone in your life that I should know about? Because this dinner party might not be the only time I need you to pretend to be my girlfriend. I promise not to take up much of your time, though. I know you already have a big art project you're working on, and the work for our committee will only add to that."

Juni's eyes shifted to the side, like she wasn't comfortable with what she was about to tell him. When she finally spoke, her voice was little better than a whisper. "No one is waiting for me."

He believed her, but he also suspected there was an unhappy story behind the hint of pain packed into her simple statement. Now wasn't the time to press for more information. It wasn't as if he wanted to share all the details of his past with her. Heck, he'd never even told Titus or any-one else much about his life before moving to Dunbar, and he'd known them far longer than he had Juni. It wasn't that he thought his friends wouldn't understand. The bigger worry was that their feelings about him would change when they learned the truth about his past. It wouldn't be the first time that had happened.

"So let me make sure I understand what the deal would be." She held up the index finger on her right hand as she reviewed the pertinent in-formation. "First, I need a solid reason to avoid rushing home to help my cousin. You're provid-ing that by offering me a contract to do design work for your committee that will have a provi-sion that requires I remain in Dunbar until the work is completed, mainly because of the short turnaround it requires."

When he nodded, she held up a second fin-ger. "In return, I will be your fake plus-one on at least one occasion to help convince your family that your engagement to Jasmine is truly over. Once they accept that, you and I will have our own amicable 'breakup,' leaving both of us free to move on."

He leaned back in his chair, trying to look more relaxed than he really was. "Got it on the first try. What do you think?"

"I think I'll be making a trip into Seattle to buy a dress."

RYDER LEFT JUNI'S place not long afterward. She needed to get back to work, and he was due at the fire station in an hour. As he walked back over to his place, he poked and prodded at the agreement they'd hammered out, trying to decide how he really felt about it. He had managed to deal with both of their problems at the same time, which was at least some indication that his plan going in had actually worked.

The biggest win was that he now had a date for his mother's dinner party, which was a huge relief. Also, thanks to the work he'd hired Juni to do, she had a legitimate excuse to stay in Dunbar rather than moving back home. That meant it was a win-win situation. But if that were true, why was he feeling a bit uneasy to the point of full-on guilty about it?

Probably because he knew that each of them was holding back some pretty significant information. From what he did know about Juni, she wasn't anyone's pushover. It took guts to move across the state on her own to advance her career. He suspected if anyone else tried to run roughshod over her plans like her cousin had, Juni would've come out of her corner swinging. There was also the matter of the lack of a man in her life. He could be wrong, but he suspected there was someone she had been interested in and that interest hadn't been reciprocated.

He couldn't very well point fingers at her for protecting her privacy. As far as Juni knew, Ryder was a small-town guy who helped rescue kittens and put out fires. If she had questions about how he managed to pay the bills without having a regular job, she hadn't pressed for answers. At least not so far. He'd have to tell her something of the truth before their date to give her a better idea about what to expect when they got to his parents' house.

If Titus and Shay found out that he'd 'fessed up to Juni before them, they might not take it well. On the other hand, they clearly both had secrets from their pasts that they hadn't shared with him. One reason the three of them had hit it off was that they'd quickly figured out that each of them was in some way starting over when they moved to Dunbar. Even without knowing the details, they had each other's backs. If Ryder needed them, both men would come running, no questions asked.

He'd do the same for them.

When Ryder had moved to Dunbar, he'd drawn a sharp line between his past and his present, even if his family refused to accept that this wasn't a temporary aberration, a small blip on the radar that would return to normal soon. His best efforts to explain to his parents why he'd chosen to build a new life for himself in a place like Dunbar just didn't compute for them. They kept insisting that he should do so much more with his life.

He'd tried that once, and it had almost killed him. Honesty made him admit that the mistakes of his past were what made his new, much less stressful life possible. Money wasn't everything, but having earned enough to live on forever while still in his twenties was a gift. For that, he would always be grateful, but there was no way he was going back to that rat race.

It would destroy him completely next time.

And on that happy thought, he dialed his mother's number, hoping against hope that it would go to voicemail. Luck was with him this once. "Hi, Mom, I just wanted to let you know that I'll be bringing a date to your dinner party. I can't wait for you to meet her. You don't need to call me back. I'm on duty tonight and will be out of touch."

With that chore done, he made one more call, which also went to voicemail. "Hi, Shelby, I thought you'd like to know that Juni agreed to do the artwork for us. It's my night to be at the fire station, but I'll check in again with you tomorrow. I wasn't sure if you'd like Juni to attend our next meeting or if the committee should come up with some ideas first."

Having covered all the necessary bases for the

day, he got his gear together and loaded it into the van. With that done, he called in an order to the café to pick up on the way. The other volunteers didn't seem to mind making do with canned soup or frozen meals while on duty but not him. He rarely settled for anything less than Titus's excellent cooking if he could help it.

Feeling much better about life in general, he backed out of his driveway and headed into town. As he passed by Juni's place, he realized he was glad he didn't have to fake excuses to see her for the foreseeable future. Weirdly enough, it was the closest he'd had to a relationship in a long time. With luck, they could have fun together without any of the complications of pursuing anything serious.

Yeah, a fake date and a fake contract left them both free to pursue their individual dreams with no inconvenient strings attached. He'd fought hard to build a solitary, more peaceful life. It had taken him nearly six months just to regain his health, and he wasn't about to put himself at risk again. No more trying to survive the constant push and pull of too many people making demands on him. That was all he really wanted.

And if he kept telling himself that, maybe he'd eventually believe it.

CHAPTER SIX

IT HAD BEEN two days since Ryder had shown
up on Juni's doorstep with doughnuts and a job
offer. Last night, he'd called to invite her to the
next Dunbar Days committee meeting at city
hall. He offered to pick her up, but she'd opted
to drive herself. She still needed to do something
about finding a dress. Since she was already giving work a pass for the morning, it only made
sense to head for Seattle when the meeting let
out. If she also did some grocery shopping on the
way back, she'd have all her errands done and
could concentrate on her artwork that evening.

As she walked past the windows on the front
of the small building that housed what passed for
city government in the small town, she paused
to check her appearance. While she seriously
doubted anyone would expect her to show up
in full-on business attire, she hadn't wanted to
veer off too far in the opposite direction. After
discarding several outfits, she'd settled on black
slacks paired with a forest green silk shell that

made her hazel eyes look more green than gold. Her hair was pulled back in a simple ponytail, and she'd limited her makeup to mascara and the barest hint of lipstick.

As usual, deciding which shoes to wear had taken a lot of thought. Due to her less than impressive height, she usually wore heels in a futile attempt to look taller and feel more confident when attending a business meeting. Today, though, she'd opted for flats. Again, she wasn't trying to impress some high-powered executives, but a small-town committee made up of volunteers. Not to mention only one person knew she was being paid for this gig, so they wouldn't be in a position to judge her too harshly for choosing comfortable footwear.

Besides, she had to navigate the mall after the meeting ended. There was no way she wanted to do that in three-inch heels, especially since she needed a knee-length dress, not a formal. She didn't have to worry about making sure the dress didn't drag on the ground if her shoes weren't the right height. Her only hope was that she could find something appropriate that wouldn't break the bank and would also be suitable for other occasions in the future.

"You must be Juni Voss."

She'd been so lost in thought, she hadn't noticed anyone approach. She turned to face a handsome man who looked to be about her age of twenty-six, give or take a little. "I am."

He held out his hand. "I'm Max Volkov, another one of the committee members. I was really pleased when Ryder told me that you agreed to do the artwork for us. I hope he didn't strong-arm you into agreeing."

"No, but he did show up with a bribe in hand. Evidently I'm a sucker for doughnuts and coffee." She smiled to reassure him that all was well as she shook his hand. "It's nice to meet you."

"The pleasure is all mine," Max said as he checked his watch. "We should probably head inside. Shelby appreciates promptness."

After they filed inside the building, he resumed talking. "You and I may end up working together on some on the advertising graphics. Since I'm a freelance writer by profession, they asked me to do the press releases and social media posts for the celebration. Normally, I write articles about local history and places of interest. Right now, though, I'm working on my first book. Trying to, anyway."

Although he sounded a little embarrassed by that last admission, Juni was impressed. "That's great. I've always admired people who can write. Where did you get the idea for the book?"

Max's expression instantly brightened. "Well,

that's really interesting. Have you visited the museum here in town?"

She shook her head. "I plan to, but I've been busy getting settled into my cabin and working. It's definitely on my agenda, though."

"You should go if for no other reason than to see the Trillium Nugget, a huge chunk of gold that was discovered in the area about a hundred years ago by my great-grandfather. He—"

Before he could finish the sentence, another voice joined the conversation. "Please don't get him started on his book, Juni. We'll never finish the meeting on time if he starts waxing poetically about his great-grandfather's adventures back in the day."

As he spoke, Ryder stepped out of a nearby room and planted himself firmly between her and Max as they continued down the hall. "I'd suggest waiting until you can read the book, but only if you have a large glass of your favorite alcoholic beverage close at hand. That's what I plan to do."

She elbowed Ryder in the side as they walked. "Don't be rude. Lots of people claim they want to write a book someday, but very few ever do. I'd be honored to read a book written by someone I've actually met."

Instead of being insulted by Ryder's snide remarks, Max laughed. "Thank you for saying that, Juni, but he's right. Once I get started talking about Grandpa Lev, I tend to forget that not everyone is as excited about his story as I am."

Halfway down the hall, Max led the way into a conference room. Juni recognized Shelby Peters, but the other two women were strangers to her. She turned to Ryder, expecting him to introduce her since he was the one who had asked her to be there. Instead, he walked around to the far side of the table and sat down. When she hesitated to follow suit, Max stepped in to lead her toward the other women. "Juni Voss, I believe you've already met Shelby."

The tall redhead smiled and stepped forward with her hand out. Juni shook it and returned the smile. "Yes, we met when she set me up with a post office box right after I moved to town."

Shelby took over from there. "Juni, this is Bea O'Malley. She owns the combination coffee shop and bakery in town."

This was someone Juni planned to get to know much better. "Nice to meet you! I've been lucky enough to have one of your bacon-maple bars. It was amazing! I will definitely be stopping by your shop soon and often."

The older woman beamed with pride. "I'm glad you enjoyed it. Those and my apple fritters get rave reviews from a lot of folks here in town. When you get a chance to come in, your first order will be on the house as a token of appreciation for you helping out the committee like this."

"Thank you, but that's not necessary."

Juni just barely managed to avoid giving Ryder a guilty glance. She had promised to keep their contract secret, but her conscience wasn't comfortable with people thinking she was donating her time free of charge when she wasn't. She hadn't realized that it could get awkward when she'd agreed to keep the information to herself.

Meanwhile, Shelby was waiting to make one more introduction. "Juni, this is Ilse Klaus, the mayor of Dunbar."

"It's nice to meet you, Madam Mayor."

The older woman cackled at that. "No need to get all formal with me, Juni. Call me Ilse. Everyone else in town does."

"Ilse it is, then."

With all of the niceties out of the way, Shelby made shooing motions with her hands. "Okay, folks, let's get started. The sooner we get through the agenda, the sooner we can all go home."

Once everyone was seated, she passed around sheets of paper with a bullet list of topics. Juni scanned it quickly, noting that her name was at the top of the list. She hoped that meant she only had to stay long enough to hear what they had in mind for the advertising. If so, she could get an early start on her shopping expedition.

"Since Juni was nice enough to join us this morning," Shelby said, "I thought we should start off talking about the advertising. Does anyone have any suggestions?"

Juni raised her hand just enough to get Shelby's attention. "I did some rough sketches last night. I studied the photos posted on the town's website from previous celebrations. I also looked at pictures of Dunbar Mountain and local flora and fauna. The drawings aren't very detailed, but I thought they might at least give us a starting point for discussion."

She handed the stack to Shelby to look through first. After glancing through them, the other woman smiled as she passed them on to Ilse. "Juni, to be honest, I had no idea what to expect and certainly didn't have any brilliant ideas myself. Having said that, these are amazing."

Ilse had already handed them off to Max. "You've got talent, young lady. Well done."

Max flipped through the pages twice before sliding them across the table to Ryder. As he did, he gave her a considering look. "I'm thinking that when it comes time for me to start working on a cover for my book, I will be calling you, Juni. You've definitely caught the feel of Dunbar in those sketches."

She never knew quite how to respond when

someone said something so nice about her work. "I'll look forward to hearing from you."

By that point, Ryder had the pictures spread out on the table in front of him. He remained silent as he leaned forward to study them. She wasn't sure why it was his opinion that would carry the most weight with her. Seeing his expression remain so serious had her gripping the edge of the table. It wasn't until he finally looked up to make eye contact with her that she could actually breathe again.

"I was already impressed with the caricature you did of me in the tree, but these are absolutely perfect." He stopped to tap two of the pictures with his fingertip. "Either of these would get my vote."

Ryder finally smiled at her, his approval shining in his blue eyes. "But, Juni, if you consider these rough sketches, I can't wait to see the finished product."

By that point, she knew she was blushing. "Thank you, everybody. I'm glad you like them."

She got a spiral notebook and a pen out of her purse. "So, let's start with those two and talk about what changes or additions you would like to see."

The ideas came flying in from everyone at the table. She listed each of them and asked for clarification on a few points. "I think I have everything that was suggested. I'll take the drawings back home and incorporate as many ideas as I can. In case for some reason I can't attend your next meeting, maybe Ryder would be willing to pick them up to show you."

He nodded. "That should be no problem."

Shelby looked around the table. "If no one else has any questions for Juni, we'll let her escape before we move on to the boring stuff."

Ilse shook her head. "I don't have any questions. I just want to thank you again for coming today. People's eyes will pop out when they see the new graphics."

Juni gathered up her stuff. "I'll be going then. See you all again soon."

To her surprise, Ryder immediately hopped up from his seat. "I'll see you out."

Without giving Shelby a chance to protest the delay that would entail, he walked out with Juni. When they stepped out onto the sidewalk in front of the building, she asked, "Did you think I couldn't find my way back down the hall?"

"No, I wanted to thank you for putting so much effort into those pictures. They're so much better than I imagined they'd be."

She knew he meant that to be complimentary, but it didn't feel quite that way. "Thanks... I think. Did you think I'd use a box of old crayons and draw stick figures?"

"Not at all, but you've only had a couple of days to work on them. You must have taken a lot of time away from the illustrations you're supposed to be focusing on. I don't want you to sacrifice that work for the sake of the town."

Okay, so that was his issue.

"Don't worry about it, Ryder. It actually helps me to have something else to think about, especially if I get stuck on a drawing. Concentrating on other ideas somehow magically frees up my subconscious to work on my main project. After I finished these sketches, I got a lot of work done on the book illustrations. I sent the newest ones off to the author and her editor this morning. Until I get their feedback, there's not much more I can do."

"That's good to hear, but promise to let me know if it gets to be too much."

"Will do. Now, you should probably head back inside before Shelby hunts you down."

He laughed. "Knowing her, she'll call her police chief husband and have him haul me back to the meeting. Where are you off to after this?"

"I'm going dress shopping for the dinner party."

Ryder winced. "I'm sorry—I feel bad that you have to buy something special to wear."

"I have something back home that would do. I could even ask my aunt to pack it up and ship it to me, but I don't want to do that. She's already not happy with me for not coming home to help Erin. If she thinks I'm over here going to fancy parties, it will only stir the pot again."

He started to reach for his wallet. "At least let me pay for the dress."

Okay, that was a firm no. "Absolutely not. I can buy my own clothes, Ryder. It's not like I won't be able to use it for other occasions in the future."

He didn't look much happier, but at least he didn't argue. "I hope you find something you like."

"Me, too." She started to walk away but turned back. After giving his faded T-shirt and ragged jeans a long look, she asked, "Am I right that I need a cocktail dress, something understated but not casual?"

"Oh, yeah. Mom never goes casual when she invites all the movers and shakers over for a party. I'll be wearing my tux."

So he actually owned a tux? That sure didn't fit the image she had of him. He drove a beat-up van, apparently didn't own a pair of jeans without holes in the knees, didn't always shave and lived in an A-frame cabin similar to the one she was renting. Hardly the kind of lifestyle that would require having a tuxedo hanging in the closet. But then she'd already begun to suspect that there was far more to Ryder Davis than met the eye.

"Well, I'd better go if I want to get done before afternoon rush hour hits Seattle."

She'd only gone a couple of steps when he spoke again. "I'm feeling peckish for some good barbecue. If I pick some up, want to have dinner with me tonight?"

Was he asking her for a real date? Because that's how it sounded. She wasn't sure how she felt about that idea, but then he added, "That will give me a chance to catch you up on everything else we cover in the rest of the meeting in case it impacts your artwork."

Feeling both relieved and disappointed at the same time, she agreed. "Sounds good. I never feel like cooking after a shopping expedition. Should we eat at my place or yours?"

"Call me when you get home, and I'll bring over the food."

"Okay, I'll see you then."

The door of city hall slammed open, and Shelby stepped out. "Sorry to interrupt, but I'm on a tight schedule."

When she disappeared back into the building. Ryder smiled at Juni. "I guess I'll see you later."

Rather than stare after him, she walked a short distance down the street before giving in to the impulse to look back. Sadly, she'd waited too long, and he was already out of sight. Maybe that was a good thing. Theirs was a business relationship, nothing more, and that's all she wanted it to be. After all, she'd moved to Dunbar to establish her independence and focus on her career, not her social life. She was okay with that.

Really.

CHAPTER SEVEN

BY THE TIME Juni had prowled through half a dozen stores, her feet hurt, her head ached, and she was ready to cancel the deal she'd made with Ryder for lack of anything suitable to wear. Well, unless he called to say that the dress code had just changed so she could wear jeans and a T-shirt to his mother's dinner party. She might have even backed out of the date if she hadn't dragged her weary self into one last shop tucked away in the back corner of the mall. To her immense relief, they'd had the perfect little black dress displayed on a mannequin right inside the door.

And miracles of miracles, they not only had it in her size, but it was on sale.

Because the expedition took far longer than she'd expected, traffic was heavy and slow-moving all the way back to Dunbar. As soon as she walked inside the cabin, she kicked off her shoes, changed into sweats and flopped down on the sofa more than ready to be done for the day. Unfortunately, artwork didn't draw itself, so she really shouldn't give into the urge to take a well-deserved nap.

Glancing toward her desk, she muttered, "I promise I'll get started soon. I just need a few minutes to catch my breath. Half an hour at the most."

That was the last thought she had until her phone rang and jerked her out of a sound sleep. She managed to sit up and found herself squinting around the room as she tried to make sense of the situation. Why was it so dark? Pushing herself up off the couch, she hunted for where she'd left her phone, which went silent just as she unearthed it from the depths of her purse.

One glance at the screen had her moaning. Not only had she dozed off, she'd slept for hours. She'd promised to let Ryder know when she got home so he could bring dinner over. No wonder he was calling. She wrote a quick text to ask him to give her fifteen minutes before heading her way. Before she could hit SEND, there was a knock at the door. "Great. So much for having time to comb my hair and wash my face."

Opening the door, she pasted on a smile before greeting her guest. "Ryder, sorry I didn't answer the phone in time. I was about to text you."

She waggled the phone in her hand to lend credence to her claim. "I accidentally fell asleep on the couch when I got home from shopping."

He studied her for a few seconds without making any move to come inside even though she'd stepped back out of the way to give him room to pass. Finally, he frowned. "Would you rather I give you half of the food and leave?"

She couldn't help but laugh. "Do I look that bad?"

His mouth quirked up in a hint of a grin. "You do know there's really no good answer to that question."

"That bad, huh?"

His expression remained serious, but there was a definite twinkle in his eyes. "Well, let's just say you look like maybe you really needed that nap."

"How tactful of you." She stepped farther away from the door to turn on some lights. "Actually, I'm glad you called. I never intended to sleep that long. I'd hoped to get some work done after I got home. Finding the right dress took longer than I expected, which meant I hit rush-hour traffic on the way back."

Ryder grimaced. "I'm sorry the meeting this morning and the shopping trip ate up so much of your time."

"Don't worry about it. Come on inside. I don't know about you, but I could use an energy boost about now. I missed lunch, and barbecue will hit the spot. Before that, though, I'm going to go run a brush through my hair so I don't look so much like a zombie. I'll be right back."

"There's no rush. Take your time." Ryder headed straight for her kitchen, calling back over his shoulder, "I'll get this heated up."

She probably should've told him to wait and let her play hostess considering it was her place, but she didn't protest. It only took her a minute to make herself look human again, so she got back to the kitchen in time to help set the table.

Except for the meat, Ryder hadn't bothered with serving dishes. Instead, he'd stuck spoons in the various containers and set them on the table. Juni thought that was a fine idea, because she was always down with limiting the number of dirty dishes she'd have to deal with. After setting plates and silverware on the table, she asked, "What would you like to drink? I have pop, milk and maybe one beer in the fridge."

"Actually, I'd be satisfied with ice water."

He took a seat at the table while she fixed their drinks. She also grabbed the roll of paper towels to use as napkins. The restaurant had stuck a few in the bag, but she figured extra wouldn't hurt considering they were having barbecued ribs, which were finger food as far as she was concerned.

As she sat down, she took a deep breath. "Everything smells wonderful."

"It's from the best barbecue joint in the area. They have this huge smoker out back, and you can smell the smoky goodness a mile before you get close to the restaurant. The sides are also top-notch. I wasn't sure what you like, so I got several. Salads are on your left. The containers on the right are three different kinds of baked beans."

When he finally had everything arranged to his liking, he passed her a platter piled high with ribs, pulled pork and burnt ends of brisket. She took some of each and then studied the salads. "It all looks so good and way too much for two people."

He laughed as he put a similar selection of food on his own plate. "I know, but I am a firm believer in the wonder that is leftovers."

As he spoke, he picked up one of the ribs with his fingers and admired it. "With luck, we should have enough extra to feed each of us another lunch or dinner tomorrow. I love not having to cook every day."

"You're a wise man."

"Nice of you to notice." He pointed to her plate. "Now, eat while it's hot."

"Yes, sir."

RYDER WAS GLAD that Juni was enjoying their impromptu dinner. Her coloring had definitely improved since he'd first arrived, even though she'd been pretty adorable all rumpled and groggy from her unexpected nap. The day had clearly taken a lot out of her, and he felt bad about that, especially since everything she'd done had been for his benefit.

He probably should've insisted on leaving her half the food and gone back home rather than taking up more of her time. However, his conscience was bothering him for not having been totally honest about what was going on between him and his family. It wouldn't be fair to let her get further involved without knowing the minefield they might be walking into at his parents' house.

Juni deserved to hear the truth while there was still time to let her back out of the deal if that's what she decided to do. If so, he'd still ask her to finish the artwork for the festival committee and see that she got paid for her time. He would also continue to run interference with her cousin as long as Juni needed him to.

He wasn't looking forward to the conversation, but he couldn't put it off any longer. When she finally pushed her plate out of the way, he got up to start cleaning up the mess they'd made. "There's dessert, too, but I figure we might want to hold off on that for a while. For now, if you'll

point me in the direction of any storage containers you have, I'll divvy up the leftovers."

She pointed toward the small bank of cabi-
nets on the far wall of the kitchen. "They're in
the bottom left. But are you sure you want to
leave some with me? You could have two meals
if you took everything. After all, you're the one
who bought it."

"I'm sure."

It didn't take long to get the leftovers pack-
aged up and put away in her fridge. Then he
fixed them each another glass of ice water and
set out the two small containers of bread pudding
he'd picked up for dessert. "We'll heat those up
when we're ready to eat them. While we wait, I
thought we should talk about the dinner party."

Juni sat up straighter, a worried look in her
eyes. "Why? Is something wrong?"

He sat back down, angling himself so he
wasn't looking directly at her. Some things
were difficult enough to talk about without the
added pressure of watching for signs of pity in
the listener's reaction. "Not exactly wrong, but
I should probably share some background about
what's going on. If you would rather not attend
the party with me afterward, I'll understand. I
just need to figure out where to start."

When she didn't say anything, he risked a
quick look in her direction. As soon as he did,

she offered him a small smile. "Maybe at the beginning? If I have questions, I'll ask them when
you're done."

"Good idea." He closed his eyes and let his
mind drift back to the past. "From middle school
on, I was the quintessential nerd with a heavy
dose of computer geek on the side. To be honest, there wasn't a subject in school I actually
liked except technology. My grades were good
only because my folks wouldn't have it any other
way. They're both college professors, and scho-
lastic excellence was a matter of family pride.
If I didn't maintain an A-average on my own,
they hired tutors to bring me back up to speed."

He sighed as the memories played out in his
head. "The extra time that took seriously ate
into my computer time, so I made a more con-
certed effort to earn good grades on my own.
Anyway, to get to the point, somewhere along
the way I went from playing computer games to
creating my own."

His pulse picked up speed as he remembered
the heady feeling of being so good at something he really loved. "I managed to earn my
associate's degree while still in high school, because that's what all of the overachievers in my
family do. They mostly grow up to be lawyers,
doctors or academics. Once I started classes
at the university, I focused on taking as many

computer-related courses as I could, throwing in some math for grins. When I sold my first game, I realized that I needed to take some business classes, too. By going summers and taking an extraheavy load of classes, I graduated at twenty."

Juni let out a low whistle. "Impressive. Sounds like you were pretty driven."

The note of surprise in her voice had him grinning. "I take it that doesn't quite fit the image that you have of me and my current lifestyle."

She didn't bother to deny it. "No, it doesn't, but then I can't exactly claim that I know you all that well. Until now, you've never told me much about your past, not that I'm complaining. I haven't shared much about mine, either."

No, she hadn't, but he wasn't going to press her for details now. She'd tell him what really brought her to his neck of the woods when she was ready. For now, he needed to get on with his depressing tale.

"Anyway, when I graduated, my folks expected me to do something more impressive with my life than creating animated stories about epic battles. That I was making a really good living at it didn't seem to matter. If anything, I think they were a bit embarrassed about my job, but I did it anyway. When it got to the point that I had more work than I could handle, I started my own company. In fact, that's how I met my ex-fiancée. Jasmine was a junior attorney at the law firm that handled all the paperwork for setting up my business."

"So she's really successful on her own."

"Yeah, and she's beautiful, too. For someone like her to be interested in dating a geeky guy like me was a huge ego boost. My parents loved her, and Jazz fit right in with the family. Better than I ever did, that's for sure. I don't think it surprised anyone when we got engaged."

Lost in his past, he hadn't noticed Juni moving her chair closer to him. When her hand settled over his, the gentle touch jarred him back into the present. "Sorry, I didn't mean for this to turn into a pity-poor-Ryder party. To be honest, after all this time, most of this stuff feels like it actually happened to someone else."

"You don't need to go on. I think I have some idea of what you're trying to tell me."

Funny, as much as he didn't like talking about this stuff, he found himself really wanting Juni to know everything. Rather than dwell on why that was, he picked up the narrative. "Pretty much to everyone's surprise, my company took off, mostly because I lucked out and managed to hire some extremely talented people. Together, we created some innovative games that sold amazingly well, and the money kept pouring in. Between working eighty hours most weeks while trying to keep up with the social events that Jazz insisted we needed to attend, I was living on adrenaline and caffeine. I sure wasn't getting much sleep or downtime.

"As you can guess, all of that took a toll, to the point that one day I collapsed at work. I was leading another in an endless series of meetings when suddenly I hit the floor unconscious. According to the ER doctor, I was dehydrated, malnourished and had the start of a bleeding ulcer. And, oh yeah, I was on the verge of all that stress doing permanent damage to my heart. The bottom line was that if I kept up that lifestyle, I could be dead before I was forty. That was probably an exaggeration on his part, but maybe not. Regardless, it was a wake-up call for me."

He stopped to sip more water. "By that point, I'd rejected several offers from a major competitor to buy out my company. I reached out to see if they were still interested without even discussing it with my parents or Jazz. The company jumped at the chance. Heck, they didn't even quibble about the sale price I named or the terms I insisted on that ensured my employees were well taken care of. I personally netted an obscene profit from the deal. More money than any twenty-something kid should've earned for playing computer games for a living."

Juni's hand dropped away from his. He missed that small connection, but it didn't surprise him that she needed a little distance to absorb everything he'd just told her. Finally, she spoke. "That's an incredible story, Ryder. I'm impressed. So few creative people manage to make a living doing something they love."

The tightness in his chest loosened, making it easier to breathe. There was a reason he didn't often share this story. Most people focused on the money he'd made, but not Juni. She understood what it meant to succeed against all odds in any kind of artistic endeavor.

She was still talking. "Do you miss it? You know, the design work."

"Sometimes, but I don't miss the deadlines and unrelenting pressure to keep producing."

After a brief silence, Juni leaned in closer again. "I take it your parents and fiancée didn't agree with your decision to sell the company."

His laugh had nothing to do with humor. "Not in the slightest. Even worse, they didn't understand why I wouldn't jump right back into the rat race even if I didn't want to do design work again. That's when I realized Jasmine loved that lifestyle more than she loved me. I expected Mom and Dad to question my decision, but that Jasmine couldn't understand how I felt came as a huge shock. I had no choice but to end the engagement. I did it as gently as I could, but it still hurt both of us. Even so, I firmly believe it was the right thing to do."

"How does she feel about that now?"

"To be honest, I have no idea. We haven't actually talked about it since. All I can say is that she has stayed closely involved with my parents, especially my mom. I suspect they both hope eventually I'll get tired of what they see as the limited opportunities in a town the size of Dunbar and come slinking back to the fold."

"Are you even tempted to give in to family expectations?"

Considering her recent problem with her cousin, he thought she might be asking for personal reasons that had nothing to do with him. "Not really. They act like there is a much larger distance between Dunbar and Seattle than a hundred miles, but then they are really thinking about a cultural divide. Even I will admit the entertainment opportunities here in town are few and definitely more rustic."

That thought amused him. "I should really take you to Shay Barnaby's tavern sometime soon. I can ask Titus to bring Moira and Shay's wife, Carli, and we'll make a night of it. The food is basically pub grub, but good. Shay sometimes has a live band perform, but most nights folks just feed quarters into an old jukebox and play dance music."

She wrinkled her nose. "Okay, but be advised I'm not the best dancer."

"Duly noted, but we'd still have fun. That's more than I can promise about Mom's dinner party. I hesitated to unload my past problems on you, but I thought I should warn you why things can get pretty tense when I appear at one of her command performances. I'll also understand if you want to back out of that part of our deal. I'll still be your demanding and difficult client as promised."

Juni sat in silence for several seconds, probably mulling over everything he'd told her. "No, I'll be your plus-one. It wouldn't be fair of me to let you run interference with my family and not do the same for you. But while we're talking about stuff, you should know I feel bad the other people on the festival committee think I'm volunteering my services when I'm really not."

He hadn't thought about that. "That doesn't have to be a problem. I can tell them that someone offered to cover your fees."

"You mean you'll admit that you're paying me?"

No surprise that she'd figured that out. "I'd rather not. I wasn't kidding about not wanting people to start hitting me up for donations. Not even my closest friends here in town know about my past job."

That clearly puzzled her. "Why not? I can't imagine it would make a difference to Titus."

She wasn't wrong. "When I first moved here, I was understandably a little gun-shy about such things. Interestingly, neither Titus nor Shay like to talk much about their pasts. If I started confessing everything, they might feel obligated to do the same when they'd just as soon not."

She slowly nodded. "I can see that. Sometimes it's hard for people on the outside looking in to understand the effects of certain family dynamics."

With that intriguing statement, she stood up. "I'll heat up our desserts. After that, I really need to work."

He'd rather stick around to see if he could pry a few secrets out of her. Curiosity had him wanting to know more about what made Juni Voss tick, but now clearly wasn't the time. He wanted her to trust him, and that wouldn't happen if he didn't take the hint that she'd had enough of his company for one night. "Sounds good. It's getting late, and I have a few things to take care of myself. I'm scheduled to drive for the shelter bright and early in the morning and help out at the fire station in the afternoon."

That she looked relieved only proved he'd correctly judged the situation. They made quick work of eating their desserts. When Juni finished off the last bite, she leaned forward and looked around the room as if checking to make sure they were still alone.

Finally, she said, "I have one more question."

"Which is?"

"Am I right that you don't particularly want Titus and that Shay guy to know you actually own a tuxedo?"

Cute. "Pretty much."

He could only imagine the grief they'd give him if they found out, especially because he actually owned three of them as well as a nice selection of bespoke suits.

Meanwhile, Juni patted him on the shoulder. "Don't worry, big guy. As long as you keep me supplied with bacon-maple bars, your fancy wardrobe will be our secret."

"It's a deal."

Bless the woman, that small bit of teasing went a long way toward easing his stress from sharing dark memories from his past. He was still chuckling as he walked back home. Maybe the dinner party wouldn't be a complete disaster after all.

CHAPTER EIGHT

JUNI WAS A COWARD, pure and simple. There was no other excuse for how she'd been ducking calls from both her aunt and her cousin ever since Ryder had hung up on Erin. She already knew what they were going to say, so what was the point in listening to a lecture from Aunt Ruby and a lot of whining from her cousin?

But a text message put an abrupt end to Juni's procrastination. Either she had to return Aunt Ruby's call, or the woman was going to turn up on her doorstep to have a discussion in person. Bowing to the inevitable, Juni made herself a cup of chamomile tea to help calm her nerves and called her aunt.

While she waited for the call to go through, she propped her phone on its stand and sipped the tea. Ruby must have had her own phone close at hand, because she answered on the second ring. "It's about time you called, young lady. You know how I worry when we don't hear from you on a regular basis."

"Sorry, Aunt Ruby, but I was on the go almost all day yesterday. It started off with a meeting in town with my new clients. They wanted to see my sample sketches in person so they could give me direct feedback. You'll be glad to know that they really loved my work and only asked for a few changes. They're scheduled to meet again in the next few days and want to see the updated versions then. After the meeting, I had to drive into Seattle. By the time I got home and had dinner, it was too late to call."

After a brief silence, Ruby asked, "What was in Seattle?"

How much should she tell her? "I needed to buy a dress for a dinner party I plan to attend with a business associate. I didn't pack anything dressy when I moved here, and there aren't any clothing shops in town that would've had anything appropriate. The good news is that I not only found the perfect dress, but it was on sale."

She hoped that last part would please Aunt Ruby. The woman loved a good bargain. The ploy clearly didn't work. "So you went shopping while I sat here worried sick about you."

Talk about guilt trips. Juni wished she'd opted for something stronger than tea, but it was too late for that. "I'm sorry, Aunt Ruby. I didn't mean to worry you."

"Fine. I'm just not used to having you live so

far away." Then she sighed. "That's enough about that. I want to know why you let some stranger hang up on Erin. Who is he and what was he doing in your house?"

"Just as he told Erin, Ryder is my newest client. We were meeting to discuss the work a local group has hired me to do. After we came to an agreement, I did the preliminary sketches and needed their feedback. That's why I met with him and his associates yesterday morning."

"Well, I think it was pretty rude of him."

"You know how intense and focused these business types can be, Aunt Ruby. And in his defense, Erin did call in the middle of my workday. The job I'm doing for him is on a short time line, so we needed to get right to work on it."

"Family should always come first."

Oh, brother.

"Yes, family is important, Aunt Ruby, but there was nothing about Erin's call that couldn't have waited until evening or even the weekend. She wouldn't have interrupted Uncle Colby or even Phillip while they were at work to talk about an event that is months away."

Ruby started to protest but stopped herself. No doubt she'd been about to point out that Juni worked from home. It had taken a lot of effort on Juni's part to convince everyone in the family that even though she worked from home that her job was real. In fact, their attitudes had been a major factor in her decision to make the move to Dunbar in the first place.

Her aunt finally continued. "I will remind Erin that we all promised that we'd quit barging in when you were working. Having said that, though, I think it's understandable that she was excited about getting engaged and wanted to share the news with you as soon as possible."

"I understand that, Aunt Ruby, and I am happy for both her and Phillip."

Sort of, anyway. No one ever seemed to remember that Juni had dated him first. They'd been seeing each other for over two months when Phillip had accepted Juni's invitation to join her family for Thanksgiving dinner. Looking back, that had turned out to be a major miscalculation on her part—or maybe not. Evidently some things were just meant to be. Phillip had apologized long and hard as soon as he realized he wanted to date Juni's cousin instead of her.

At least he'd had the courage to be honest with her. It would've been far worse for everyone involved if he'd felt obligated to keep dating Juni while having strong feelings for Erin. After Phillip broke the bad news, Erin had also come to Juni to ask her permission to date him. She'd made it clear that family came first. If

Juni wasn't comfortable with the situation, Erin would break it off with him immediately.

It had hurt to lose her first real boyfriend to someone else, but even Juni could see how Phillip and her cousin had simply clicked. That was three years ago, and the couple had been inseparable ever since. It had never been a matter of *if* Erin and Phillip would get engaged but *when*.

Meanwhile, Aunt Ruby finally got around to the real reason behind her desire to talk to Juni. "So I know that Erin asked you to help her organize the wedding. I realize that might not be easy for you, considering everything, but it would mean a lot to her."

Okay, here came the tough part. Juni had to take a stand and then stick to her guns. "I'm sorry, Aunt Ruby, but that's not going to happen. Like I told Erin, I'm thrilled to be her maid of honor. That means a lot to me. It will also be fun to shop for the perfect bridesmaids' dresses."

She let that much sink in before continuing. "However, I can't organize everything from this distance, and I have contractual obligations to remain in this area that I can't ignore. I also honestly believe it would be smarter to hire a professional who has all the right connections to ensure that Erin's wedding is the absolute best it can be. Even if I still lived there, I wouldn't know who the best people were for the job.

One poor choice and who knows what could go wrong. I don't want to be responsible for ruining her special day."

Juni crossed her fingers that would convince her aunt that Erin should look elsewhere for someone to direct the extravaganza she was bound to want for her big day. When her aunt didn't immediately respond, Juni suspected she hadn't yet won the battle. Ruby's next comment proved her right.

"But you've always been the organized, take-charge one in the family, Juni. There's no reason you wouldn't be able to handle this."

Sure there was, starting with the simple fact she didn't want to. Knowing that might sound selfish, she settled for pointing out the logistics of the situation. "Except I don't live in Crestville anymore, Aunt Ruby. My work is here."

"Don't you do most of your work online?"

"Not this time. Both of my clients prefer to deal in person, so I have to stay here in Dunbar for the foreseeable future. I'm sorry, but I have deadlines to meet. If I don't do the work, I don't get paid. That's how it is for people who are self-employed."

"I suppose it is." Her aunt shook her head and finally surrendered, at least for the moment. "I'll talk to Erin. She'll be really disappointed, but I guess it can't be helped."

Juni knew she shouldn't feel guilty, but it was hard not to. She never liked to disappoint her aunt. Ruby and her husband had stepped up big-time when she'd needed them the most. "I promise I'm not doing this lightly. These two contracts really are important to me. If the author and publisher are happy with my artwork, it could lead to other jobs."

Finally, Ruby smiled just a little. "They'll love your drawings. We all know how talented you are."

That was nice to hear. "Thanks for saying that, Aunt Ruby. And I promise I won't go so long between phone calls."

"Good. You know how I worry."

Yeah, she did. To lighten the conversation, Juni redirected it. "How is the new quilt for the church auction coming along? Did you make a final decision on the colors?"

The ploy worked. Ruby immediately held up two squares from her last project so Juni could see them. "I went with the peach and cream for one square and soft blues and greens for the other one. I think they'll look great together. I really like the pattern, too. It's a variation on a traditional design."

From there, they moved on to talk about the new pastor at the church and how well she was doing. After that, they chatted about more family stuff. Evidently, Uncle Colby's physical had gone well, except he still needed to exercise more. No surprise there. The doctor told him the same thing every year.

Aunt Ruby finished by telling her about the latest escapades in Uncle Colby's ongoing war against the varmints that kept chowing down on his vegetable garden. The plants were getting eaten almost as soon as they broke through the soil. It was an annual problem, and he'd tried all kinds of things to protect his precious vegetables.

"I hope his latest efforts work better than what he tried last year."

"Honey, we all do. I love that man dearly, but it does get tiresome listening to his constant complaints at dinnertime about marauding deer and ravenous bunnies."

Juni was about to ask another question when she heard a knock at the door. "Aunt Ruby, I'd better go. Someone is at the door."

Ruby immediately leaned closer to the phone, her face filling the screen. "Make sure you check to see who is out there before you open the door, Juni. Call the police if you don't recognize them, and call me back regardless. I want to know that you're okay."

Enough was enough. "I promise I'll text you."

Then she disconnected the call before her aunt

could do more than sputter. Bless the woman, her heart was in the right place, but at some point she needed to accept that Juni was an adult who could look after herself.

Even so, she did peek out the window. She half expected to see Ryder standing on her porch since he was the only visitor she'd had to date. To her surprise, though, it was Shelby Peters. Juni quickly unlocked the door. "Hi, Shelby. Come on in."

"I probably should've called first, but Ryder thought it would be all right if I stopped by as long as I came armed with bacon-maple bars."

When she held out a bag from Bea's bakery, it was hard not to drool. "I wish I could tell you he was wrong, but Bea's pastries buy a whole lot of forgiveness."

That had Shelby laughing. "So true. Her apple fritters are my personal weakness, a fact that my husband exploits all too often."

Juni led the short distance to her small living room area. "Have a seat, and I'll fix us something hot to drink. Do you want tea, coffee or hot chocolate?"

"Coffee, if it's not too much trouble."

"No trouble at all. I usually make a fresh pot about this time of day. I often work pretty late into the evening and an extra dose of caffeine gives me a late morning boost of energy."

Shelby made herself comfortable as she looked around the cabin with obvious curiosity. "You know, I've driven by these A-frames all my life, but this is the first time I've ever been inside one. The previous owner let them get pretty run-down, but someone else bought them a while back and really fixed them up. I don't think I've ever heard the identity of the new owner, but I definitely like what they've done with the place. I have to admit I've been curious about who it might be."

"I wish I could help you with that, but I've only dealt with the property manager. The name on the lease was an LLC, so it only has the company name on it."

"Oh, well. Maybe someday I'll solve the mystery."

Juni put the coffee on to brew and then brought plates and napkins into the living room and set them on the small coffee table in front of the sofa. After sitting down on the opposite end of the couch from Shelby, she asked, "So what brings you to my doorstep today?"

"I've actually been meaning to stop by ever since I first met you at the post office. You know, to welcome you to Dunbar. But between my jobs and being on the festival committee, more time slipped by than I had realized. We don't get a lot of newcomers to Dunbar, and the ones we do get tend to be retirees. It was nice to see someone closer to my own age move in. We can always use some fresh blood in town."

As she spoke, Shelby put a maple bar on each plate and set one in front of Juni. It was tempting to dive right into eating the pastry, but it would probably be more polite to wait until she could serve her guest some coffee. "I'm actually glad my cabin is out here in the woods. If I lived closer to that bakery, I'd be in there every day. That would have an adverse effect on my waistline for sure."

"It's a common problem." Shelby laughed and shook her head. "It can cause other problems as well. My husband probably wouldn't appreciate me telling you this, but when he first moved to town he got in the habit of walking down to Bea's at exactly the same time every morning for coffee and one of her pastries. There aren't all that many eligible men in the area, especially one as good-looking as Cade. That's why all of the single ladies in town—and a fair number of the married ones—would stop everything to watch him stroll down the street. There's just something about a man in a uniform."

She grinned as she fanned her face with her hand. "To tell the truth, I still stand at the window to watch him go by. Back before we started dating, I thought it was funny seeing him pretend he didn't notice all the attention he was getting. It still is, in fact, although I have more mixed feelings about it. I trust Cade implicitly, but some of those women can be pretty determined. Early on, they even started bringing him hot meals every day. The poor guy had to resume cooking for himself after he and I started dating and the casserole brigade suspended operations."

Okay, that was pretty funny, but then Juni figured every small town probably had its quirks. Crestville, where her family lived, certainly did.

Shelby's smile turned a bit sly. "You should know that Ryder gets his own fair share of the ogling these days. I'm guessing it's those broad shoulders and gorgeous blue eyes."

Was she implying Juni should be jealous? It wasn't as if she and Ryder were dating or anything.

"I hadn't really noticed."

Her guest snorted at that. Besides, Shelby wasn't wrong about Ryder being attractive, especially his eyes and smile. "Okay, maybe I noticed, but we're just neighbors."

Shelby arched an eyebrow and studied Juni for several seconds. "You might have started out that way, but the two of you seem to spend a lot of time together. From what I've heard, he's taken you to breakfast at the café and introduced you to his friends, brought you treats from Bea's bakery and picked up barbecue for your dinner last night."

Boy, gossip spread quickly in Dunbar. Still trying to downplay her interactions with Ryder, she said, "That makes it sound more serious than it is. The breakfast was a thank-you for me baby-sitting two kittens for him when he got called into the fire station unexpectedly. The pastries were a bribe to get me to do the artwork for the festival committee. And the barbecue..."

She stopped there. He'd offered to buy her dinner because he knew she was losing more of her workday going shopping for that dress. While he hadn't exactly asked her to keep their upcoming dinner date at his parents' house to herself, she didn't figure he really wanted people to know about it.

"And the barbecue?" Shelby prodded.

"He was just being nice."

That wasn't exactly a lie even if it wasn't the full truth. It was a relief when Shelby let the subject drop. "I probably shouldn't tease you about Ryder. I know I didn't much appreciate people poking their noses into my business when Cade and I were going through a rough patch, especially when he tossed me in jail."

Juni almost choked on a bite of her maple bar. "He what?"

Shelby shrugged her shoulders. "That's a long

story. We sort of backed each other into a corner and things got out of hand. It all worked out eventually, though. That's all that matters."

After checking the time, she grimaced. "Whoops. I'm due back at work soon, so I had better get to the real reason I stopped by today."

She leaned down to pull a trade paperback out of her purse and handed it to Juni. "This is for you. A group of women here in town have a book club that meets monthly. That's the current selection we're reading, and the next meeting is in three weeks. I thought since you're living here now, you might like to come and see what you think. We have pretty lively discussions and great refreshments."

Juni took the time to read the cover copy on the book, which had been written by a bestselling fantasy author. She'd actually been meaning to read it, but she hadn't gotten around to getting a library card since the move. It was definitely tempting to accept Shelby's invitation, but she wanted to be up front about her status here in Dunbar. "I'm only here because a client requested that I move to this area while I'm doing the artwork for her book. Even though we mostly interact by phone or email, she preferred that I be close enough that we could meet in person occasionally. Since it was such a great opportunity, I agreed. But that's why I only have a six-month lease on this cabin. I'd love to give the book club a try as long as you understand that I will likely be gone in a few months."

"I have no problem with that, and I'm sure the other members won't care." Her smile turned sly. "Besides, maybe you'll decide to stay once you make more friends in town. Just look how many people you've met in the short time you've been here."

That was true, although that was mostly because of Ryder. "I'll start reading tonight."

"Since you're getting a late start, don't worry if you don't completely finish it. That happens to all of us at one time or another. We still come to the meetings anyway."

With that, Shelby stood up. "I'd better be going. I hope you enjoy the book. I have your email address from the paperwork you gave us at the planning meeting, and I'll send you the info on the meeting and directions to my house."

"Thanks again for the maple bar and the invitation."

After closing the door, Juni leaned against it and considered what had just happened. Even though she'd primarily moved to Dunbar for her job, she'd also jumped at the chance to see what it would be like to live completely on her own for the first time. Even when she went away to college, the school had been only a short drive from her hometown. She did feel guilty about worrying her family, but she hoped the separation would convince them she was an adult and more than capable of taking care of herself.

She hadn't expected to get drawn into the community and was surprised how pleased she was that everyone had been so welcoming. She did a quick head count of the locals she'd met so far, starting with Shelby, Carli and Moira, all of whom were around her age. The mayor and Bea were both a lot older, but they'd been really nice to her as well. Titus and Shay had also gone out of their way to make her feel welcome.

And finally, there was Ryder with those broad shoulders and blue eyes Shelby mentioned. She wasn't lying when she'd said that they were just neighbors. What she hadn't admitted even to herself up until that moment was that she wouldn't mind being so much more than that.

Rather than get all tangled up in the implications of what that might entail, she marched herself back over to the computer and concentrated on how best to illustrate what Sabrina's bears were up to now.

CHAPTER NINE

RYDER HAD A serious problem, one he wasn't sure how to handle. He had just left a meeting at the shelter about the booth they planned to have at the festival in Dunbar. While they had a core group of reliable volunteers, there were never enough people to staff everything on the schedule. As it turned out, there was another event the same day as the one in Dunbar. It was a much bigger festival that could potentially bring in more donations as well as additional opportunities to find homes for more dogs and cats.

No one had wanted to make the call to back out of either festival, but it was unclear how they could do both. Another complication was that Ryder was already scheduled to drive the fire truck in the parade, which would take at least an hour. In the end, he had offered to see if he could find someone from outside their organization to cover the booth in Dunbar for him during that time. He had a particular person in mind, but he wasn't sure how Juni would react if he tried to volunteer her services again.

All he could do was ask her, which was why he was hovering just inside the tree line on her side of the woods as he tried to work up the courage to go knock on her door. And that had him feeling like a complete fool. Seriously, the worst thing that could happen was that she might simply say no. If so, he would accept her decision and then try to find someone else who might be able to help. Shay's wife was a possibility, but there was a good chance that Carli already had other commitments that day. If she wasn't available, he'd have to see if maybe Shay could drive the truck for him.

While he continued to waffle, his cell phone buzzed. Seeing his mother's name on the screen didn't improve his mood. "Hi, Mom. What's up?"

"I'm calling about the message you left for me about the dinner party. I apologize for the delay in getting back to you. My friends and I went out of town for one of our spa getaways. You might remember that one of the rules when we go is that we have to shut off our phones for the duration."

He knew the spa visit was something she and several of her sorority sisters from college did a couple of times a year. "I hope you had fun."

"We did, but that's not why I called. It's the fact that you've decided to bring a plus-one to the dinner party without telling me when I first invited you to come."

There was no mistaking the note of frustration in her voice. Knowing it probably wouldn't work, he tried to placate her. "I thought you'd want advance notice, Mom. For sure, I know you wouldn't have appreciated me showing up with an extra guest without giving you fair warning."

The ensuing silence wasn't a surprise. He mentally counted off the seconds as he waited for her to continue. It didn't take long.

"If I were serving a buffet or just hors d'oeuvres, an extra guest wouldn't be a problem. However, we're doing a sit-down dinner this time. I didn't know you were seeing someone new, so I assumed you'd be coming alone. You certainly didn't mention this person the last time you stopped by the house."

There was a reason for that. He hadn't yet met Juni when he had dropped by to visit his folks. Not that he was going to tell his mother that. "We've only recently started dating, but I thought you'd like to meet her."

"Well, I still wish you'd asked before inviting her. You know that I spend a lot of time on my guest list to make sure the people I invite are compatible and, well, that the number of men and women is even."

"So let me guess, you thought it would be all right to pair me with Jasmine again even though I've told you not to do that anymore."

Sounding more than a little defensive, his mother pushed back. "Your father and I consider her a friend of the family. She's not seeing anyone right now, and as far as we knew, neither were you. It only made sense to seat the two of you together. I also planned to ask you to bring her to the party since parking is rather limited in our area."

"Just so you know, I would have refused. That's what Uber is for." Ryder leaned against a handy tree to marshal his thoughts about what to say next. "Before I hang up, I have a couple of things I want to say. First, you should've asked me if I would prefer to choose my own date for your party. Second, if you insist on inviting my ex-fiancée, make sure she brings a date of her own. I'm sure she could find someone who'd love to spend some time with your important friends. Finally, in the future, if her name is on the guest list, leave mine off."

When she started to sputter in protest, he cut in. "Mom, I know you think you're doing the right thing by trying to get the two of us back together, but I'm not interested. I've moved on, and Jazz wouldn't be happy with the life I'm living now."

They both knew that was true. "I should've made it clearer before now how I felt. If you still want me to attend the party, fine. I'll come, but I will be bringing Juni. Leave it up to Jasmine if she still wants to attend. If she does, then put another leaf in the table and tell her to bring a date. Problem solved."

No one could pack more disappointment in a sigh than his mother, but at least she knew when to surrender. "Fine. Please remember that your father and I simply want you to be successful and happy."

"That's just it, Mom. I am."

Then he hung up before she could say anything else.

JUNI WATCHED RYDER from the window in the loft of the cabin. If he was aware of her scrutiny, he gave no indication of it. She'd only gone upstairs to retrieve the book she'd left on the bedside table last night. Her intention had been to read it while she ate a bowl of her homemade tomato soup for lunch. But before she headed back down the steps, she happened to spot her neighbor lurking beside one of the big cedars that surrounded her cabin.

She thought maybe he was headed her way,

but then he stopped to answer his phone. Even from a distance it was easy to tell that the call wasn't going well. He kept running his free hand through his hair and eventually he leaned back into the tree as if that was all that was keeping him upright. She'd recently had her own experience with phone calls like that. The one with Aunt Ruby had definitely had some ups and downs, but it was nothing compared to Erin's latest call.

The bottom line was that some people couldn't take no for an answer. Evidently Erin had called the top-rated wedding consultant in her area, only to find the woman was already booked for the weekend of the wedding. Erin had made it clear that if she couldn't have the best, then she wanted Juni. Where was the logic in that? Nothing had changed since their last call. Juni still had work to do in Dunbar and wasn't leaving town until her lease ran out, if then.

Finally, she'd firmly, and mostly politely, told Erin to call more coordinators. Someone was bound to be available. Crossing her fingers that that was true, she'd hung up and turned off the phone again. And unless she was mistaken, Ryder had just done that same thing. In fact, he raised his arm as if preparing to throw his phone as far as he could send it. She breathed a sigh of relief when he jerked his hand back down and stuffed the phone in his pocket.

He took a couple of steps toward her cabin, but then abruptly turned around as if heading home. That inexplicably spurred her into motion, sending her charging down the steps and out the front door. As soon as she reached the porch, she yelled his name. When he didn't respond, she took off in the direction of his cabin, stopping to call his name again. This time he stepped back into sight.

"You bellowed?"

Noting Ryder's smile didn't quite reach his eyes, Juni was sure he wouldn't appreciate any questions about whatever had just happened between him and the person on the other end of that call. Desperate for an excuse, she could only manage to come up with one that was pathetic at best. It was worth a try, though. "Yeah, I happened to see you from the upstairs window. I made a pot of tomato soup this morning. It's a new recipe, and I'd like to get your opinion. Also, for what it's worth, I make a mean grilled cheese sandwich, too. What do you say?"

"Look, I'm not sure that's a good idea." He retreated a step back in the direction of his house. "It's not that I don't appreciate the invitation, but I'm not in the best of moods. I wouldn't be good company."

She should probably accept his refusal and walk away, but he looked like he needed a friend more than solitude right now. She reached out to tug on the sleeve of his flannel shirt. "I don't care about your mood. All I want is your opinion on the soup. You don't have to be cheery to do that."

It was a relief when he relaxed enough to let her lead him toward her place. "What's so special about this soup?"

"It has different spices in it than any other version I've tried before. I'd like to know what someone with a discerning palate thinks in case I decide to serve it to company sometime."

"Two questions. Am I not considered company? And will it hurt your feelings if I don't like it?"

By that point, the corners of his mouth had quirked up in a hint of a more genuine smile. "No, you're not company. I already said you were a discerning palate. Also, if I didn't want your honest opinion, I wouldn't have hunted you down and dragged you back home with me."

"Fair enough."

When they walked into her cabin, she pointed him toward her desk. "While I prepare the food, you can look at the updated versions of the artwork for the festival committee. I won't be long."

As she put the sandwiches together, she kept

a wary eye on Ryder while he studied her drawings. She didn't really care if he liked her soup, but she very much cared about his opinion on her artwork. He thumbed through the five drawings quickly and then did it again, this time pausing to take a closer look at each one. Finally, he spread them out on her desktop and sat down in her chair as he continued to study them.

Her stomach was tied up in knots by the time he finally looked in her direction. "Well?"

He glanced at them again. "I can't decide which one is the best. They're all that good."

She let out her breath in one big whoosh. "Thank goodness. For a minute there, I thought you were trying to think of a tactful way to tell me you were disappointed in how they turned out."

He stood up and headed her way. When he got there, he tugged the butter knife out of Juni's hand and set it on the counter. Then he gently turned her to face him and pulled her in close for a hug. "I don't know how you could ever doubt your amazing talent when everything I've seen of your work has been so impressive."

"Thank you, but I think all artistic people have moments of self-doubt." As she spoke, she let herself relax into his gentle hold and gave him a quick squeeze. "It's nice to be reminded that others see value in my work."

"I worked with a lot of graphic artists in my prior life. Some of the best in the business." He stepped back just far enough to put his palm under her chin to tilt her face up toward his. "I'd put your work up against theirs anytime."

When she started to speak, he placed a single fingertip across her lips. "And, no, I'm not just saying that."

Her cheeks flushed hot. How had he guessed that was exactly what she was thinking? Ryder answered her silent question. "Like you said, all creative people have moments of doubt. Even when I was at my most successful, I kept wondering if everything I had accomplished had been a fluke, the kind of once-in-a-lifetime thing that would never happen again. Looking back, I wish I had been smart enough to relax and enjoy the creative process instead of defining my success by the size of my bank account."

Then he leaned in closer, enough so she could feel his breath against her skin. His gaze intensified as he whispered, "You might want to learn from my mistakes. Enjoy the ride and don't let your insecurities interfere with the process."

He continued to study her, leaving her wondering what else he was thinking right now. "Ryder?"

He smiled just a little. "You are amazingly

talented, Juni, not to mention you have the kind of beauty that makes me want to…"

When he didn't continue, she asked, "To what?"

Ryder cupped the side of her face with his hand, his mouth curved up in a soft smile. "I want to kiss you. What do you say?"

Right then she couldn't think of a single thing she wanted more. She whispered, "I want that, too."

Her breath caught in her chest at what happened next. Ryder's lips slowly brushed across hers—once, twice—and then settled in place for a real kiss. She rose up on her toes to slide her hands around his neck as she lost herself in the wonder of it all.

It was hard to tell which of them broke it off, but at least Ryder didn't immediately release his hold on her. That might have hurt her feelings. Instead, he rested his forehead against hers for several seconds before finally backing away. She let her hands drop back down to her sides as she also retreated a step.

"I, um, better go fix that soup and sandwich I promised you."

Without waiting for him to respond, she got busy at the counter. And if her heart was racing and her hands a bit shaky, well, she kept that tidbit of information to herself.

CHAPTER TEN

RYDER RETURNED TO Juni's desk to study the artwork again. It was more of an excuse to put some
space between them than any real need to remind himself how talented she was. He risked a
glance in her direction to see how she was han-
dling what had just happened, but it was hard
to tell. Right now she was laser-focused on the
skillet in front of her as if cooking two grilled
cheese sandwiches was the most important thing
in the whole universe.

As if sensing his scrutiny, she looked up long
enough to frown at him before reaching for a
spatula to flip the sandwiches. When she almost
missed the skillet with one of them, he turned
away before she could see him grinning. Good
to know that he wasn't the only one who'd been
rattled by that kiss. His reaction—or overreac-
tion, if he was going to be honest—was as much
of a surprise as the fact he wanted to test those
waters again and soon.

He hadn't lied when he'd told Juni he hadn't

been involved with anyone since he and Jasmine had gone their separate ways. That was due in part to the lack of opportunity in a town the size of Dunbar. He also wanted to figure out where this new life of his was headed before he tried sharing it with anyone else. He'd already hurt one woman he'd cared about and had no desire to do that again.

But somewhere along the line, Juni had managed to slip past the walls he'd erected around his personal space. He wasn't sure how that had happened, but it was time to take a definite step back to think about the possible consequences. Getting emotionally involved with her hadn't been part of the deal. Besides, as far as he knew, she still intended to move back to her hometown when she finished her current contract with that author. He liked Juni a lot, but he wasn't looking to uproot his life again when he was finally getting it back on track.

The bottom line was that a repeat performance of what had just happened wouldn't be fair to Juni or him. It would only complicate their original agreement, and he didn't want to risk either one of them getting hurt in the process.

"Lunch is ready. We'll eat in here."

Ryder quickly schooled his expression into something approaching neutral. "I'm looking forward to tasting the soup and also finding out what makes your grilled cheese sandwiches so special. Titus will want to know if he has unexpected competition from a new cook in town."

She rolled her eyes as she set a mug full of soup and a small plate that held his sandwich in front of him. "The bread is homemade, and I use my own special pimiento cheese blend. It has sharp cheddar for flavor and Monterey Jack for creaminess."

One bite had him sold on the sandwich. "This is delicious. I've never tasted one with that exact flavor profile before."

Juni settled into the chair across from him but made no move to start eating as she waited for him to try the soup. Again, it surprised him. There was a slight hint of warm spice with the barest touch of heat. So good.

"Don't worry. I won't be telling Titus anything. It would destroy him to find out that I prefer your soup to his." He pointed at her with his spoon. "You wouldn't want to be responsible for making the toughest guy in town cry, would you?"

That had her laughing. "He might look tough, but I've said before that I suspect he's a real marshmallow inside."

That assessment of Titus almost caused Ryder to snort soup out of his nose. "Seriously? Have you ever really looked at him? No one messes with Titus. Heck, when he first moved to town, rumor had it that he'd learned everything he knows about cooking while working in a prison kitchen."

Juni's eyes widened in shock. "Seriously? He's an ex-con?"

Okay, now Ryder was treading on thin ice. He knew the rumor wasn't true, but Titus didn't exactly share a lot of details about his past even with his closest friends. "No, he's not. I already told you he went to culinary school before coming here. The point is that most people didn't hesitate to believe that story. I know for a fact he faced off against three rowdies who'd dared to threaten Moira, and they all immediately backed down. Then there's Shay. He's built like a tank and served for years with recon marines, some of the toughest guys around, and even he says he'd hesitate to take on Titus."

She cracked up laughing and gave up all pretense of trying to eat. "You're spinning tales trying to see how gullible I am. That's not what they're like at all. I've seen how Titus treats Moira, not to mention that enormous dog of his. Shay's a family man who adores both his wife and the boy they've adopted."

"You keep telling yourself that if it makes you feel better." He picked up the other half of his sandwich. Before taking a bite, he had one more thing to say on the subject. "But if you stick around Dunbar long enough, you'll eventually see the other side of their personalities. Both men are protectors to the bone, and they won't stand for anyone threatening people they care about."

Juni finally started eating her lunch. From the way she kept glancing in his direction between bites, it was clear that she had something she wanted to say but wasn't sure if she should. He'd give her all the time she needed to make up her mind. If she still hadn't spoken up by the time he was ready to leave, he'd find some way to pry it out of her.

As it turned out, he didn't have to. When she pushed her mug and plate to the side, Juni leaned forward to put her elbows on the table and threaded her fingers together. "So, I have a confession to make."

"Which is?"

"I didn't invite you over to taste my soup. That was only an excuse to stop you from going back home. Correct me if I'm wrong, but I think you were coming to see me for some reason when you got a phone call that upset you."

It was amazing how well she could read him. Leaning back in his chair, he considered how much to tell her. "My mother called. She finally got around to responding to the message I left on her voicemail telling her that I was bringing you to the dinner party as my date."

"Let me guess. She wasn't happy."

"Not particularly, but please don't take it personally. Evidently having an extra person will mess up her seating chart."

"There's more, isn't there?"

"Yeah, there is. The real problem is she planned to ask me to bring Jasmine to the party and take her back home afterward. Something about the available parking being pretty limited. In reality, that would be Mom's way of manufacturing another opportunity for me to suddenly realize that I made a huge mistake in breaking off the engagement."

Juni nodded as if his explanation didn't surprise her. "And do you want that opportunity?"

On some level he found that question a bit insulting. Did she really think he was the kind of guy who would kiss one woman while wanting to go back to dating someone else?

"I do not and have made that clear on numerous occasions. I've also asked Mom to leave me off the guest list if Jazz is invited."

Too restless to remain seated, he carried his dishes over to the sink and came back for Juni's. Considering how volatile his mood was right now, he really should've refused Juni's invitation to lunch. Before he could apologize for snapping at her, she stood next to him and leaned against the kitchen counter while he rinsed the dishes and put them in the dishwasher.

Her smile was sympathetic. "I figured it was something like that. I recognized that particular look on your face even from a distance."

He wiped his hands on the dish towel and carefully hung it back up to dry. "What look is that?"

"The one I see in the mirror when I have to remind myself yet again that I really do love my family. You know, even when they're driving me crazy."

Yeah, they did have that in common. "So who called you this time?"

She took his hand and led him back to the couch in the living room. "Both my aunt and my cousin. Not at the same time, but with pretty much the same message."

"Let me guess. Your cousin still wants you to manage her wedding. Your aunt is caught in between, but mostly wishes you weren't living so far away."

"Got it right on the first try."

When he sat on the couch, she surprised him by sitting down right beside him rather than positioning herself on the other end. Figuring they could each use a little comfort, he wrapped his arm around her shoulders and tugged her in closer to his side.

Since Juni was still in Dunbar and not packing her suitcase, he could probably guess the answer to his next question. "What did you tell them?"

"The same thing I told them before. I need to be where I am because of work, and that Erin should hire a professional."

"Think they've given up?"

She glanced up at him. "Has your mother?"

"Point taken."

"Moving on. Why were you headed my way in the first place?"

He winced. "Well, about that… You see, I'm looking for someone who might be willing to work at the animal shelter's booth for a couple of hours or so at the festival. The problem is that we've been invited to host another adoption event on the same day. It would provide our group with some much needed exposure."

"And staffing both in one day is stretching your resources to the max."

"Exactly. We don't have all that many volunteers to begin with, and most will be needed to ferry around the animals and then supervise when people are checking them out. We try to do that away from the main crush of the crowd to keep from stressing out the cats and dogs."

"And where will you be during the time

this unknown someone would be covering the booth?"

At least she was taking the time to ask questions instead of immediately refusing to even consider helping him out. "I was asked to drive the town's new fire truck in the parade. Some of the rest of our crew are going to have their kids riding along on the back of the truck to throw candy to the crowd. As soon as the parade is over, I'll come right back to the booth for the rest of the afternoon."

That he was double-booked didn't seem to surprise her. "The town I'm from is a little bigger than Dunbar, but I know people there have to wear multiple hats on some occasions. What would you need me to do at the booth?"

"You'll do it?"

"Why not? I would need some coaching about the shelter and everything they do, but that should be easy enough. Besides, I can always show up early enough to watch you in action."

"That would be great, Juni. I'll owe you another meal at Titus's."

"It's a deal. Two hours of my time in exchange for one of his meals is more than fair."

Now that they had that settled, another idea popped into his head. "Speaking of meals, I've mentioned before that you might like to check out Shay's place. As it turns out, I'm not sched-

uled at the fire station or the shelter this weekend. Would you be interested if I can set up
something for this Friday or Saturday evening?
I can check in with Titus, Max and Cade Peters
to see which would be the better night, and then
let Shay know to expect a crowd for dinner. I'm
sure his wife, Carli, will join us, too."

Rather than jumping at the chance, Juni
looked a bit worried. "That sounds like fun, but
aren't you concerned people might get the idea
that we're dating for real?"

Good point. "I'll make sure they all know that
I'm just showing you the sights here in Dunbar."

That had her laughing. "I drove past the tavern the other day. I'm not sure that it would be
classified as a tourist attraction by anyone's stan-
dards."

She wasn't wrong. "Actually Shay has done a
lot to upgrade the interior of the place. He's gone
so far as to add a pretty extensive wine list and
improve the menu. The good news is that you
won't need another new dress for the big night."

Juni swiped the back of her hand across her
forehead. "Whew! Thank goodness for that. I'm
not ready to face another massive dress hunt.
Hanging out with your friends does sound like
fun. Just let me know which night and what time
I should be ready."

"I will."

Feeling far better than when he'd first arrived, he decided it was time to go home and let her get back to work. "Send me the files on the artwork when you get a chance. I can't wait to show them to the others."

"I just need to switch out the colors on a couple to offer the committee some choices. Once they reach a final decision, I'll get it all polished up. Max also needs to let me know the dimensions he wants for the various places he plans to advertise. I'll have to tweak things a bit to make them look right in different sizes."

That all made sense. "I'll make sure he gets the information to you as soon as he can."

He gave her shoulder a quick squeeze. "Thanks for dragging me out of my funk, Juni. Next time you get one of those calls, feel free to come running. I can't promise to top your grilled cheese sandwiches or the soup, but I would be glad to pick up one of Titus's pies or some of Bea's pastries for purely medicinal purposes."

She got up and held out her hand to tug him up off the sofa. "That's mighty generous of you. You should know that I might stoop to faking a call or two for one of those bacon-maple bars."

"I stand forewarned."

He led the way toward the door. If he'd been smarter, he would have kept going instead of stopping to thank her one more time. Because he hadn't actually left, they ended up standing in the doorway, feeling awkward.

Was he tempted to kiss her again? Yes.

But should he? That was the real question. Before he could come up with the answer, she took the matter into her own hands. Grabbing a handful of his shirt, she tugged him forward and down closer to her height. Then, with a wicked grin, she gave him a quick kiss on the lips and immediately released her hold on him.

"Thank you?" was all he could think to say.

"Well, you were making a big deal out of nothing, Ryder. What happened earlier was a simple kiss. Nothing more."

Then she made shooing motions with her hands. "Now go. I have work to do."

He did as she ordered even though he didn't believe her assessment of the situation. That last kiss might have been a simple gesture between two friends. The earlier one, though, was something else altogether. And when he figured out exactly what that was, he'd be revisiting the subject. For now, he had calls to make. He'd start with the shelter to tell them he'd found someone to help with the booth on the day of the festival. Next, he'd make sure Max knew to touch base with Juni.

Finally, he'd stop by to see Titus and start the ball rolling for a night of fun at Shay's tavern.

Images of holding Juni in his arms out on the dance floor had him wishing the weekend wasn't still two days away. His conscience kicked in long enough to remind him that to maintain the appearance that they were really just friends, he should probably limit the number of slow dances to one or maybe two.

But even so, as soon as he stepped inside his cabin, he found himself saying, "Alexa, make a note. Remind me to get plenty of quarters for the jukebox."

CHAPTER ELEVEN

JUNI STRUGGLED NOT to fidget as Ryder maneuvered his rattletrap van into the crowded parking lot at the tavern. He had to circle through the aisles twice before finally finding a spot at the farthest edge of the lot. She really shouldn't have been surprised that the place would be packed on a Saturday night considering the nightlife opportunities in Dunbar were rather limited.

"You doing okay over there?"

She had been watching the flow of people walking toward the entrance where there was a neon sign that simply said Barnaby's. Turning to face Ryder, she bit her lip and pondered if she needed to make a small confession. Deciding it was probably a good idea, she pointed toward the tavern. "I should probably tell you right now that I've never set foot in a place like this."

Judging by the puzzled look he gave her, that bit of information must have come as a bit of a shock to him. "Never? Not even when you were in college?"

"Nope."

She turned her attention back to their destination. "To be honest, I didn't have much of a social life when I was in school. You're not the only one who carried an extra heavy class load in order to graduate earlier than normal. Add in working two jobs to pay my bills, and I didn't have much time for partying."

He studied her for several seconds before speaking again. "If you'd rather not do this, I could develop a quick headache. No one would question it. They all know how delicate I am."

Okay, that was cute. "No, I wouldn't want to disappoint your friends, especially when you worked so hard to make this happen. Besides, I've actually been looking forward to this evening. I just thought you should know that I might need you to coach me on the proper etiquette."

He cracked up laughing. "I'm not sure there is such a thing as etiquette at Barnaby's. As long as people treat Shay's staff with respect and don't start any fights, it's pretty much anything goes. Later in the evening, he might have to confiscate a few sets of keys from people who shouldn't be driving after a night of heavy drinking. Some folks take offense at that, but not many are foolish enough to argue with Shay. Considering the chief of police and another one of his officers will be in attendance tonight, things should stay pretty calm."

He waited a beat and then added, "But just in case, if I tell you to dive under the table, do it without hesitation. You can ask questions after things settle back down. Understood?"

Was he kidding? Somehow, she didn't think so. Snapping off a salute, she said, "Understood, sir!"

Her response had him smiling, but then he turned serious. "I've never been here when things got out of control, but I promise I will keep you safe. Okay?"

When she nodded, he got out and came around to open the van door for her. They wound their way through the parked cars to reach the entrance to the bar. The closer they got, the more she could feel the heavy throb from the music playing inside. Ryder leaned in close enough for her to hear him. "You ready for this?"

Maybe not, but that wasn't going to stop her. "Yeah, I am."

The gentle touch of Ryder's hand on her lower back as he guided her inside went a long way toward calming her nerves. She wasn't sure why she was so jittery. After all, she knew most of the people they were supposed to be hanging out with for the evening. Police Chief Cade Peters and the owner of a local bed-and-breakfast,

Rikki Volkov, were the only two she hadn't met before.

Ryder gave her a second or two to get her bearings once they were inside. Then he nodded toward the far corner on the right. "Shay said he would reserve tables for us next to the dance floor."

Evidently Titus had been watching for them, because he stood up and waved. Ryder immediately took her hand and said, "Stick close to me."

Running interference for her, Ryder used his big body to plow a clear path through the crowded room. It was a relief when they finally reached their assigned seats. They ended up sitting between Shay and Carli on one side and Max and Rikki on the other. Titus and Moira took seats along the opposite side next to Shelby and her husband.

Ryder made the few necessary introductions. "Thanks for coming tonight, everybody. Seeing as Juni is new to the area, I thought it was time to introduce her to all of the cultural opportunities here in town. I told her that this place is famous for its fine pub grub cuisine and extensive wine list."

Even Shay laughed at Ryder's assessment of his tavern. He gave Juni a quick bow. "We only offer the finest of sweet potato fries and hot wings made to your personal heat preference, and the wine comes in actual bottles, not boxes."

Juni grinned at him. "Bring it on. I can't wait to try everything."

With that, Shay signaled one of the servers to head their way. She made quick work of taking their drink orders and then circled back a few minutes later to take their dinner orders. While they waited, Ryder took his jacket off and hung it on the back of his chair after pulling a sandwich bag full of quarters out of the pocket. He tossed it on the table where the coins landed with a solid thunk. When she gave him a puzzled look, Ryder directed her attention toward the far edge of the dance floor. "They're for the jukebox. I promised you a night of good food, good company and a lot of dancing."

There was a gleam of amusement in Titus's eyes as he pulled a nearly identical baggie from his own pocket. "Like minds and all of that."

At that point, Max was frowning at both of them. "Hey, nobody told me about this. Now what am I supposed to do?"

Cade started laughing as he added his own supply of quarters to the pile. "Don't worry, Max. We won't care if you dance to music we pay for."

The other man continued to look outraged. "That's not the point. I don't want my wife thinking I'm too cheap to pay for the privilege of dancing with her."

Rikki gave her husband a quick kiss. "Don't let it upset you. We can bring the quarters next time."

Shay dangled his key chain in the air. "Personally, I don't have to worry about bringing quarters. Since I have the key to the jukebox, I'll just retrieve everyone's quarters from the machine and use them again."

Shay's wife, Carli, beamed at him. "Clever man."

Ryder glared at him. "So let me get this straight. We not only pay you to feed us, but we also foot the bill for your entertainment."

The other man gave him a smug look. "Yep, pretty much. It's genius, don't you think?"

Ryder held his hand out flat and waggled it in the air. "Only if by genius, you really mean sneaky."

Juni listened to the interchange, enjoying the easy banter between friends. She could get used to hanging out with this group. A second later, Carli leaned in closer. "Shelby told us how thrilled the festival committee is with the artwork you've done for them. The mayor and Bea have also been raving about how perfect it is and how talented you are."

It was hard not to blush. "They're very kind.

They actually gave me some really clear suggestions about what they were looking for. That always makes my job so much easier."

Max had been listening to their conversation. "That reminds me. I finally have the dimensions ready for you. I'll send them to you first thing in the morning."

"Sounds good."

Then he clapped his hands and rubbed them together. Smiling at his wife, he said, "Enough about business. How about a quick dance before the food arrives?"

"I'd love to." Rikki gave him a teasing grin. "But how are you going to pay for it?"

Max immediately gave Ryder a pointed look and held out his hand. "You organized this evening but failed to provide me with all the pertinent details."

Pretending to be much put-upon, Ryder reached for his stash of coins. "Fine, this round will be my treat."

Then he tugged Juni up from her chair. "But Juni gets to pick the first song."

It didn't take her long to choose a song that she liked. The opening strains filled the air as Ryder led her onto the dance floor. The rest of their group was already out there. Juni had warned Ryder that she wasn't the best dancer, but as it turned out, following his lead was easy. By the time the song was halfway over, it was as if they'd been dancing together forever.

She wasn't the only one who looked disappointed when the song ended, but Titus took care of the problem. He fed more money into the machine, guaranteeing they could keep dancing until their food arrived.

By the time the third song came to an end, two of Shay's servers had arrived at the table with trays piled high with food. All five couples returned to their places and dug right into their meals. It took only a couple of bites to confirm Ryder had not exaggerated about the quality of the food Shay offered. Her burger was perfectly done with just the barest hint of pink in the middle, and the sweet potato fries were crispy on the outside while still creamy on the inside. Coupled with an extra spicy ketchup, they were delicious.

Ryder reached over to steal one of her fries in exchange for one of his onion rings. "Having fun?"

Juni smiled and nodded. "Very much so."

"That's good."

"Would you like another glass of wine?"

She wasn't much of a drinker, but this wasn't a night for caution. She wasn't driving, and she could always nurse the second glass of wine for a while. "Yes, that would be nice."

He caught the eye of their server as she walked

by. "We'll take another round, but make mine a glass of pop this time."

Juni noticed that several of the others switched to nonalcoholic drinks as well. Considering two of them were police officers, maybe that shouldn't have been a surprise. When Ryder finished the last bite of his bacon burger, he asked, "You ready to spend more of my quarters?"

"Sure."

This time he chose the music, a mix of country and rock. They started toward the dance floor, but he did an abrupt about-face. "I'll be right back."

He quickly fed more quarters into the machine before returning to her side. "I wanted to make sure we had enough good music to dance to before Shay starts picking the songs."

"You don't like his taste in music?"

"Didn't you notice all those disco songs he has on there? Since it's his bar, I have to think that he's the one who decides what kind of music gets loaded on the machine. I keep picturing him in a white suit and making some fancy moves out there on the dance floor."

Ryder shuddered and frowned up at the ceiling. "He probably has a mirror ball hidden somewhere up there for nights like this."

Their host had overheard the conversation and took offense. "Don't blame that music on me.

Those songs were requested for the last karaoke night. You haven't lived until you've seen four of the local truckers decked out in their finest flannel shirts and jeans while clomping around in steel-toed boots doing their best Bee Gees imitation. It was even more impressive that they actually nailed all of the right dance moves. I can't imagine how long they'd been practicing."

The image he described was hilarious. Juni grinned at him. "I can honestly say that I'm sorry I missed that."

"Don't worry. From what I hear, they plan to do an encore performance at the next karaoke event. You can find the date on our website. Even if you don't want to participate, it's a real hoot watching the performances."

When she gave Ryder a hopeful look, he gave an exaggerated shudder. "Okay, we'll come unless I have to be on duty at the station that night."

Then he gave her a stern look. "But you're going to have to drive, because I'll need a whole lot more than one beer to enjoy their performance."

She took that as a challenge. "Well, we wouldn't want them to have all the fun. What song should you and I do?"

He almost choked. "No way, lady. You're not getting me up on that stage with you."

Shay snickered. "Chicken."

After a brief hesitation, Ryder accepted the challenge—with a few provisions of his own. "Just for that, Shay, I'm going drag you up there with me. That means you and I will need to get matching shirts."

Carli cracked up at the shocked look on her husband's face. "You'd both look good in blue."

Shay clearly hadn't been expecting his wife to join in on the fun. "Why would I want to do something like that?"

By that point, Titus and Cade had joined the group. After exchanging glances, Titus answered the question. "Because your lady wants you to. That's reason enough."

Moira looked at Juni and then at the other three women in the group. When each of them nodded at her, she smiled up at her husband. "I'm sure I'm speaking for all of the ladies when I say we'd love to see you five guys performing up there together. In fact, I'd pay good money to watch that. It doesn't have to be disco, of course. Some good old-fashioned Motown would be fine with us."

By that point, the men were looking a little sick. A few seconds later, the women cracked up. Realizing they'd been had, the men all grumbled but finally gave in and grinned back. Shay pulled Carli in close for a kiss. "Very funny, lady."

"Yeah, it was." She didn't look the least bit sorry as she gave him a gentle shove toward the dance floor. "Now, let's dance."

At the same time, Ryder led Juni to an open space a short distance away. She looked around to make sure they weren't within hearing distance of the others. "I really like your friends."

He shook his head. "Actually, I'm not sure introducing you to those ladies was a good idea. They're going to encourage you to get into all kinds of trouble. Or maybe it's the other way around. Now that I think about it, you started it by suggesting you and I needed to perform. Seriously, until Moira started laughing, she had me convinced that the five of us were going to have to buy matching gold suits and learn some fancy choreography."

"At least you wouldn't have been on stage by yourself. Of course, if you stand behind Cade and Titus, you would be almost invisible."

He looked insulted. "That's mean. It's not my fault that they're both built like defensive tackles. Regardless, I'm a better dancer than either of them."

To prove that, he twirled her out and then back in again. She loved it. "Yeah, you are, but I wouldn't say that so loudly. If they get the idea that you're dissing their dance skills, you might end up having to prove your claim on stage. And if that happens, I promise to be in the front row cheering you on."

He laughed and twirled her again. "Good to know."

RYDER COULDN'T REMEMBER the last time he'd had so much fun. The whole group alternated between dancing to a few songs and sitting at the table while telling tall tales and laughing. It was interesting to see how easily Juni managed to fit in with his friends. She chatted effortlessly with everyone, listening with interest to the wide-ranging conversation even when they were talking about people and events that weren't familiar to her. It wouldn't take her long to carve out a permanent niche for herself in Dunbar if she were to decide that's what she wanted.

He'd have to consider what he thought about that possibility. He wasn't looking for any kind of long-term commitment these days, and it seemed unlikely Juni would want that either. After all, she'd made the move to Dunbar to further her career while establishing her independence from her family. She would no doubt move on after she finished her current contracts. Why else would she have only asked for a six-month lease? But what if she changed her mind and wanted to stay longer? That might not be possible if the cabin was already booked by someone else. Just in case, he made a mental note to tell his property manager to take her A-frame off the market for the foreseeable future.

A few seconds later, Juni nodded when Carli asked her a question. The two women got up and headed in the direction of the restrooms. Shay slid over into Carli's chair. "So you and Juni."

"What about us?"

Not that he necessarily wanted to hear what Shay had to say on the subject. His friend studied him for a second before answering. "I think she's good for you."

Ryder tracked Juni's progress through the bar until she disappeared from sight. "You didn't phrase that quite right. I'm pretty sure what you meant to say is that she's too good for me. If so, you won't get any arguments from me."

"I don't deny that, but then I also know Carli is also too good for me. I'm pretty sure Max, Titus and Cade would all say the same thing about their wives, but the key is to try real hard to make sure they don't figure that out anytime soon."

Even if the guys actually felt that way, Ryder suspected the four women counted themselves lucky to have found good men who clearly adored them. They'd all gone through some rough spots along the way, and he was glad each of his friends had found such happiness.

Things were different for him and Juni. They were only helping each other out with family problems. He suspected Shay wouldn't approve if Ryder told him the truth—that his relationship with Juni was a business arrangement.

"So are you going to keep seeing her?"

"Next weekend she's going to a dinner party at my folks' house with me."

That had Shay sitting back in his chair, his eyes wide with surprise. "So it's serious enough that you're taking her home to meet the parents? That is pretty quick work."

Okay, Ryder hadn't thought through how that announcement would sound. "No, that's not what I meant. You asked if I was going to keep seeing her, so I told you the next outing we have planned. My mother and father are having some of their business associates and friends over for dinner. I asked Juni if she would mind being my date for the evening."

"You never talk much about your family."

"No, I don't." And he wasn't about to start now.

"I'm guessing there's a reason for that."

When Ryder didn't offer to explain, Shay looked more resigned than angry. "Okay, I get it. We all have stuff we don't talk about. I'll just say one more thing before I shut up. Juni is a nice woman. Make sure she knows what she's walking into."

"We've already had that conversation."

Although the more he thought about it, he wasn't sure any kind of explanation would prepare Juni for the situation. It wasn't the first time he thought he should give up and cancel the date for Juni's sake. He could survive one last evening sitting next to his ex. He'd also insist on reimbursing Juni for the dress she'd bought. She'd probably fight him on that, but it would only be fair.

She was on her way back. Without thinking, he was up and moving to head her off before she reached the table.

"Let's dance."

"Sure."

Determined to keep the tone of their evening light, he made sure the next round of songs were fast-paced, the kind that were right for two people who were just friends. Three dances later, they returned to their seats, both a little out of breath. Once Juni was seated, Ryder excused himself to make a quick trip to the men's room.

When he returned, the other four couples were all out on the dance floor, leaving Juni alone at the table. Well, not completely alone. A pair of brothers who owned a local trucking company had taken advantage of his brief absence to move in on his woman…his date…no, make that his friend. No matter how he defined their relationship, the situation had him seeing red. He marched toward the table, his fists clenched at his sides.

Juni saw him coming before her companions did. At first she looked happy to see him, but her expression quickly morphed into one of confusion. Trace, the guy on her left, turned to see what had caught her attention. When he spotted Ryder, he leaned in close to his brother and muttered, "Logan, trouble is headed our way."

They immediately moved to stand shoulder to shoulder a couple of feet behind Juni's chair. She twisted in her seat to see what they were up to before turning her attention back toward Ryder. When he got within a few feet of the table, she offered him an edgy smile. "Ryder, I guess you already know Trace and Logan Calland. They've been nice enough to keep me company while you were gone."

He crossed his arms over his chest and glared at each man in turn. "I bet they have."

By that point, Juni wasn't looking at all happy. "What's that supposed to mean?"

Realizing he was treading on thin ice, he forced himself to relax. Evidently, his effort was only marginally successful since the two brothers immediately took a step back. Trace held up his hands. "Sorry, Ryder. We didn't know she was spoken for when we stopped to say hi."

Shay suddenly appeared out of nowhere and positioned himself an equal distance between Ryder and the other two men. "Is there a problem here?"

Trace and Logan immediately retreated until they had their backs to a nearby wall. "We don't have a problem, Shay. In fact, Logan and I were about to call it an evening. We've already paid our bill. If it's okay, we'll be going now."

Shay shot Ryder a dark look. "You got any problem with that?"

"Nope, not at all."

As the two brothers sidled farther away, Ryder parked himself between them and Juni. It was a jerk move, but right now he couldn't seem to help himself. Trace looked back one last time and mouthed the word *sorry* before following his brother out into the night. Ryder nodded to let him know the message had been received.

Unfortunately, from the way Juni was glaring at him right now, he was going to have to do some apologizing of his own. "I'm sorry, Juni. I was out of line."

"Yes, you were. For the record, after I told them I was here with someone, they were both perfect gentlemen. That is more than I can say about you right now."

She sat back in her chair and frowned. He cringed at the chill in her voice, especially knowing Shay was listening. "I guess I'm even more out of practice on how to act in public than I thought."

After studying him for another second or two, she finally relaxed. "Just don't do it again."

Rather than continue the awkward conversation, he held out his hand. "Want to dance?"

He breathed a sigh of relief as soon as Juni put her hand in his. "Sure."

Shay brushed past Ryder, leaning in to whisper, "Just friends, huh?"

Ryder ignored him and led Juni out onto the dance floor. About halfway into the next song, the music cut off with a screech as if someone had pulled the plug on the sound system. Suspicious that hadn't been an accident, Ryder looked back toward the jukebox where Shay and Titus were busy shoving quarter after quarter into the slot. When they were finished, they leaned against the wall and crossed their arms over their chests, sporting smug smiles.

It was no surprise that the next song that came over the speakers was a country ballad with lyrics about saying goodbye to the right woman and living with regrets. He deliberately turned his back to his now ex-friends and held out his arms to Juni, leaving it up to her if she wanted to slow dance with him. His pulse stuttered when she didn't hesitate, and they swayed to the gentle rhythm. Considering how right it felt, giving into the temptation to hold her probably wasn't the smartest thing he'd ever done.

But that didn't stop him from making the same mistake three more times before the night was over.

CHAPTER TWELVE

IT HAD BEEN a week since their night at Shay's tavern, but Juni figured tonight was bound to be a far different experience. For starters, they were traveling in a much more elegant vehicle. Not for the first time, she trailed her fingers across the buttery soft surface of her seat, loving the sensuous feel of real leather. She still couldn't wrap her head around the fact that Ryder owned a Jaguar. While she didn't know enough about classic cars to guess the exact year of this one, she recognized expensive when she saw it. The dark green exterior and tan leather interior exuded sophistication.

Where did he keep the car hidden? There was no garage on his property, and she'd never seen the Jag parked in his driveway. While she could understand him using his beat-up van to run errands for the animal shelter, why keep this beauty stashed away? It had to be much more fun to drive.

Ryder glanced in her direction when she

reached out to run her fingertip along the side of the wooden steering wheel. "I'm guessing you have questions."

She couldn't help but cringe a little as she jerked her hand back to her side of the car. "Yeah, I do. Let me start by saying I'm not complaining about your van. It's practical and perfect for everyday use."

Her assessment clearly amused him. "Don't forget reliable. That van has never failed to start and gets me wherever I need to go. It also has a much simpler engine and drivetrain. I can do most of the maintenance on it myself."

He patted the steering wheel. "This baby, on the other hand, insists on a specialist's care."

"Exactly." She hesitated before continuing. She didn't want to insult him or hurt his feelings. "It's just that I almost offered to drive tonight. My car isn't fancy, but I thought it might be more…comfortable than the van."

"That's probably true, and I'm guessing it also doesn't smell like cats." By this point, he was grinning. "But I think what you really meant is that you thought my parents might be happier if we arrived in a vehicle that doesn't have rust as one of its primary colors."

There was no use in denying it. "Pretty much."

"You're not wrong. In fact, I'm pretty sure that if we showed up in the van, either they or the homeowners' association would have had it towed before we even reached the front door."

"So do you only use this car for special occasions like your mom's party?"

"That and the occasional road trip. I keep it garaged in a nearby town that has one of those big storage units. I rarely drive it during the winter months because I don't want to risk damaging it when driving conditions are bad. Since we're well into spring now, I had it serviced so we could arrive in style tonight."

He patted the dashboard as if the car was a beloved pet. "This is one of the few things I kept from my previous life. I've thought about trading it in for something more practical—maybe a new SUV with four-wheel drive. That would certainly be more sensible living this close to the mountains."

"It would be a real shame to do that. Being sensible is highly overrated, especially if it would mean getting rid of a beauty like this. She's a once-in-a-lifetime kind of car."

"So my Jag is a 'she'?"

Juni let her hand glide over the leather again. "Well, yeah. She's sleek, beautiful and I'm betting really fast."

"She is that."

Juni whooped with excitement when he gunned the engine and sent the car ripping down the rural highway in a quick burst of speed. He laughed at her reaction as he gradually brought their speed back down to somewhere in the vicinity of the speed limit.

"Can we do that again?"

He grinned and granted her request. "Why, Juni Voss, I would never have guessed that you're an adrenaline junkie!"

"I'm not usually, but how often will I have the chance to tear down the road in a classic Jag? I don't think there was anything like it in the town where I grew up. If there had been, I'm pretty sure the owner would have driven it in the Fourth of July parade just to show it off."

Ryder looked intrigued by that idea. "You know, maybe I should drive this instead of the fire truck at the festival."

"Better yet, you could charge people for taking a ride in it and donate the money to the shelter."

"You might have something there." Then he shook his head. "On second thought, maybe not. My friends wouldn't be content with me giving them a ride. They'd insist on getting behind the wheel themselves, and that's not happening. I've seen how Titus tears down the highway on that motorcycle of his when he thinks the cops won't catch him. Heck, I even hesitated to let him drive my van. There's no way I'd let him behind the wheel of this baby."

Wait a minute. "Are you saying they don't even know you own a Jag?"

"I don't use it around town. It's not very practical for everyday driving."

That was true, but she suspected he kept the car hidden because it would raise a lot of questions about his life before he moved to Dunbar. "I won't tell anyone."

"Don't worry about it. They're bound to find out eventually. I'll have to think about the best way to make the big reveal." He reached over to give her hand a soft squeeze. "Can you imagine the look on Shay's face if I were to arrive at the bar in this? Or maybe I should blast through that stretch of highway outside of town where Moira likes to set up a speed trap. I'm sure the first thing she'd do after writing me a big, fat ticket would be to call Titus and then Cade. Of course, if I really wanted the news to get out to everybody at once, I could always park it in front of Bea's coffee shop. Titus claims she's the unofficial town crier of Dunbar, Washington."

"I can just see that. I stopped in for one of her apple fritters and some coffee earlier this week. I was amazed by the amount of news she shared with her customers. I was there less than half an hour, and I couldn't believe everything I learned about what was going on in town. None of it was mean-spirited or anything, but she sure knows a lot about a whole bunch of people. I guess that's life in a small town."

"It is indeed."

After that bit of wisdom, they lapsed into silence. She couldn't help but notice that Ryder's grip on the steering wheel gradually tightened once they left the rural highway behind and merged onto the westbound interstate. His tension continued to worsen the closer they got to Seattle.

When he flipped on the turn signal and pulled over into the exit lane, he drew a sharp breath. "Juni, I'm going to apologize in advance for dragging you into this. If you'd rather not go, I'll understand. I can still call my mother and tell her…something. I don't know what. Car trouble might be believable."

"It will be fine, Ryder. We've come this far. Let's see how it goes. If all else fails, I can develop a handy migraine. Like you, I'm delicate."

Some of his tension eased as he shot her a quick smile. "It's a deal."

RYDER DIDN'T KNOW how Juni could be so calm when he felt like he was about to jump out of his skin. His parents would be polite to her. He knew that for a fact. His father especially would enjoy talking to an artist. He dabbled in watercolors, and both of Ryder's parents were enthusiastic supporters of the arts in the Seattle area.

"Are you ready?"

Juni's question jerked Ryder back into the moment. He'd managed to snag a parking spot that ensured the Jag wouldn't be blocked in by other cars. That might be important if he and Juni needed to make a quick escape from the party.

Sadly, he'd delayed as long as he could and turned off the engine. It was time to head inside. "Yeah, let's go. I think we're hitting the sweet spot of not arriving too early or too late."

Juni tangled her fingers in his. "We'll be fine."

The front door swung open as soon as the two of them stepped onto the porch. Ryder was surprised that his mother had chosen to greet them personally. She usually had a maid stationed at the entrance to usher in new arrivals while she saw to her other guests.

Her smile might have looked completely natural to anyone who didn't know her well, but there was definitely a hint of tension there. She tipped her head up and to the side. "I'm glad you could make it, Ryder."

He dutifully kissed her on the cheek and then stepped back. "Mom, I'd like you to meet my friend Juni Voss. She's the graphic artist I told you about."

"It's nice to meet you, Ms. Voss."

"Thank you for inviting me tonight, Mrs. Davis." Juni smiled and held out her hand. "And please call me Juni."

His mother nodded as they shook hands. Now that the obligatory niceties had been observed, she led them past the entry and into the living room to join the other guests. "I'll go fetch your father. I know he will want to meet Juni right away. Ryder, why don't you get the two of you something to drink?"

"Good idea, Mom."

He waited until she walked away to nudge Juni in the direction of the bar that had been set up in the back corner of the room. "What would you like? Wine? A cocktail of some kind?"

Feigning disappointment, he then whispered, "Unfortunately, Mom won't stoop to serving beer at her shindigs no matter how many times I've asked her to."

Juni rolled her eyes. "White wine will be fine."

When they reached the bar, the bartender offered them a practiced smile. "What will it be?"

"A glass of white wine for the lady. I'll have some of my father's best scotch on the rocks. Make it a double."

When Juni arched an eyebrow and gave him a pointed look, he surrendered. "Fine. Let's pretend I was only kidding."

Turning back to the bartender, he grumbled, "Make it a single."

He handed Juni her drink and then picked up his own. A movement near the door caught his attention. "Here they come."

Juni sipped her drink as she watched his parents making their way through the scattering of guests . "You take after your father. For sure, you both rock the whole tuxedo look."

"Brace yourself."

Juni snickered, but quickly schooled her expression to something more serious when his parents made their final approach. Ryder performed introductions. "Dad, this is my friend Juni Voss. I'm sure Mom told you that Juni is an artist."

His father offered Juni a genuinely warm smile. "She did indeed. I'd love to hear all about it."

Ryder was glad to see that his father's greeting was more sincere than his mother's had been. For her part, Juni took it all in stride and seemed completely relaxed when she responded. "Currently, I'm doing the illustrations for a children's book. I'm also doing some graphic artwork for a local festival."

Ryder joined the conversation. "She did a great caricature of me. I liked it so much, I had it framed."

She smiled up at him. "How often do you get

to draw a picture of a firefighter standing up in a tree?"

His father looked at Juni and then at Ryder as if trying to decide if they were serious. "Okay, I'll bite. What were you doing up in a tree?"

"Trying to catch a kitten."

His mother blinked in surprise while his father's smile dimmed for a brief second before he asked, "So, how did this little adventure turn out?"

"I took the kitten and its brother to the local shelter to be cared for."

Someone else unexpectedly joined the discussion. "So you're still playing fireman and working at an animal shelter."

Ryder managed not to jump at Jasmine's question. He'd been so focused on his parents that he'd failed to notice her approach. Juni turned to face her, her expression flat. "I'm pretty sure that 'playing' isn't the right word to describe what volunteer firefighters do. They save lives, fight fires and respond to all kinds of emergencies, so it's not a game. It's actually dangerous but critical work."

Whoa, he never expected Juni to leap to his defense, and she probably didn't realize she was swimming with sharks right now. He slipped his arm around her waist, gently tugging her into his side, conveying without words that she was under his protection.

Jasmine rudely ignored her, but maybe that was for the best. "Nice to see you again, Ryder."

He acknowledged her comment with a small nod, but then turned his attention back to his parents. "I'm sure you two need to greet more of your guests. I'm going to show Juni the view from the back deck."

After setting what was left of his drink on the bar, he took Juni's hand. "Lake Washington is especially beautiful at sunset."

"I'd love to see it." She smiled at his parents but not Jasmine, which wasn't surprising. "If you'll excuse us."

They walked through the house without speaking, cutting through the kitchen to reach the back door. Once they made it outside, he drew a deep breath of the cool evening air. "I'm sorry…"

Juni stopped him. Resting her head against his arm, she sighed. "No apologies needed. Your parents were perfectly pleasant, and you're right about the view. The lake is beautiful."

He noticed she still hadn't said anything about Jasmine. "Would you like to leave now?"

"There's no use in upsetting your mother on my account. We'll hang around, eat what I'm sure will be a spectacular meal and then make our escape."

She stared out at the water for several seconds. "I get that parents can drive you crazy sometimes, but there's not a day that goes by that I don't wish I could have one more day with mine."

He hated the pain in her voice. To offer her some bit of comfort, he wrapped his arm around her shoulders. "You've never talked about them before. What happened?"

"A car accident thanks to bad weather and slick roads. Aunt Ruby and Uncle Colby stepped up and took me in. I'll always be grateful for that." Her eyes looked so darn sad when she glanced up at him. "So, like I was saying, don't burn bridges. You never know when something might happen that would prevent you from ever rebuilding them."

That was probably good advice. Before he could say so, a bell chimed.

"That's Mom's signal that dinner is about to be served. Let's go find our places."

JUNI COUNTED HERSELF LUCKY. She'd half expected to end up seated next to Ryder's ex-fiancée. The last thing she wanted was to make small talk with that woman. Jasmine was everything she was not—tall, gorgeous and sophisticated. Rather than dwell on her, she concentrated on watching how well Ryder fit in with the other guests at the table. It was as if he'd slipped on a completely different persona along with his tuxedo.

Although she'd never admit it to him, she preferred the man he'd been the other night at Shay's bar. While Ryder frequently smiled, sitting there in his mother's dining room, he never once laughed. Maybe these people were too focused on appearances to ever kick back and simply enjoy themselves. So far, she'd been introduced to a local judge, a couple of college professors and even a state senator. Definitely not the kind of crowd she normally hung out with.

At least the woman on her other side made an effort to be friendly. After finding out Juni was an artist, Brenda told her about a group she'd recently gotten involved with that was working to raise funds to support creative arts programs in local schools. In the past, the group had purchased musical instruments, art supplies, sheet music, and even costumes for musicals and plays. A short time into their conversation, Ryder put his arm across the back of Juni's chair and leaned forward to ask some pretty pointed questions about the group.

Delighted to share her enthusiasm for the project, Brenda immediately launched into a more detailed explanation about the work they were doing. When she was finished, Ryder smiled and passed her a business card. "Here's my contact information. Send me the details. No promises, but I will get back in touch one way or another after I have a chance to review everything."

Clutching the card as if it were priceless, Brenda smiled at Ryder. "I'll send all the information to you ASAP."

"I'll be watching for it."

Brenda thanked Ryder again before turning her attention back to her own dinner companion. As soon as she did, the man seated on Ryder's other side cleared his throat to draw their attention. Before introducing himself, he offered both Ryder and Juni a slick, polished smile. "I'm sure your parents have mentioned me, Mr. Davis. They knew I wanted to meet you. I'm George Sterling. I've been involved in local politics at the city and county levels, but I just announced my campaign to become state representative from my district. I'm sure you know how expensive politics have gotten to be."

He paused briefly for Ryder to comment. When he remained silent, the man continued. "So far, I've been fortunate to meet people willing to step up and support my efforts. I've assured them that they won't be sorry. When I'm elected, they know their voices will be heard."

Juni wasn't naive but she would have thought a professional politician would've been more… subtle? Maybe discreet was closer to the mark.

This guy had to know that any number of people at the table might be listening in on his blatant sales pitch. Regardless, he showed off that same insincere smile again as he said, "So, Mr. Davis…or perhaps I can call you Ryder? After all, we're all friends here. Would you like my campaign manager to get in touch with you next week?"

Ryder had yet to respond to anything the man had said. When he finally did, it was short and to the point. "The answer to both of your questions is no. You may not call me Ryder. In fact, don't call me at all. I'm not interested in anything you're selling."

All of the conversations at their end of the table abruptly went silent for a brief moment as the other guests looked at the flustered politician with either sympathy or amusement. He was still sputtering when Ryder angled his chair to face Juni more directly, pointedly turning his back to him. Smiling at her, Ryder asked, "My salmon was delicious. How was your chicken?"

She rested her hand on his knee. He might look calm, but the muscles in his leg were bunched tight with tension. Did this kind of thing happen to him all the time? If so, no wonder he dreaded his mother's invitations. "The chicken was wonderful. I've never had it stuffed with crabmeat before, and the cream sauce was the perfect accent."

By that point, he looked a little more relaxed. Even more so after the politician excused himself and left the table. Without acknowledging his departure, Ryder continued talking. "Wait until they bring around the desserts. It's always hard to choose. The good news is that Mom serves them in mini sizes so her guests can try several."

He looked around as if to make sure no one was listening, which of course they all were. "I've been known to order seconds of any that are particularly good."

She grinned at him. "Any chance there will be bacon-maple bars?"

There, that had him laughing. "I doubt it, but I'll be sure to suggest Mom try them at her next party."

The rest of the meal passed peacefully, which was a relief. If anyone else had thought to hit Ryder up for money, his cold response to the politician must have had them thinking better of the idea. After the dessert cart had come and gone, the two of them made their escape back out onto the deck to enjoy the night air.

"How are you holding up?"

Juni stared out at the water. "I'm doing fine. The meal was wonderful, and Brenda and her companion were really nice."

"Yeah, they were."

The temperature outside had dropped after the sun went down, leaving it a little too cool to be comfortable. When she shivered a little, Ryder immediately stripped off his tuxedo jacket and draped it across her shoulders. While she appreciated the extra warmth it provided, she asked, "Are you sure you don't need it?"

"No, I'm fine. If I go grab us some coffee, will you be okay out here alone? I won't be gone long."

"That sounds good. I'm sure no one will bother me out here."

As it turned out, she was wrong about that. As soon as Ryder disappeared back inside the house, the last person she wanted to talk to stepped out onto the deck. Jasmine made a pretense of looking around before turning her full attention to Juni. She crossed the short distance, stopping just close enough to force Juni to have to tip her head back to look the much taller woman in the eye.

"If you're looking for Ryder, he'll be back in a minute."

"No, actually, I was hoping to have a moment alone with you."

By that point, Juni figured her smile was about as genuine as the politician's had been. "Well, you found me."

"I realize that I was probably a little rude earlier. I never introduced myself. My name is Jasmine Broderick. I'm a special friend of the family."

Her smile was hard around the edges, brittle and cold. "I'm guessing you already know that Ryder and I were engaged. After he sold his business, we put our engagement on hold while he decides what he wants to do next. After all, he has so much to offer the world. You can understand why his current lack of direction is so upsetting for everyone."

Juni tugged Ryder's jacket closer around her. The chill running through her now had nothing to do with the evening air and everything to do with the snark in the other woman's voice. If Jasmine thought Juni wouldn't respond in kind, she was wrong, and Juni couldn't wait to prove it to her.

But before she could do exactly that, Ryder reappeared. He brushed past Jasmine to hand Juni her coffee. "I added extra cream. Mom likes her coffee pretty strong."

She sipped it. "Perfect. You always know just how I like it."

Jasmine flinched, the only sign that she didn't like being reminded that Juni was the one Ryder spent his time with these days.

Meanwhile, he turned to give Jasmine a hard

look. "I couldn't help but overhear what you said to Juni. Were you lying to her or to yourself?"

She backed up a step. "I was simply introducing myself, something you should have done earlier, all things considered."

"And what things would those be? Do I really have to remind you that we didn't put anything on hold? We broke up. That hasn't changed and won't. What I choose to do with my life is no longer your concern and hasn't been for a while now. While we're at it, my parents' feelings on the subject are also none of your business. In the future, keep your opinions to yourself. Ms. Voss is my guest, and I won't stand for anyone being rude to her. Now, if you'll excuse us, we have a long drive ahead of us."

Juni didn't need to be told twice that it was time to head back inside. They'd made it as far as the door when Jasmine spoke again. "I'm an invited guest here myself, you know."

Ryder didn't bother to look back in her direction. "But not mine, and that's all that matters."

Juni struggled to slow his headlong charge through the house, figuring he needed to get his temper back under control before he found his parents. No doubt Jasmine would eventually fill them in on her version of their encounter, but Juni was sure Ryder wouldn't want to stick around to hear what his parents had to say on the subject.

Out of desperation, Juni grabbed Ryder's arm and jerked him to a stop. She took both of their coffee cups and set them on a nearby table. "Now, stand still and simply breathe."

He did as she ordered, closing his eyes before drawing a slow breath and then letting it out. He did it again before speaking. "I'm sorry about all of that. I should never have dragged you into this."

Instead of arguing the point, she removed his jacket and held it out. "Put this back on. You don't want to look disheveled when you talk to your folks."

When he slipped it on, she reached up to straighten his tie and then brushed her hands over his shoulders and down his lapels. "No apologies necessary. Not to sound like we're back in grade school, but she started it."

That comment had him chuckling. "And I finished it."

"If you hadn't, I would have." Juni shrugged. "Besides, neither of us did anything wrong. Considering her earlier actions, it's obvious that woman came tonight spoiling for a fight."

"And we gave her one."

He smiled down at her. For a second, she

thought he might kiss her, but the arrival of his parents put a stop to that idea.

"Ryder, there you are. I think Jasmine was looking for you."

They both turned to face his mother, who had stepped into the alcove with them. She frowned slightly when she noticed Juni's hand was still resting on Ryder's chest. Ryder must have noticed, too, because he covered her hand with his and entwined his fingers with hers.

"Don't worry, Mom. She found us."

"That's good. I think she wanted to apologize for her comments right after you first arrived."

Ryder gave a bitter laugh. "No, Mom, that wasn't her intention at all. Instead, she cornered Juni when I stepped away to get us some coffee and was incredibly rude to her. She fed her a pack of lies, even claiming that our engagement was only on hold until I figure my life out. Which, by the way, I already have."

His mother frowned and slowly shook her head. "I'm sorry, but that doesn't sound like Jasmine. She wouldn't have—"

Ryder slashed his hand through the air to cut her off. "Which means you think I would lie about what happened."

"No, not at all. You said you weren't there to hear everything that was said. I'm sure Juni misunderstood the situation."

"Tell yourself that if it makes you feel better, but I won't listen to excuses for Jasmine's appalling behavior."

Luckily Ryder's father stopped her from defending Jasmine again. "Marjorie, please. We weren't there, and Juni is our guest. Regardless of what was or wasn't said, we owe her an apology if the situation made her uncomfortable."

That's all it took to have his wife back down. "You're right, of course. Juni, I'm awfully sorry that the conversation was upsetting. I hope both of you will forgive us."

Ryder didn't look as if he wanted to do that, but Juni didn't hesitate. "Of course, Mr. and Mrs. Davis. Again, it was nice to meet you, and I really enjoyed the dinner and chatting with several of your guests."

People were approaching the foyer, no doubt ready to call it an evening as well. "Looks like some folks would also like to say their goodbyes, so we'll be going now."

Ryder opened the door for Juni, letting her make her escape first. As he walked past his mother, she met Ryder's gaze, her expression a little uncertain. "We'll talk soon."

He simply nodded and walked out.

CHAPTER THIRTEEN

"WHAT'S WRONG, JUNI? Didn't you sleep well last night? That's the third time you've yawned in the past couple of minutes."

Juni watched as Aunt Ruby leaned in closer to the phone on her end to get a better look at Juni's appearance. Whatever she saw definitely had her frowning. "It's after ten o'clock, and you're still in your pajamas. You haven't even combed your hair."

Her aunt was right on both counts. That's because Juni had still been in bed when the phone call had dragged her out of a sound sleep. She'd briefly considered letting it go to voicemail, but ignoring her aunt never worked. Ruby would have waited a short time and tried again. That's why Juni stared at her coffeemaker and waited impatiently for it to finish brewing. She desperately needed a huge dose of caffeine if she was going to survive this phone call.

The two of them always talked on Sunday, but nowhere near this early. If her sleep-clogged brain had understood Aunt Ruby correctly, Uncle Colby had a bad cold and hadn't felt up to going to church. With free time on her hands, Ruby had decided to call Juni earlier than normal. Realizing her aunt was still waiting for a response, Juni managed to mumble, "Sorry, Aunt Ruby, but I was still in bed when you called."

Evidently that was cause for alarm. "What's wrong, honey? Are you coming down with something, too?"

"No, I'm fine." Juni reached for the biggest coffee mug she owned. "Really."

"But we never sleep this late."

That might be true for Ruby and her husband, but not for Juni. She loved to sleep in whenever she could get away with it. When at long last the coffeemaker beeped, she grabbed the carafe and started pouring. "Give me a second, Aunt Ruby. I'll be right back with you."

She set the phone aside long enough to finish fixing her coffee. After adding enough milk to take the edge off the heat, she downed a huge gulp, picked up the phone again and headed into the living room to settle into the corner of the couch. Once she was covered up with a blanket, she took one more drink before rejoining the conversation, knowing it was likely to become an inquisition as soon as she admitted why she'd slept so late.

"Sorry to keep you waiting. Now to answer your question, I'm extratired because I was out later than usual last night. That's all."

The silence on the other end of the conversation didn't last long. "What? Where were you? Who were you with?"

"I'm sure I mentioned that a business associate had been invited to a dinner party in Seattle. He needed a plus-one and asked if I would consider going with him. That's why I bought that dress I told you about."

Ruby's eyes narrowed. "I suppose this is the same business associate who hung up on Erin."

There was no use in denying it. "Yeah, but I would appreciate it if you didn't judge Ryder by that one incident. I promise he's really a nice guy and very well thought of here in Dunbar."

"It sounds like you like him, too."

Probably more than she should, but that wasn't something she was going to admit to her aunt. "I do. For one thing, he's been really supportive of my work. He's the reason I got the contract to do all of the graphics for the town's upcoming festival. That will be a nice addition to my portfolio."

The next question was predictable, which had Juni smiling. "Do you know anything about his people?"

Family was everything to Aunt Ruby. "Actually, I've met both his mother and father. The dinner party was at their house."

"Oh, that's nice. What kind of food did they have?"

Aunt Ruby was always interested in new ideas of what to serve whenever she needed to feed a crowd. Juni was pretty sure last night's entrees wouldn't make the list. "Well, I had a chicken breast stuffed with crabmeat and topped with a white sauce. Ryder had the salmon."

Ruby looked disappointed, but then she was a casserole kind of gal at heart. "That all sounds pretty fancy."

"It was, sort of. To be honest, I would have rather had your shepherd's pie. You know me and my sweet tooth, so it won't surprise you that my favorite part was the desserts. Ryder's mom likes to serve everything in really small portions. That way her guests can have more than one kind without feeling too guilty about it." She laughed. "I'm almost embarrassed to admit I had two different fruit tarts and a chocolate macadamia nut cookie. In my defense, Ryder was even greedier. I'm pretty sure he had one of everything. I suspect he would've gone back for seconds on a couple, but his mother gave him one of those looks. You know, the one that says enough is enough."

At least Aunt Ruby laughed about that. "I like

the idea of small portions of several different flavors. Maybe I'll try it at the next quilting guild meeting."

"I bet they'd love that."

Trying to sound oh-so-casual, Ruby asked, "So are you and this Ryder fellow actually dating now? Is that why he took you home to meet his parents?"

Juni wasn't sure how to answer that. Their official agreement was business only. The reality was turning out to be a little murkier than that, because they enjoyed hanging out together a little too much. The problem was the short-term nature of their relationship. When her contract on the illustrations was complete, her family fully expected her to move back home to stay. Getting emotionally attached not only to Ryder but his friends as well would only make it harder to leave Dunbar behind.

"No, we're not dating. Last night wasn't exactly a family gathering kind of party." How best to describe it so that her aunt would understand? "The other guests were a combination of family friends and business associates with a few local politicians thrown into the mix. It was more of an opportunity to do some networking."

Ruby looked confused, but then she'd probably never attended a function like that. Of course, neither had Juni before last night. Finally, her aunt asked, "Did you enjoy spending that much time with a bunch of strangers?"

"Actually, there were a couple of people I really liked. One woman was particularly interesting. She and I happened to be seated together at the table. Brenda is working to raise money for a group that supports the arts in local schools. We had a lovely discussion about the importance of creative outlets for kids. I think Ryder may even make a donation to the cause."

"I'm not surprised you and this lady really hit it off."

Ruby looked away from the phone and frowned. "Oops, I'd better go. Your uncle is calling. You know how he gets when he's sick. I have to go hold his hand and offer him some sympathy. Before I do that, maybe I'll fix him another cup of tea laced with honey and a little shot of brandy."

Her voice dropped to a quiet whisper. "We'll both have an easier day of it if he sleeps most of the time."

Juni snickered. Uncle Colby was normally the strong guy everyone depended on. But at the first sign of a sniffle, he took up residence in his recliner, covered up with a comforter, and indulged in a major pity party. "Tell him I'm sorry he's not feeling well and that I love him. You, too."

"We love you right back. Go back to bed if you need to. Sorry I woke you up."

"Not a problem. I'm up now. It's past time for me to eat breakfast and get some work done."

Ruby looked as if she wanted to say something but wasn't sure if she should. Finally, she jerked her head in a quick nod and then spoke. "One more thing, Juni. This is the first time in ages that you've shown this much interest in someone. I know you say it's all business, but that's not how it sounds when you talk about Ryder."

When Juni started to protest, Ruby held up her hand to cut her off. "Maybe I'm misreading the situation. If so, fine. However, should you and he eventually decide there is more to this relationship than just business dinners and contracts, we're going to want to meet him."

Then she hung up, leaving Juni staring at a blank screen.

RYDER STARED OUT his front window and prayed for patience. He really wasn't in the mood to rehash the events of the previous night. "I'm sorry Jasmine was upset, but I did warn you that inviting both of us to the dinner was a bad idea."

His mother rarely lost her temper, but she was clearly on the edge of doing so. "I thought at the very least you could be an adult about it."

He fought the temptation to point out once

again that Jasmine had gone out of her way to be rude to Juni. Rather than rehashing the whole affair again, he settled for making his position clear on the subject. "I will repeat what I told you before. If you insist on inviting my ex, don't bother inviting me. Problem solved. If you want to see me, fine. We'll get together when it's just going to be you, me and Dad."

Hopefully, she'd take that as the peace offering he meant for it to be. Unfortunately she wasn't ready to let the matter drop. "We'd love to meet you for lunch or dinner whenever you have time, but there's still a problem. Because of her job, Jasmine has become a regular part of our social circle, Ryder. Her law firm handles various personal legal affairs not only for your father and me, but with a number of our friends as well. Avoiding her completely isn't possible."

"Then make sure Jasmine knows she's only there as a business associate and not part of a relationship that ended two years ago."

Rather than respond to that suggestion, his mom switched gears. "Did your companion enjoy the evening?"

"Her name is Juni, Mom, and she did. She and Brenda Jefferson especially hit it off. I guess that's only logical since they have a common interest in promoting the arts in schools."

"Oh, that's right. Brenda mentioned that she'd

enjoyed talking with her. By the way, she was really thrilled that you asked her to send along information about that charity she's involved with."

"The file arrived earlier this afternoon, but I haven't had a chance to look at it yet."

"I'm sure they will appreciate anything you can do to help them."

"We'll see. I told her I wasn't making any promises, but that I would let them know one way or another after I read through everything. A lot of these groups have really good intentions, but they don't always have their ducks in a row when it comes to the execution."

"I trust your judgment when it comes to this sort of thing, so let me know what you decide. If you find it to be a worthwhile cause, your father and I will consider making a donation as well." After a brief hesitation, she continued. "I understand that you also spoke with George Sterling."

Ryder didn't even try to hide his disdain. "Only very briefly, mainly because I didn't like anything he had to say. I don't like politicians whose primary loyalty is to the people who donate to their campaigns rather than their actual constituents. I made it very clear that neither he nor his campaign will get a dime from me. I'm pretty sure he wasn't happy about that."

"Interesting. Again, I'm happy for your input.

Several of our friends are supporting him, but I've had my own misgivings about that man. He's a little too slick for my taste."

"Mine, too."

At least the two of them had finally found one topic they could agree on. It was definitely time to end the call. "I'd better go, Mom. I have something I need to do."

"Something like chasing a kitten up a tree?"

Her tone was teasing, but he was pretty sure she didn't really find that whole incident all that amusing. "No, that was a one-off."

Hopefully, anyway. "That reminds me. I meant to text you a photo of that caricature Juni drew of me to memorialize the moment."

"I'll be watching for it. Talk to you soon."

"Bye, Mom."

As soon as she hung up, he dutifully snapped a shot of the picture on the wall and sent it to her. Within seconds, she replied, saying it was cute and that Juni definitely had talent.

He shoved the phone back in his hip pocket and grabbed his keys. Titus had asked him to stop by the café to pick up another load of donated pet food for the shelter. His shift at the fire station wasn't until that evening, which left him several hours to kill. That had him thinking about Juni and wondering what she was up to. Maybe she'd like to grab something to eat at the café and then ride along with him to the shelter. If she had enough time in her schedule, they also could walk some of the shelter dogs on the trail that wound through the woods behind the building. He should probably call her first, but it was just as easy to walk over to her place.

Less than five minutes later, he was knocking on her door. It swung open within seconds. When Juni stepped into sight, he had to fight hard not to start laughing. This wasn't the first time he'd come knocking only to find her still in pajamas and looking as if she'd just crawled out of bed. She rubbed her eyes and then glared at him. "Don't laugh. When my aunt called for our weekly chat, I was still in bed asleep. I haven't even had a chance to eat breakfast yet."

He leaned against the door frame. "Poor baby, that's a rough way to kick off your morning. As a matter of fact, I also just got off the phone with my mother. Must be the day for it."

"How did that conversation go?"

"Started off rough but got a little better."

"It's probably too much to hope that your folks eventually realized that we weren't the problem last night."

He shrugged. "Evidently part of the issue is that Jazz's law firm has a lot of connections with my parents and their circle of friends. So even though she is my ex, she's still a business associate. I told Mom if she wanted to keep the peace, she needs to leave me off the guest list on the occasions they have to include her."

Juni looked skeptical that would actually happen, and she wasn't wrong. The issue was definitely a work in progress. Time to move on. "So, I was wondering if you were busy today."

She finally stepped back, giving him room to enter the cabin. "What do you have in mind?"

"Titus called. He has a whole bunch of donated pet food he needs me to pick up. I thought we could have a late breakfast at the café and then deliver the food to the shelter. While we're there, we can take some of the dogs for a walk. There are always a bunch who need the exercise, and it's a nice day for a short hike. What do you say?"

Juni glanced toward her computer and frowned. "I really need to work. I'm scheduled to meet with the author this week."

"If it makes a difference, I have to be back by late afternoon myself. I'm on duty at the station early this evening." He offered her his most winsome smile. "After breakfast, we can also stop at Bea's before heading to the shelter. Occasionally I take a box of doughnuts for the staff and volunteers to share."

"Are you buying extras for the two of us? If so, are we talking bacon-maple bars?"

Okay, that worked. Juni now looked considerably more interested in the plan. Nothing like the possibility of a bacon-maple bar to smooth the way. "If she has any left when we get there. Otherwise, you might have to settle for an apple fritter."

"You are a sneaky man, Ryder Davis," Juni complained as she threw her hands up in the air in surrender. "How am I supposed to resist such temptation? Have a seat while I get dressed. The coffee is fresh if you want some."

Then she walked away still muttering under her breath. It was probably better that he couldn't make out what she was saying about him right then. After helping himself to some coffee, he snuck a peek at the pile of drawings on her desk. This particular bunch were the illustrations she was doing for the children's book. Once again, her talent dazzled him.

The bears were absolutely adorable. She'd managed to give them each a distinct personality and such expressive faces. No doubt both kids and their parents would love them. In fact, he could already imagine all kinds of merchandise featuring the various characters. Heck, even he'd like a T-shirt with the family of bears on it. He could also picture Shay, Carli and their six-year-old son, Luca, wearing matching sweatshirts with the papa, mama and baby bears emblazoned on the front.

"What are you smiling about?"

He showed her the picture he'd been looking at. "I was thinking if the book takes off, the merchandising of the illustrations could earn everyone involved a small fortune."

Her cheeks turned rosy as if she were embarrassed by the praise, but pleased by it all the same. "That's nice of you to say."

"I'm not simply being nice, Juni. I meant every word." He set the picture back down on the stack. "Now, we'd better get going if you're going to get back in time to work."

Juni quickly locked up and followed Ryder outside. It seemed perfectly natural when she slipped her hand into his as they cut through the woods back to his house. It occurred to him that once again they were further blurring the line they'd drawn regarding the nature of their relationship. They were supposed to be friends, nothing more. Continuing to become more and more entangled in each other's lives was probably a bad idea, especially if they wanted to make a clean break of it when Juni left town.

But even knowing that, he couldn't bring himself to end that small physical connection with her until she climbed into the van.

CHAPTER FOURTEEN

THEY MADE THE trip into town in short order. After parking in the alley, Ryder poked his head in the back door of the café to let Titus know he was there. The other man wiped his hands on a towel. "Give me a minute to put this dough into the fridge to proof, and I'll be out to help you."

"Don't bother. Juni is with me, and the two of us should be able to handle it. After we get everything loaded, we'll be in to grab some breakfast before we make the delivery."

Titus tossed him his keys. "See you in a few."

When Ryder unlocked the storage shed, he was impressed by the amount of kibble Titus had managed to collect. Juni let out a low whistle. "Wow, that's a huge pile of pet food. I'm impressed."

"The shelter goes through an awful lot of the stuff, especially since they also supply the volunteers with food for the animals they foster at home. When the shelter gets more than they can immediately use, they sometimes share it with another shelter in the area. I'm not sure how Titus manages to collect as much as he does, but it makes a real difference in the shelter's budget."

He picked up a pair of thirty-pound bags and headed for the van. After stacking them inside, he turned back and almost ran into Juni carrying two of the smaller bags. He added them to those already inside the van and followed her back to the shed for another load. Between the two of them, they made pretty quick work of transferring everything. When they were done, he locked both the van and the shed.

Juni looked up and down the alley. "Don't we need to park somewhere else while we eat?"

"No. Not much traffic passes through here, and the van is pretty much out of the way. Besides, we won't be here all that long."

Rather than walking around to the front of the café, he led her up the steps to the back door. "Titus won't mind if we come in through this way."

Inside the kitchen, the short-order cook looked back over his shoulder and nodded. "Head on in and find a table. The specials today are the cinnamon bread French toast and a Greek omelet."

"They both sound great, Gunner."

Ryder stopped to pet Ned, who was curled up in his bed on the far side of the room. Before walking away, he grabbed a couple of the treats

Titus kept handy for his furry friend and offered them to Ned. The huge dog wolfed them down, thumping his tail to express his thanks.

Gunner made a disgusted noise. "With as much as that dog eats, it's a wonder that he can even walk. You people have spoiled him rotten."

Titus walked into the room just in time to hear the conversation. "Like you're any better. I filled that jar yesterday evening, and I've only given Ned three treats. Even with what Ryder just fed him, the jar should still be close to full. Want to explain why it's half-empty?"

"Your wife came through earlier."

Titus's gravelly laugh rang out. "I'm going to tell her that you're blaming her when we both know you toss that mutt a treat every time he looks in your direction."

Ryder figured it was better to stay out of the argument. The last thing he wanted to do was offend the two men who were going to be cooking his next meal. "Come on, Juni. Let's go find a table while these two hash out their differences."

Titus washed his hands at the sink. "I'll be out in a minute to take your orders unless you already know what you want."

"What do you think, Juni? Do you want to study the menu or are you ready to order?"

She didn't hesitate. "I'd like the Greek omelet with coffee to drink."

"I'll have the same."

"Your food should be ready soon. I'll bring it along with a fresh pot of coffee." Then Titus pointed toward the far side of the diner. "Take the table over by the window."

"Thanks, man."

Juni headed out of the room. Ryder started to follow her, but Titus stopped him. "Can you wait a second? It won't take long."

"I'll be there in a minute, Juni."

"No problem."

When she was gone, any hint of humor disappeared from Titus's face. The change brought Ryder up short. "What's wrong?"

"Nothing's wrong, but a couple of guys here in town have asked me and Shay if you and Juni are a thing. They've seen her around, and they're interested."

Ryder's own mood took a downward turn. "Was it the Calland brothers? Because if it was them, I thought I made it pretty clear how I felt about the subject."

"They're here, but they're not the only ones who have been asking. I just thought you should know. The problem is that I don't know how she feels about your relationship. If you're really just friends, then you have no right to fend off any other contenders, and she can date anyone she wants."

Titus leaned in closer, meeting Ryder eye to eye. "If it's something more, you need to make sure you two are on the same page."

This was not a conversation Ryder wanted to be having. "Since when do you write an advice column, Titus?"

The other man didn't appreciate the snide remark, but at least he didn't go on the attack. "Yeah, I'm aware that I'm the last person who should be giving anyone advice, bonehead. I'm simply saying from the outside looking in, you and that lady have something good going on. You need to figure out where this friendship is headed before you manage to mess it up bigtime. Now, go sit down. Last time I looked, the Callands were still finishing up their breakfasts."

Ryder hadn't fully unpacked everything Titus was trying to tell him, but right now he was flashing back to the night at Barnaby's, seeing Trace and Logan talking to Juni. Once again, his temper instantly flared red hot, a sign that Titus was right on target with his assessment of the situation. Ryder really needed to get his head on straight when it came to Juni. He had no real claim on her and probably would have to back off if she suddenly decided she wanted to date someone else. As long as Ryder himself wasn't interested in anything permanent, he had no right to tell her she shouldn't see someone else.

It took him several deep breaths to get his blood pressure back down to somewhere close to normal. "Thanks for letting me know, Titus."

The other man's big hand came down on his shoulder. "Like I said, I'm no expert in relationships. Heaven knows my own mistakes cost me and Moira ten years that we could've had together. I suspect you've been through some stuff, but all of that's in the past. Don't let it screw up your future, too. Now, go before she thinks you've abandoned her."

All Ryder could do at that point was nod and head out into the café. It was a huge relief to see Juni was sitting alone when he finally located her in the crowded room. She must have been watching for him, because she smiled and waved to make sure that he saw her.

As he wound his way between the other tables, he spotted the Calland brothers. They were seated on the opposite end of the room. It wasn't clear if either of them had noticed Juni walk in, but Ryder could breathe more easily.

By the time he sat down, he had himself under control. Or at least he thought he had, but Juni had clearly noticed something wasn't right. "What's wrong, Ryder? Did Titus share some bad news?"

Yeah, but not the kind she was thinking. "No, he just wanted me to know that a couple of guys in town had been asking about me. Everything is fine."

For now, anyway.

She glanced past him toward the kitchen door. "Looks like our food is already on its way."

Good. At least while they were eating, he wouldn't have to deal with questions about the nature of their relationship. As soon as Titus set down the plates, Ryder picked up his fork and dug right in.

JUNI BUCKLED HER SEAT BELT. "That was fun. I'd love to do that again."

She and Ryder had made several trips around the trail that looped through the woods behind the shelter, taking a different bunch of dogs each trip. It had been a while since she'd spent so much time outside, and the exercise had done her a lot of good. Their four-legged companions had enjoyed the excursions as well. Ryder had suggested that they let the dogs set the pace, allowing them to sniff and explore to their hearts' content along the way.

Juni had felt a bit guilty when it came time to leave and the dogs had to return to their kennels. At least all of them had seemed content to curl up on their beds and settle in for a nap. "I hope they all find homes soon."

"The shelter has a pretty high success rate for

placing them in good homes. In fact, it's where Shay and Luca found the two dogs they adopted. The original plan was to adopt just one, but they couldn't bring themselves to separate the pair since the dogs were brothers. It's turned out well for all concerned."

"How did you get involved in the shelter?"

"Through Titus. He noticed my van and asked if there was any chance I'd be willing to haul some food to the shelter. He used to take it in the back of his truck, but it doesn't have a cover over the bed. It happened to be raining like crazy, and he didn't want the food to get wet. I delivered the stuff and checked the place out for myself. I'd been looking for something to get involved in for a while, and it fit the bill."

"I bet they appreciate everything you do to help out." She smiled at him. "For sure they were excited about the box of doughnuts you left in the staff room. I didn't have the heart to steal one of the fritters for myself."

"I'm sure they appreciated your restraint."

"I hope so." She sighed. "I have to admit I can't stop thinking about Millie, that yellow Lab mix. If I were going to stay here permanently, I'm pretty sure I'd be back at the shelter filling out adoption paperwork. She was such a sweetie."

"No reason you couldn't adopt her even if you

are planning on moving back home. The shelter doesn't insist the dogs have to stay in this area. I know your aunt wouldn't allow pets because of your cousin's allergies, but don't either of you have your own apartments?"

"Erin shares a place with a friend from college, but I was still living at home until I came here. After college, I moved into the mother-in-law apartment in my aunt and uncle's basement. They wouldn't let me pay rent while I paid off my student loans. Now that I'm out of debt, I plan to find a place of my own. But until that happens, I wouldn't have anywhere to leave Millie until I get settled in."

He shrugged. "You could always leave her with me for the short term if you're really serious about wanting to give her a permanent home. It's a major decision, and I know it's something you need to think about. Just know I'm willing to help if you need me to."

She appreciated him preaching caution, but remembering Millie's big brown eyes and playful nature made it hard not to ask Ryder to turn back around. Another problem occurred to her. "I'd also have to ask the property manager I've been dealing with what my landlord's policy is about having pets. The subject didn't come up when I rented the cabin since I didn't have a pet to worry about at the time."

By that point, they were on the road that led to their cabins. "You don't have to worry about that. Your landlord won't have a problem with it."

That he spoke with such confidence surprised her. "Do you actually know him? Or I guess it could be a her. Shelby was asking me if I knew who owned the cabins. Seems she's really curious about who bought them a while back."

Something about the amused look on Ryder's face had Juni jumping to an interesting conclusion. "It's you, isn't it?"

"What makes you say that?"

"I'm right, aren't I?"

"Yeah, I actually own several properties in the area. Although Cade doesn't know it, he rented one of my places when he first moved to town. He loved it so much, he kept nagging my property manager to see if I would be willing to sell it to him."

"Did you?"

"Yeah, I did. I used the money from that sale to buy the A-frame you're living in. It worked out well for everybody."

Then he changed topics. "But about Millie. You obviously need time to think things through. It's hard to do that if you're worried about someone else adopting her in the interim. I'll call the manager of the shelter and ask her to put a hold on Millie for a week."

"I wouldn't want you to break any rules for me."

"Don't worry about it. We've done it before. Let me know when you make a decision." He pulled into her driveway and stopped. "Thanks for going with me today. Have fun playing with your crayons, but do try to stay in the lines."

She gave him a soft punch on his arm. "I'll have you know my kindergarten teacher used to hold up my artwork as an example to the other kids."

Then she looked around as if to make sure they were alone and whispered, "The secret is having one of those big boxes of crayons with a built in sharpener."

He laughed. "Noted. I'll have to pick up a box the next time I go shopping."

"Thanks for getting me out of the house for a while today. I tend to get lost in my work and forget to do healthy things like exercising and breathing fresh air."

"I'm not trying to unduly influence your decision regarding Millie, but having a dog will remind you of such things on a regular basis. Lab mixes like her need regular exercise, which translates into you getting some at the same time."

She opened the van door. "I'll add that to the pro side of my list of things to consider."

By that point, she was down on the ground.

"Just so you know, I'll be gone tomorrow morning, and I'm not sure when I'll be back. I'm meeting Sabrina Luberti at her home. We're going to go over all of the illustrations I've done so far and talk about any changes she might want."

"Are you worried about that?"

"Not exactly. So far her requests have been pretty reasonable, and she's liked the tweaks I've made at her request. It's just that this will be our first in-person meeting, and I've always found it easier to take criticism or suggestions from a distance."

"You'll do fine, Juni. Everyone likes you."

She crossed her fingers and held them up. "I hope so. From what her editor told me, they're hoping this will be the first book in a whole series about the same bears. It could mean long-term employment for me."

"Call me when you get home. We'll either celebrate or commiserate, whichever is appropriate."

"It's a deal."

He waited until she was inside before driving away. She waved from the front window and then put on the requisite pot of coffee that she'd need to power her evening's work. There were several preliminary sketches she wanted to touch up before her meeting with Sabrina. They were her first thoughts on scenes that came later in the book. Experience had taught her that Sabrina liked to have several options to consider before making a final decision on how things should look. Most often, she picked a few details from each version, which Juni would then blend together into one cohesive whole.

But before she could bring herself to concentrate on the work she had under contract, she found herself drawing a picture of the front of the animal shelter. When that was done to her satisfaction, she surrounded it with a circle of small portraits of the dogs she and Ryder had walked today. It was the kind of thing she did when she needed to think something through, but normally she only made a rough sketch. The process usually helped settle her mind so she could concentrate on the work at hand.

This time, though, she couldn't seem to stop, drawing sketch after sketch until the paper was filled with images of would-be pets who were hoping for homes. One dog stood front and center—Millie. Rather than stuffing the finished product into her portfolio, she called Ryder and left a message on his voicemail.

"Look, I know you're on duty tonight. I just wanted you to know that I've made up my mind about Millie. I'll be making an appointment at the shelter to start the adoption process. Let me know if you want to come with me."

After a brief hesitation, she added, "Stay safe out there tonight."

With her decision made and her message delivered, she finally got to work.

CHAPTER FIFTEEN

ON IMPULSE, Juni pulled over onto the shoulder of the road half a mile short of her destination. Seeing as she was a little early for her in-person appointment, it wouldn't hurt to take a moment to gather herself. While she and Sabrina Luberti had only talked on the phone or through online meetings, there was no logical reason to think that being in the same room with the author would be any different.

However, right now Juni's mind was being anything but logical.

She checked her appearance in the rearview mirror one more time. She rarely wore more than minimal makeup. However, she'd taken a little more effort with her appearance this morning, using a brighter shade of lipstick, a little more mascara and a touch of eye shadow. After some deliberation, she'd decided to slick her hair back in a high ponytail rather that wearing it down around her shoulders. She'd also tried on and rejected three different outfits before deciding business casual was the right way to go. Pairing her favorite navy slacks with a lightweight cream sweater and low heels looked professional but understated.

After touching up her lipstick one last time, Juni took a calming breath and gave herself a pep talk. "You can do this. You already know Sabrina likes your artwork. That's all that matters. There's no reason to think something will go wrong. It's not like my whole career is on the line here."

Breathe in. Breathe out.

"Don't forget. Ryder also likes your work."

Of course, he didn't have any say in the matter, but somehow knowing Ryder had the caricature she'd drawn of him hanging on his living room wall helped settle her nerves. "Okay, let's do this."

Five minutes later, she stood on Sabrina's front deck with her portfolio in hand. She had been curious to see what the author's home would look like. From the kind of books Sabrina wrote, Juni had expected a cozy cottage or perhaps a Victorian-style house with a lot of gingerbread trim painted in a rainbow of colors. Boy, had she missed the mark! As it turned out, the house was ultramodern with lots of glass and sharp angles.

Perched at the top of a steep rise, it offered an incredible view of a small valley and the mountains to the east. If Juni lived there, she would spend all of her time trying to capture the incredible beauty on canvas or paper. Oils would be perfect for the deep green of the forest with the snowcapped mountains forming the backdrop. On the other hand, watercolors would be the better choice to capture the soft light of dawn as it crept up and over the mountain ridge to flow down into the valley to banish the last of the night's shadows. The possibilities were endless.

She turned away from the amazing vista when the door behind her opened and Sabrina joined her on the deck. "I thought I heard someone out here."

Juni smiled. "Sorry, I was about to ring the bell when I got caught up in the amazing view."

The comment clearly pleased the other woman. She walked across the porch to lean against the railing and stare out into the distance. "My late husband and I took one look at this place and knew we'd never want to live anywhere else. We used to enjoy a glass of wine out here when the weather permitted. Even now when I'm writing and hit a rough spot, I come out to admire the view—rain or shine—and somehow I always find the inspiration I need."

Juni held her face up to the warmth of the sun. "I can see why. I was just trying to decide whether I'd have better luck capturing all of this beauty with oils or watercolors."

Sabrina continued to study the scene in front of them. "I'd love to see what you come up with. At our best, we authors can create vivid images and evoke powerful emotions with our writing. But words aren't the only way to capture an image and the feelings it inspires."

She offered Juni a wry grin. "Also, it's a lot more convenient to look at a piece of artwork on the wall than it is to get out a book and hunt for the right descriptive passage."

Juni nodded. "That's so true. Although I have to admit that I've reread some of my favorite books so often that they fall open to the best parts."

"I have a few books that are well trained like that." Sabrina stepped back from the railing. "Let's head inside. I thought we could enjoy some tea and scones before we get down to business."

"That sounds lovely."

Juni followed her inside, stopping by the door long enough to follow her hostess's lead by slipping off her shoes before going any farther.

Sabrina led the way into the kitchen. She motioned toward the antique round oak pedestal table in the corner. "Make yourself comfortable. The light is better in here than in the dining room, so I thought this is where we'd hang out. Just so you know, I can hardly wait to see your newest sketches."

The tea Sabrina had brewed was Earl Grey, one of Juni's favorites. Its citrusy flavor partnered well with scones topped with lemon curd.

"You didn't need to go to all of this trouble," Juni said, "but I'm glad you did."

"It was no trouble at all." Sabrina added another dollop of the curd on top of her scone. "I love to bake but don't do it often since I'd end up eating it all myself. It's hard to resist that much temptation."

Juni laughed. "My aunt bakes all the time, so there was always something sweet and carby around. I thought I might be able to wean myself from craving sugary treats when I moved to Dunbar. Sadly, it hasn't worked out that way. There's a café in town that offers huge, freshly baked cinnamon rolls that are to die for as well as some amazing pies. If that's not bad enough, there's also a bakery that serves up fresh apple fritters and bacon-maple bars."

Sabrina's eyes widened. "Seriously? Bacon on a maple bar?"

"Yeah, I know it sounds weird, but they are amazing. You can't go wrong with a still warm doughnut covered with maple icing and a strip of smoky bacon."

The other woman still didn't look convinced. "If you say so."

Juni offered her a wicked grin and waggled her eyebrows. "I could always bring you one the next time I come."

Assuming she got invited back.

Sabrina pondered for fewer than five seconds before deciding to accept the offer. "I don't need to develop another bad habit, but I'm always up for trying something new. I'll probably regret it, but please do me a favor and don't tell me the name of the bakery. If their pastries are as good as you say they are, I'd probably be making a daily trip to Dunbar to buy more."

"It's a deal."

THEY LINGERED OVER the last of the tea and scones, but finally it was time to get down to business. When all of her earlier tension came surging back, Juni instantly regretted that last scone. She did her best to hide her nervousness by carrying the dishes and empty teapot over to the counter while Sabrina wiped down the table to make sure there was nothing that might damage or stain Juni's artwork.

"Okay, let's see what you've got."

Juni nodded. She'd had enlargements made of her computer sketches at a local print shop so Sabrina could see the artwork in greater detail than on a laptop screen. After removing the stack of the prints from her portfolio, she set it aside and spread the illustrations out in the order they would appear in the book. When they were arranged to her satisfaction, she retreated to the other side of the room to let her client view them without having Juni hovering over her shoulder.

Sabrina murmured under her breath as she picked up the first sketch and studied it before moving on to the next. Time seemed to drag on forever, but it couldn't have been more than a few minutes when she finally returned the last drawing to its place in the lineup. By that point, Juni's pulse was pounding in her head. Worse yet, her hands were shaking enough that she clasped them behind her back to hide them from sight.

Why wasn't Sabrina saying anything? Positive or negative didn't matter. The waiting was worse. Sabrina reached out to straighten one of the sketches and then turned to face Juni with a huge smile on her face.

"I don't know how you've done it, Juni, but it's as if you've somehow plucked the exact images out of my mind. I might ask for a few minor tweaks at some point, but I know my editor is going to love them as much as I do."

Juni knew she should accept the compliment with some degree of professional confidence.

That wasn't going to happen. Instead, she could only ask, "Really?"

"Really."

Sabrina crossed the distance between them and gave Juni a quick hug. "I know just how you feel. I still panic every time I send a new proposal to my editor, wondering if I still remember how to write a book. You'd think that at some point we'd gain enough confidence in our talent to get past all of that."

Juni huffed a small laugh. "Maybe that's what motivates us to keep trying to improve our skills. You know, so that someday we'll finally master the one thing that will grant us some semblance of confidence."

"I wouldn't be surprised." Sabrina stepped back and quietly said, "Let's sit down and talk about what comes next."

As Juni resumed her seat at the table, she swallowed hard, trying to clear the huge lump of tension currently lodged in her throat. The solemn expression on Sabrina's face at that moment maybe meant not all the news was going to be good. Doing her best to brace herself for whatever was about to come, she said, "Okay, I'm ready."

Sabrina met her gaze briefly before turning to study the sketches again. "I love your work. I meant every word I said—when I see these, it's as if I'm looking at the images in my own head. I will admit I was a bit hesitant when my editor said they wanted me to work with a relatively inexperienced illustrator on this series. She really loved the samples you submitted to them. As it's turned out, I'm glad I listened to her."

Juni had to ask, "Why not use the same illustrator who did your last books? I've looked at them, and the artwork was great."

"Yes, it was. However, Jason's career has really taken off, and he gets more job offers than he can handle. It was going to be at least a year before he could get around to doing the artwork for my current book, much less the sequels I already have planned."

There wasn't much Juni could say until she figured out where Sabrina was headed with this. Even so, she nodded if for no other reason than to make it clear she was listening. As soon as she did, Sabrina moved on. "One of the reasons I liked working with Jason was that he was local. We didn't get together often, but we met to talk about everything at least once on each book. I know most of the time that illustrators and authors don't meet in person, but I've always preferred to do that. Call me old-fashioned, but it's easier to convey what I'm looking for when we can share a cup of tea or coffee and talk things out."

•

"I can understand that."

Although it was a lot to ask. As a single woman with no kids, Juni was relatively unencumbered and free to make the move at least for a short time. That hadn't stopped her aunt and uncle from doing their best to talk her out of accepting the contract that would take her so far from home. She understood where they were coming from and knew they weren't controlling as much as overprotective. They were the same with their daughter.

As a result, Juni had debated long and hard about her decision to move to Dunbar. In the end, she'd decided the chance to work with such a successful author didn't come around all that often. It was also a chance to prove she was no longer the broken little girl she'd been after her parents died and she'd been sent to live with people she'd barely known. Even so, her aunt and uncle might still be resistant to her getting her own place when she returned, but that was a problem for another day.

Meanwhile, Sabrina was still talking. "I do want to thank you again for accommodating my little foible."

"I was glad to do it."

Sabrina gave Juni a considering look. "I suppose it would be too soon to ask if you might be willing to extend your stay in the area beyond the original six months. I already have the next three books in this series under contract, but I've also been working on another idea. It will be a while before I get the concept nailed down to the point that I'll be ready for my agent to submit the proposal to my publisher. It will also take some time for them to decide whether they want to buy it. Until that happens, there would be no reason to start talking about the artwork."

Juni bit her lip to keep from making any kind of commitment until she gave the matter some serious thought. "First, I'm honored that you like my work enough to want to continue collaborating with me, but I would like some time to think about it."

Sabrina studied her for several seconds. "That's probably a wise decision on your part, Juni. I want to be clear, this is not a do-or-die situation. I can't expect you to change all your plans because of a project that I can't guarantee will actually succeed. I really just wanted to let you know about the possibility. For now, we can concentrate on the remaining bear books. My editor has finished reading the text for the second book and sent it back for a few revisions. As soon as she accepts the changes, I'll send along the file so you can start working on preliminary sketches for that story. Otherwise, I promise I'll keep you posted about the other project as things move forward."

"I appreciate that."

It was time to head back to the cabin. As Sabrina helped her pack up the artwork, Juni said, "When I get home, I'll send you the digital files on these so you can decide what tweaks you want done. After I've finished, I'll send the updated files to you and the editor."

Sabrina followed her out the front door. "By the way, I meant what I said earlier. If you try your hand at painting a picture of the view from my deck, I would love to see it."

"You'll be the first."

On second thought, she'd more likely be the second considering how often Ryder managed to sneak a peek at Juni's work. She waved at Sabrina one last time before driving away. It was a huge relief to not have to make an immediate decision. At the same time, knowing that she might have work lined up for the foreseeable future had her wanting to celebrate big-time. She'd always shared any good news with Aunt Ruby and Uncle Colby, but they would be upset if she decided to remain in Dunbar a lot longer than originally expected.

And that was a problem. Yes, she was grateful for everything they'd ever done for her. That said, she needed to follow her dreams wherever they led her. Right now that meant living in Dunbar. One way or another, she would eventually have to have that conversation with them but not yet. There was no reason to get them all riled up if the second project didn't pan out.

No, she wanted to share the news with someone who wouldn't immediately start listing all the reasons why she shouldn't even consider the offer. So rather than driving straight back to her cabin, she would make a quick detour through Dunbar and pick up something special from Bea's. Then she'd stop at Ryder's place for a brief celebration before returning home. He wouldn't mind if she showed up unannounced. Heaven knew he'd done the same on more than one occasion.

Half an hour later, her plan fell apart because Ryder wasn't home. He hadn't said anything about being on duty at the fire station when they'd spoken the day before, but maybe he'd been called in unexpectedly. He could also be helping at the animal shelter while they finalized everything that needed to be done ahead of the festival on Saturday. Either way, it was disappointing to have missed him. It was also a reminder that the nature of their relationship did not include an obligation to keep each other in the loop when it came to their day-to-day activities.

It was tempting to hang around for a few minutes to see if he'd return, but she really did need to get back to her own place and work. That left only one question—should she leave him a note or send him a text that she had a treat with his name on it at her house? In the end, she decided against it. If he happened to show up later of his own accord, the apple fritter would still be good.

And if he didn't, well, she could always eat it for breakfast.

CHAPTER SIXTEEN

THE DAY OF the festival dawned cloudy and damp, but blue sky had started to peek out from the clouds by the time Ryder and Juni arrived at the park. He'd spent the previous evening with other volunteers setting up a row of booths. The animal shelter was only one of several local charities and organizations that used the festival as a chance to connect with the community. Other booths were for local vendors, craftsmen and artists wanting to sell their wares to friends and neighbors.

As soon as Juni spotted Bea's booth down the way, she got excited. "Hey, look who's open for breakfast! Even better, the line is really short right now. Why don't you start unloading the van while I get us some fresh coffee and something to eat?"

Ryder set down the box of forms and brochures and reached for his wallet. "Sounds good."

Juni waved him off. "My treat this time."

"Two sugars and cream. Biggest size she has. Order me two if she only has small cups."

"Got it."

She disappeared into the early morning crowd while he went back to work. A few seconds later, Titus wandered over. "Need any help?"

"Sure thing. Can you finish opening those boxes so I can unload them? Once they're empty, I'll dump them back in the van and move it back out to the parking lot."

Titus pulled out his pocket knife and got started. "I heard earlier that the shelter has had to split its attention between two different festivals today. Does that mean you have to work the booth all by yourself?"

"Nope. I drafted Juni to help me. She's hanging out with me this morning to learn the ropes. I'm scheduled to drive the fire truck in the parade, so she'll be on her own during that time."

"Nice of her to pitch in like that. She seems to do that a lot."

Ryder arranged a neat display of the shelter's brochures on the counter. "This time, she has an ulterior motive. She's planning to adopt one of the shelter dogs today. Millie's a young Lab mix and a real sweetheart. Once we get all the paperwork filled out, I'll get her set up with everything she needs. After that, Juni will bring Millie home to the cabin, at least for the time being."

Titus looked up from what he was doing. "What's that supposed to mean?"

Ryder sighed. "That she'll be taking Millie with her when she moves, whether she goes back home to Crestville or heads somewhere else."

A time that grew closer with each passing day, something Ryder needed to keep in mind. Even so, it was hard to ignore the heavy press of regret that settled somewhere in the middle of his chest.

Titus stopped working and shot Ryder a dark look. "Please tell me you've at least told her you'd like her to stay."

"It's not my call to make. Her career is just starting to take off, and that's her focus now. She needs to be free to pursue her dreams. She moved here to establish her independence from her overprotective family. She doesn't need me trying to hold her back."

"I'm sorry to hear that." Titus picked up another box to flatten. "Forget I said anything. After our last discussion, I promised myself I'd stay out of your personal business."

"Good idea. I can only imagine how you would have reacted if I had tried to give you advice on how best to convince Moira to give you another—"

He realized Titus was no longer listening. Instead he was focused on something happening behind Ryder. When he turned to see what was going on, his blood ran cold and then hot. Juni was headed back toward the booth, but she wasn't alone. No, she was flanked by the Calland brothers and laughing at something one of them had just said. Obviously they'd completely forgotten their encounter with Ryder at the tavern.

Flexing his fists, Ryder gritted his teeth and counted to ten. When that didn't work, he doubled his efforts and counted to twenty. It was tempting—so, so tempting—to give them a quick reminder of their previous discussion. Instead, he turned his back to the trio, hoping that would help tamp down his temper.

At least Titus was there to talk some sense into him. "Steady there, Ryder. If Juni was interested in either of them, she would continue hanging out with them instead of coming back here to you. Instead, she's headed this way, and they're gone. She's almost here, so calm the heck down. If you'll remember, she didn't appreciate you running them off the last time. Don't be a jealous jerk, especially in public. Besides, it's not like you're intending to stake an official claim on her. Friends only, remember?"

Then he muttered, "Unless that changes."

That last part wasn't exactly a question, but Ryder took it that way. "Again, she's only here for a few more months, Titus. If she'd asked to extend her lease, I'd know."

"So based on your 'friends only' status, you're assuming she would've immediately told you if she'd changed her mind."

It was hard not to smirk a little when he answered, "That, and the fact that I'm her landlord."

That little bombshell left Titus staring at Ryder as if he'd grown a second head. "You're not renting? You actually own those A-frames?"

Ryder rearranged the samples of dog and cat foods that a local pet store had donated as giveaways. "Yeah, as well as several other rentals in the area."

Titus mulled that over for several seconds. "By any chance did you also own the place Cade and Shelby just bought? If so, do they know?"

"I did, and I'm not sure if they ever figured it out. All of my properties are owned in the name of my LLC, so they dealt with the corporation's attorney, not me."

By that point, Titus had an evil grin on his face. "They've made some pretty wild guesses about who sold them the house. I love knowing the answer when they don't, but it's not nice to lord it over them if I can't actually tell them."

There was no real reason he shouldn't, but Ryder still hesitated. When Titus noticed, he held up his hands. "Forget it. It's your secret to share."

Juni was almost within hearing now. He'd already shared a lot about his past with her in the short time he'd known her. Maybe it was time he did the same with someone else who had shown him nothing but friendship.

"I know we kid around about me having big bucks, but here's the thing. It's not exactly a joke. This isn't the time or place to go into a lot of details, but let's just say that I started my own business at a ridiculously young age. I made a ton of money, but it literally almost killed me in the process. I also learned that when some people find out that I'm rich, they follow me around with their hands out. It's hard to trust people when you don't know if it's you they like or if it's your bank account."

"I get that. Like I said, it's your secret to share." Titus flattened the last of the boxes. "Is there anything else I can do?"

"Nope, we're good."

Juni joined them. She set a cardboard tray down on the table. After handing Ryder a cup of coffee, she held out a second one to Titus. "I brought you a cup, too. I also bought extra breakfast sandwiches."

Her kind gesture clearly pleased Titus. "Thanks, Juni. That will hit the spot. Breakfast was quite a while ago. Moira got called out about four this morning."

She studied both men with a slightly puzzled expression on her face. "I hope I didn't interrupt something."

Ryder had been about to take a bite of his sandwich. "Why would you say that?"

She shrugged. "Because the two of you looked as if you were in the middle of a pretty serious conversation. I can go wander around for a while if you would like me to."

Titus offered up one of his usual rough laughs. "Can't say the woman doesn't have good instincts. Reminds me of Moira."

"Titus just found out that I'm your landlord. Evidently me being landed gentry came as a bit of a surprise. I don't know why he was so shocked by that."

She gave his holey jeans and faded T-shirt a pointed look. "Well, it's not like you exactly dress the part."

True enough. "So the next time I'm on the hook to do a bunch of manual labor, I should wear my tuxedo?"

Titus almost choked on his sandwich. "You own a tux?"

"No." This was getting to be really entertaining. "I actually own three."

Might as well keep going. "If I'd worn a tux today, I would've had to also drive my Jag to complete the image. However, it would have been hard to cram all of these boxes in the boot."

His friend stared first at Ryder and then at Juni as he tried to decide if Ryder was jerking his chain. "Right. You own a Jag."

When Ryder didn't respond one way or the other, Juni took pity on the man. "Yeah, he does. It's a real beauty, too. Dark green with tan leather interior. I've ridden in it. Ryder drove it the night we went to dinner at his parents' house. He was afraid their homeowners' association would tow his rusty old van out of their fancy neighborhood."

Even Ryder had to laugh at that. Then Titus's expression turned sly. "When do I get to drive it?"

"Fat chance, buddy. I might take you for a spin in it sometime, but I've seen the way you drive. There's no way I'd let you behind the wheel."

"Jerk."

"No arguments there. She's my baby, and I'd have to deck you if you managed to get her dinged up."

"You could try. I could take you in a fair fight—not that I'd fight fair."

Juni giggled. "Right now I'm picturing Moira cuffing both of you and hauling you off to the slammer."

Titus gave an exaggerated shudder. "She would, too. The woman has no patience with fools."

"And what woman is that?"

He whipped around to grin at his wife, who had just slipped up behind him. "You, of course. Ryder is being a total jerk. Did you know he's been hiding the fact that he owns three tuxedos and a classic Jag? Not only that, he won't let me drive it. He also threatened me with bodily harm if I managed to scratch it."

Moira rolled her eyes. "Can you blame him? You're my husband, and I love you. That doesn't mean I would let you drive a car like that if I owned one."

By that point, Titus was looking pretty disgusted. "I am not that bad of a driver."

Juni tactfully tried to change the subject. She held out the bag with the food she'd bought from Bea. "Moira, I bought a few extra breakfast sandwiches. Would you like one?"

"That would be great."

As Moira unwrapped the sandwich, she gave Ryder a considering look. "I never figured you for the tuxedo type, but I bet you clean up pretty well."

"Thanks." Although Ryder was pretty sure there might be a hint of an insult tucked into her assessment.

Juni laughed and pretended to fan her face. "You know, he really does. There's just something about a man in a tuxedo that does it for me. Seriously, I almost fainted when he picked me up in that Jag. It was like something out of a rom-com. You know the kind where the guy who lives next door turns out to be a prince or a duke."

By that point, Ryder was pretty sure he was blushing. On the other hand, Titus was busy glaring at the two giggling women. "Hey, I'll have you know he's not the only one who can rock a tux."

His wife reached up to pat him on the cheek. "I'm sure you can. But since I've never seen you in one, I'll have to take your word for it."

Ryder was only too glad to have the focus of the conversation switch to his friend. "You can have one of mine if you want. We're fairly close to the same size, so it wouldn't take much to alter it to fit."

Titus crossed his arms over his chest and glared at him. "Only if you'll loan me the car for an evening to complete the image."

Juni bit her lower lip, probably trying to hold back her laughter, as both Moira and Titus waited to see if he'd take the bait. Even if the trio was ganging up on him, Ryder knew he was surrounded by trusted friends who liked him for who he truly was, not just courting his favor in the hopes of a handout. "Fine. You can borrow my car for an evening, but you have to promise to have her home at a decent hour. I'd like it even better if it was before dark. Oh, and no drinking. You have to be clearheaded and at your best when you're behind the wheel."

Even with the limitations, Titus looked shocked at Ryder's capitulation. "Seriously, man. You don't have to do this. We were only kidding."

His wife gave him an elbow in his ribs. "Speak for yourself, big guy. I want to see you in a tux and driving a classic car."

Ryder took pity on his friend. "Let me know when you two want the keys. Also, I was only kidding about having her home before sunset. You might as well make a night of it."

Moira looked delighted by the prospects. "I'll check the schedule at work to see when I have a weekend off."

Titus captured her hand in his and brushed a quick kiss on it. "As soon as you find that out, I'll make the reservations."

Then he checked the time. "Oops, I promised Gunner I wouldn't be gone long. See you guys later."

Moira turned to follow him. "And I have to get back on patrol. Thanks for the sandwich, Juni. We'll have to get together for coffee one of these days soon."

Juni looked pleased by the idea. "I'd love that. I'm hoping to attend the book club meeting next week. I'm not quite done with the book, but I'm enjoying it."

"I enjoyed it myself. It will be a fun book to talk about."

Ryder went back to work after his friends left. When he turned around to set out some clipboards with adoption forms on them, he noticed that Juni was still watching Titus and Moira as they walked away.

"Something wrong?"

His question startled her out of her reverie. "No, not really."

He bet that was patently untrue, especially when she turned her attention to the sample pet food he'd set out on the counter in neat rows and began to rearrange them. He didn't comment, figuring the busywork gave her something to focus on besides whatever was troubling her. Rather than press for an answer, he went back to work himself. He'd have to head to the firehouse in an hour to change into his uniform and drive the truck to the parking lot where the parade would be forming up.

A few seconds later, she sighed. "Sometimes it's hard not to be a bit jealous of what Moira and Titus have together. Then there's Cade and Shelby. Max and Rikki. Shay and Carli."

Yeah, lately he'd felt that way a few times himself. In an effort to lighten the moment, he said, "I suspect it's something in the water…or more likely Titus's pies."

She responded with a small smile. "You might be on to something there. From what I gather, there have been a lot of surprise weddings since he opened his café. On the other hand, that wouldn't account for my cousin and her fiancé."

"You haven't talked about the wedding much. Did your cousin ever find someone to organize it for her?"

"Yeah, she did. Aunt Ruby says the woman they hired has everything on track. Besides the church, they've already lined up most of the vendors they need—florist, caterer, DJ and the reception hall. Now Erin is on a mission to find the perfect dress."

She huffed a small laugh. "I'll deny saying this, but it is a huge relief I'm on the wrong side of the state to get caught up in that. Aunt Ruby is really excited that Erin and Phillip are getting married, but even she is losing her enthusiasm for dress shopping. Once they do find Erin's dress, then we'll have to start shopping for the bridesmaids' dresses."

"I assume you're still going to be in the wedding party."

"Yeah, I am." Not that she looked happy about it.

He risked bringing up what might be a sore subject. "Do you like her fiancé?"

Juni's wince was painful to see, and he immediately regretted asking the question. "Never mind. It's none of my business."

"No, it's okay. It's just that I dated Phillip first." She continued fiddling with the pet food and spoke in a soft voice laced with a hint of remembered pain. "We met when I was in college. We'd been dating a couple of months when I took him home to meet the family. Over that weekend, something clicked between him and Erin."

She paused to snap her fingers. "And just like that, I was the odd woman out. I wasn't happy it happened, of course, but even I can't deny they've found something special together. They both felt terrible about it."

"As well they should." He hated that their actions hurt Juni even if she seemed to have come to terms with the situation. Mostly, anyway.

"I know they didn't mean for it to happen, and looking back, it could've been much worse. What if they'd fallen in love after he and I had gotten married? Or what if he'd married me out of a sense of obligation? All three of us could easily have ended up miserable."

She finally stacked the pet food to her satisfaction and picked up one of the clipboards and a pen. "That's enough on that subject. Water under the bridge and all of that. I'm going to fill out the adoption papers."

"Let me know if you have any questions."

He didn't expect her to have any problems since the form was pretty straightforward. Even so, he kept an eye on her as he finished organizing the booth. It occurred to him that each of them had skated pretty close to marrying the wrong person. Even if Juni hadn't officially been engaged to the guy, he suspected she'd been thinking that was a distinct possibility. He had no doubt that it had been hard for her at the time even if she'd picked up the pieces and moved on.

It hadn't been easy for him to break it off with Jasmine, but he hadn't done it on a whim. The only regret he had was that it had hurt them both even if it was the right decision in the long run. He really hoped that eventually Jazz would accept that she was better off without him. There was no way he'd ever go back to the lifestyle that meant so much to her. She truly loved her job and lived to hobnob with the influential people in the local business community. That wasn't the life he wanted, not anymore.

Dunbar had become home to him, and the people who lived there had become his friends and neighbors. More importantly, the slower pace of life gave him the time and space to think about what might come next for him. He was starting to realize he would eventually want to do something more challenging than volunteering at the shelter and the fire department. Being around Juni reminded him of how much he'd enjoyed the creative process even if he'd grown to hate the pressure he'd been under.

It was impossible to imagine Jasmine sharing the small-town life, but Juni was different. She'd quickly managed to carve out a place for herself in Dunbar, effortlessly gathering a new set of friends along the way. He might have eased the way by introducing her to the locals, but she'd managed to charm them all on her own. It was almost scary how easily she'd slipped into his life, changing things even without meaning to. Suddenly, he was sharing the secrets of his past not only with her, but with Titus.

She'd described herself as the odd woman out when it came to her cousin and her fiancé. He'd experienced some of that same awkward feeling himself as one by one his friends had fallen in love. It occurred to him that he hadn't felt that way for a while now, and he knew the minute that change had started. He'd been standing up in a tree, hoping he could capture a feral kitten and get back down to the ground without injuring either one of them. He'd had some serious doubts he'd be that lucky. Then he'd looked down and seen the answer to all of his immediate problems written in a beautiful woman's smile.

"Hey, Ryder, can you look this over and make sure I filled it out correctly?"

He'd had his back to her, not sure how much of what he was feeling would show on his face. To buy himself a little time, he picked up a stack of the flattened boxes and carried them over to the van before joining her at the counter. He gave the form a quick read. "Looks great. You shouldn't have any problems finalizing the adoption today as soon as we get done here. The director kept Millie back for you. She doesn't like to bring animals that are spoken for to adoption events."

"That makes sense, and I really appreciate it."

He handed her back the clipboard just as the shelter's van pulled up beside the booth. "Talk about perfect timing. Looks like our special guests have arrived. The volunteers will need our help getting set up. The good news is that you can be one of the first to pet the cats and dogs." Juni's face lit up, once again charming him with her ability to find happiness in every situation. Surprisingly, her smile disappeared as quickly as it had appeared.

"What's wrong?"

"I'm a bit scared, Ryder. I've never had a pet of any kind before. What if I take Millie home only to find out she's not happy living with me?"

He gave into the temptation to give her a reassuring hug along with his honest opinion on the subject. "Millie struck me as a smart dog. She took one look at you and knew she'd found her forever person. The two of you were made for each other."

There was one other truth he didn't share with her—that right now, he was jealous as heck of Millie.

CHAPTER SEVENTEEN

Juni was having a great time covering the booth while Ryder was off doing his thing at the fire station. She'd started off by having an interesting conversation with two young girls whose parents had promised to let them adopt a pair of kittens. She'd taken notes about their preferred colors and even jotted down the names the girls were considering for their yet to be chosen pets. All of that had kept them entertained while their parents had completed the necessary paperwork.

As soon as they were finished, she'd directed them to the viewing area the other volunteers had set up so people could meet the shelter animals. She'd been surprised to learn that there were more than just cats and dogs. Three bunnies, two guinea pigs and even a pygmy goat had joined the party.

The shelter had also sent along several notebooks with pictures of other animals that were available for adoption. It wasn't practical to bring them all to the festival, especially when they had another adoption event going on at a different location. The notebooks made it easier for interested parties to consider all the possible candidates.

By the time the young family walked away, the girls were positively bouncing with excitement. Juni knew exactly how they felt. It was only a matter of a few hours before she'd be bringing home a furry roommate of her own. She hadn't been exaggerating when she told Ryder how nervous she was, but knowing he would be there to help would go a long way toward calming her fears.

The only big hurdle she had left to face was breaking the news to her aunt and uncle. They still thought she'd be moving back into their mother-in-law apartment when she eventually returned home. The truth was she'd been planning on moving into an apartment of her own even before she'd decided to adopt Millie.

She needed room to breathe, to make her own decisions without being second-guessed every step of the way. If she moved back into their mother-in-law apartment, they would once again wade in on every topic whether she was in need of help or not. It wasn't until she'd moved into the A-frame that she'd realized how bad the situation had become.

That had her thinking back to the discussion

she'd had with Sabrina about the possibility of Juni extending her stay in Dunbar while they worked on the bear books. It was such a tempting proposition. Even if the separate project Sabrina was working on never came to fruition it didn't really matter. Juni did most of her work remotely anyway. Living in the woods near the Cascades wouldn't prevent her from competing for jobs all over the country. She also preferred living in a small town, especially one conveniently located so close to a major city like Seattle.

The crowd was suddenly on the move and heading for the road that wound through the park. The parade must be approaching. From what Ryder had told her, it formed at the far end of Dunbar and then traveled through the center of town toward the park. Once there, it would circle the park before reaching the end of its planned route.

She didn't want to stray too far from the booth, but she really wanted to see at least a little of the parade. It would be fun to wave at Ryder as he drove by. He and the other members of the fire department were supposed to be near the front of the parade, so she wouldn't have to wait long to see him. She could catch a glimpse of the fire truck as it went by and then hustle right back to the booth.

After scribbling a note on a piece of paper that said she'd be back soon, she took off at a slow run. When she approached the road, the Calland brothers spotted her and called her name. They were standing on a picnic table a few feet behind the people crowded along the edge of the road.

"Hey, guys! Did I miss anything?"

Trace shook his head. "Not yet. We were hoping to get here in time to get a spot at the front of the crowd, but our timing was off. That's why we staked out this picnic table. Want to join us?"

"Sure thing."

Because unless she gained enough elevation, she wouldn't be able to see anything at all. Logan held out his hand to keep her steady while she climbed up on the seat and then on the top of the table.

At that moment, the high school band slowed to a stop long enough to play a rousing march before continuing on down the road. Next came a family of five on horseback, all decked out in matching Western outfits. They stopped to do some fancy rope tricks. Then the riders waved their hats in the air as their horses reared up on their hind legs. The kids weren't the only ones in the crowd who went wild and applauded like crazy.

At long last, the fire truck rounded the corner to her left. As expected, Ryder was at the wheel. He gave the siren a short burst and drove down the road toward Juni and her two companions. She noticed he was scanning the crowd and waved her arms over her head to get his attention. As soon as Ryder spotted her, he waved back and looked happy to see her. A second later, his grin faded slightly. She wasn't sure why. Maybe he was worried about the booth being left unstaffed even for a few minutes.

By that point, the huge vehicle had come to a full stop, to give the firefighters and kids riding on the back end of the truck a chance to wave at family and friends as they threw candy to the crowd. The only one she recognized was Shay, who was decked out in his firefighter uniform and had Luca perched up on his shoulders. When she called their names, both of them waved at her in between tossing fistfuls of candy and what looked like firefighter badges to any kids who ran up to the side of the truck.

A short time later, Ryder sounded the siren again, warning everyone to retreat to a safe distance. When he got the all clear from one of the other firefighters, he eased the truck on down the road and out of sight. As much as she'd like to see more of the parade, it was time to get back to the booth.

Turning to Trace and Logan, she said, "Thanks for letting me share your table."

Before she could clamber back down, Logan stopped her. "Aren't you going to watch the rest of the parade?"

"Wish I could, but I'm covering the booth for the animal shelter while Ryder is driving the fire truck."

He gave her a curious look as he joined her on the ground. "I was going to see if you wanted to grab some lunch with me over by the food court, but it sounds like the two of you are still seeing each other."

Not in the way he meant, but even so she wasn't sure accepting Logan's invitation was a good idea. "Not exactly. Ryder and I are really good friends, not to mention next-door neighbors."

Logan kicked his smile up a notch. "So would your friend get upset if you had lunch with another friend? If not that, maybe dinner tonight?"

"Sorry, but for sure I can't do dinner. I'm adopting a dog later this afternoon, and it will be Millie's first night in her new home."

Evidently he wasn't going to give up easily. "But lunch will work?"

Yeah, but she needed to establish some ground rules. "I should probably warn you that I'm not looking to get seriously involved with anyone. I'm only living here in Dunbar on a temporary basis."

Logan took the news with good grace. "Well,

that is disappointing, but I appreciate the warning. Regardless, I'd still like to buy you lunch."

Okay, then. She checked the time. From what she'd heard, the parade had gotten off to a late start, which meant Ryder could be gone for a while yet. "How about I meet you at the food court in half an hour?"

"I'll see you there."

THE TRIP BACK to the fire station seemingly took forever. The day of the festival was one of the few occasions when Dunbar had enough traffic to cause actual delays getting through town. Ryder finally texted Juni and let her know he would be a little late getting back and to suggest that she take a break to get some lunch.

She'd responded within seconds to say she'd been about to do that exact thing. Then she added that her time in the booth was going smoothly. There'd been a steady stream of people stopping by, but so far she'd been able to answer their questions. It also seemed likely every animal they'd brought to the festival would have a new home within the next few days.

All of that was good news and relieved one area of concern as he carefully backed the truck into the garage at the station. Most of his passengers had stayed behind at the park to catch up with their families, but Shay and Luca had chosen to make the trip back with him. The boy loved fire trucks and the chance to ride in one didn't come around often. They'd also helped him make sure no candy wrappers or other trash had been left behind. The alarm could go off at any minute, and the truck needed to be ready for action.

Shay tossed the last few bits of trash in a nearby wastebasket. "Luca, I'm going to run upstairs to change clothes. Do you want to come with me or hang out down here with Ryder?"

"I'll stay here."

"Okay. I won't be long." Then Shay leaned down to whisper something in the boy's ear before disappearing up the steps.

Ryder was returning his gear to his locker when Luca tugged on his arm. "What's up, kiddo?"

"Thanks for letting me ride with you today, Mr. Ryder."

He gave the boy a quick hug. "You did a great job sharing the candy and badges with the kids along the parade route."

"I saw a bunch of my friends." He looked around to make sure no one else was listening before adding, "I threw them extras."

It was hard not to laugh at the boy's guilty confession. "That was nice of you. A guy should take good care of his friends."

"That's what my dad said."

At that point, a car pulled up outside the open door. "Looks like Carli is here to pick up you and Shay. Don't forget to take your fireman's hat with you."

Shay must have spotted his wife's arrival from an upstairs window, because he came thundering back down the steps. "You ready to get some lunch, Luca?"

The boy gave Shay a narrowed-eyed look. "Yep. Don't forget Carli promised I could pick whatever I want to eat."

"I haven't forgotten." Shay grinned at his son. "Besides, she also promised I could do that, too."

Ryder snickered at that idea. He pointed at Luca and then at Shay. "I can understand why she'd trust Luca to make good decisions, but I'd think she'd want to keep an eye on you. You'll probably pick a funnel cake topped with a gallon of chocolate sauce."

That had Luca laughing again. "Nope, she made us promise to eat something healthy or no desserts."

Shay started toward the door, his son in tow. He stopped short of the waiting car. "Ryder, I don't see your van. Do you need a ride back to the park?"

"If you don't mind, I'd appreciate it. My van was blocked when I got ready to head for the station to get the truck. I flagged down Moira, and she gave me a lift here. I just need to lock up."

He sat in the back seat with Luca as Carli drove through back streets to avoid the traffic on the main street through town. She glanced at him in the rearview mirror. "Now that the parade is over, can you kick back and relax for the rest of the day?"

"No, I'm working at the booth for the animal shelter. Juni has been covering for me, but I'm going to take over as soon as I get back."

"That was nice of her."

"It was, but she also has an ulterior motive. She's decided to adopt a dog, and I promised to get them set up with everything they'll need."

Luca had been watching out the window, but evidently he'd been listening to the conversation. "You did that for us when we adopted Beau and Bruno. They still sleep in their beds."

Both of his parents chuckled at that. Shay twisted around to look at Luca. "If that's true, how come I find them on your bed when I tuck you in at night?"

His son rolled his eyes. "The beds Mr. Ryder gave us are where they sleep when we watch television. They sleep in my bed when it's nighttime. They need cuddles."

Lucky dogs—Ryder could use a few cuddles of his own. "I'll have to tell Juni that's how these things work. She's never owned a pet before, so she has a lot to learn."

The boy took that to heart. "Tell her she can ask me if she needs help."

"I'll do that, Luca. I'm sure she'll appreciate knowing you'd lend her your expertise."

His dad looked back again. "In case you don't know, *expertise* is a fancy word that means you know a lot about taking care of dogs now. Maybe once Juni's new friend gets settled in we can arrange a playdate for her and our two."

Luca clearly liked that idea. "Maybe at the park. Beau and Bruno love to go on walks there. Can you tell Miss Juni that, too?"

"I will. In fact, you might get a chance to tell her yourself. She'll be hanging out with me at the booth this afternoon."

Well, unless one of the Calland brothers had lured her away. He wasn't sure how she'd come to be standing on a picnic table with the pair, but seeing her with them for the second time in one day hadn't made him happy. He guessed he'd find out soon enough now that he was back at the park.

After they all climbed out of the car, Ryder smiled down at Luca. "Have fun deciding what to eat. There'll be a lot of great things to choose from."

The boy looked up at him and frowned. "Aren't

you going to eat with us? You haven't had lunch, either."

Ryder did his best to reassure his young companion. "I wish I could, Luca, but I really need to get back to the animal shelter's booth. Maybe if the lines aren't too long, I'll get something to go."

That satisfied Luca, who hurried to catch up with Carli. On the other hand, Shay fell back to walk with Ryder. "Is something wrong? You're looking pretty grim all of a sudden."

"No, everything is fine. It's just been a long day."

"Yeah, right. I recognized that look all too well. Are you and Juni having problems? If so, try groveling. It worked for both me and Titus."

Shay's concern, however well-intentioned, made Ryder want to pound his head on a nearby tree. It was only early afternoon, and he'd already had two different friends sticking their noses in his personal business. With his luck, Cade and Max would be along soon to join in on the discussion.

"No, we're not having problems."

Shay turned his gaze in the direction of his wife and son, his expression making it clear they were the center of his existence. "Keep telling yourself that if it makes you feel better. But been there, done that, and wish like heck I'd gotten my head on straight a lot sooner."

Ryder was relieved they'd reached the food court. The four of them paused to check out their options. The food truck with the shortest line was the one serving gyros. Good enough. "I'm going to grab a gyro and head back to the booth. Enjoy the rest of your day."

Shay pointed toward a big tent on the other side of the clearing. "We're going to check out the barbecue."

"Have fun."

"You, too."

Ryder had only gone a few steps when the sound of a familiar laugh had him searching the crowd for its source. It didn't take him long to spot Juni. He started to head toward her but stopped when he realized she was with one of the Calland brothers. They seemed to be having a good time.

Lucky them.

Juni happened to glance in his direction. As soon as she spotted him, she pointed to the other side of the table with one hand and waved him to come join them with the other. No way that was happening. It was too late to pretend he hadn't seen her at all, so he shook his head before doing an about-face to head back to the booth.

Alone and not happy about it.

CHAPTER EIGHTEEN

ALL THINGS CONSIDERED, Ryder probably wasn't in the right frame of mind to be dealing with the public. He supposed he could always shut down the booth early and head home, but that wasn't going to happen. Once he made a commitment, he stood by it. His friends at the shelter—both human and otherwise—deserved better of him than to abandon the booth simply because he wasn't happy.

He made quick work of straightening stacks of forms and brochures, the simple action going a long way toward getting his head back in the game. Once that was done, he called the volunteer in charge of the animals they'd brought to the park.

"Hey, Ben. I wanted to let you know I'm back. How are things going?"

"Juni said she'd already shared the good news that we've had serious interest in all of the animals we brought today. I've also spoken with the volunteers at the other festival, and they've had similar results. Sounds like we'll soon have room to take more animals from that shelter in eastern Washington that's overcrowded."

"That's great news. I'm sure they'll be relieved to hear that."

"Oops, gotta go. There's a couple headed this way, and it's the third time they've stopped by. I'm thinking they're pretty serious about adopting that tuxedo cat."

"I'll keep my fingers crossed."

Feeling better about the world in general, he pulled up a chair and made himself comfortable. The shelter had posted that they'd be at the park until four o'clock, so he had another two hours before he could pack up and head home. The festival's activities lasted until well into the evening and included a fireworks display, but that much noise and the increasing crowds would only stress the animals. It was better to get them back to the shelter sooner rather than later.

He wasn't sure how the rest of the day would play out. Later tonight, maybe he'd drop in at Shay's for a burger and a couple of cold ones. That made more sense than sitting home alone and sulking. Because that's exactly what he would be doing. How many times had he reminded all of his friends that he and Juni were only friends? That he had no claim on her and didn't want one.

It wasn't fun to be the last one to realize he was lying to himself and everyone else. If he wasn't getting emotionally invested in their relationship, he wouldn't have gotten his tail in a twist over seeing her having fun with Logan Calland. He still didn't like it, but his anger had been misplaced. Juni had done nothing wrong, and neither had Logan. Instead, Ryder was the one who had crossed the line.

His mood didn't improve when he remembered that he and Juni still had plans for after the festival. He owed it to both her and Millie to make sure the adoption went smoothly. Yeah, Juni could probably manage on her own, but he wanted to be there for her. After she and her new roommate were settled, there would be time to talk about other things.

Like how he was sorry he had acted like an idiot a few minutes ago. That he regretted that the parameters of their relationship had gotten so muddied in his head, mainly because everything was so easy with her. Not her problem, just his. She'd stayed safely on the right side of the line in their relationship. For both their sakes, he needed to back off and give each of them some space. If that meant she'd be spending more time with Logan, so be it. Ryder had no right to interfere, especially if she really liked the guy.

The sound of footsteps approaching the booth

had him sitting up straighter. It was too much to hope that it was someone interested in adopting a cat or dog. He squinted up at Juni. She didn't look angry, but she didn't exactly look happy, either. He sat up even straighter and met her gaze head on.

"Did you enjoy your lunch?"

"As a matter of fact, I did."

Then she dropped a bag in his lap. "Here's yours. Since the only food truck in the direction you were originally walking was the one with gyros, that's what I got for you. Enjoy."

Without waiting for him to thank her, she walked over to the counter. For the second time that day, she rearranged the few remaining samples of pet food. He hated that she was upset with him. "Thanks for buying me something to eat. How much do I owe you?"

She gave him a dark look over her shoulder. "All you owe me is an explanation."

"About?"

Juni turned to face him, her hands on her hips. "Don't play games with me, Ryder. I could understand if you were concerned because you thought one of us should be at the booth instead of hanging out in the food court. But somehow I don't think that's why you looked so angry when you saw me there. In fact, now that I think about it, it was the same expression you had on your face when I waved at you during the parade."

She wasn't wrong.

"You're right, and I owe you an apology, Juni. I didn't like seeing you hanging out with Logan."

Especially twice in one day, not that he planned to share that fact with Juni. She was already mad enough at him. She studied him for several seconds before responding. "For the record, it was a spur-of-the-moment thing. I waited too late to stake out a front-row spot to watch you drive by, and I'm too short to be able to see over the crowd. When Logan and his brother saw me, they were kind enough to invite me to stand on the table with them."

That didn't explain how she came to have lunch with Logan.

She pointed at his sandwich. "Eat that before it gets cold."

As soon as he started to unwrap the gyro, she launched back into her explanation. "After you drove out of sight, I started to return to the booth. That's when Logan asked if you and I were still dating."

"And you said?"

"The truth—that we were friends and neighbors. I also explained that since my move to Dunbar was temporary, I wasn't looking to get involved with anyone. Despite that, he still wanted to have lunch together. We parted company with no other plans on the table. I bought your lunch and came straight back here."

She paused as if waiting for some response from him. He wasn't about to admit how happy he was that she didn't seem in a hurry to spend more time with Logan, so he simply said, "Okay."

Evidently that wasn't the response she was looking for. She stared up at the sky as if praying for patience. "Yes, it is okay, Ryder. Our agreement stated that you would pretend to be my client and I would be your plus-one at your mother's party. Nothing in that says I can't have lunch with someone else."

She narrowed her eyes and frowned. "Well, unless you decided the rules have changed. If that's the case, shouldn't I be the first to know about it?"

He set the sandwich aside and stood. "You're right, of course. I don't know what's going on with me, and I'm sorry. We are friends. Period. If you decide to date someone else, I won't interfere."

No matter how much he'd want to.

Juni asked him one more question. "Are we still on for finalizing my adopting Millie?"

That she still wanted his help had him breathing more easily. "We are."

"Good."

They were saved from more awkward conversation by the arrival of a flurry of visitors seeking information about the adoption process and what dogs and cats were available. By the time he and Juni had answered all of their questions, things were pretty much back to normal between the two of them. They probably wouldn't stay that way if he didn't get his head back in the friends-only game, but he'd take what few minutes of peace he could.

FOUR HOURS LATER, the process of finalizing the adoption was going smoothly, just as Ryder had promised. At his recommendation, Juni took the opportunity to spend more time alone with Millie in the outside visitation pen at the shelter. He'd explained mistakes sometimes happened and the prospective owners ended up bringing the dog back to the shelter. That was traumatic for all concerned, so it was better to proceed cautiously.

She and Millie played a game of fetch to let the dog work off some energy. Afterward, Juni picked out a sunny spot and sat on the ground to see what Millie would do. Her heart swelled with happiness when Millie plopped down next to her and put her head on Juni's lap. The dog's soulful eyes drifted closed as Juni stroked her soft fur and murmured reassurances that Millie was beautiful and perfect.

At the same time, she was aware of Ryder watching them from the window, patiently giving them time to get acquainted. She liked that about him. The truth was, she liked everything about him. She'd never known a man she felt so at ease with, not even Phillip. Sharing special moments like this with him simply felt right. Mainly because he understood her in ways no one else did, not even her family. If she were honest about it, on one level she even liked that he didn't want to see her with another man, because maybe that meant he was developing some strong feelings for her.

That would only be fair, since she was slowly coming to realize that her feelings for him had somehow slipped far beyond mere friendship. She wasn't even sure when that had happened, but it was now hard to imagine a future without him in it. Now wasn't the right time or place, but eventually she would have to find the courage to tell him that.

When he finally came outside, he paused to snap a couple of pictures with his phone as he slowly approached them. Millie raised her head long enough to watch him. After thumping her tail a couple of times, she closed her eyes and resumed her snuggling.

Ryder squatted down next to them and gently stroked Millie's head. "You two seem to have hit it off."

Juni couldn't quit smiling. "I think she really likes me."

"Of course she does. Millie's a smart girl. Does this mean you've made up your mind?"

"I'm still nervous, but mostly because I have so much to learn."

He surprised her by slapping his forehead with the palm of his hand. "I was supposed to tell you that Luca would be glad to share his expertise with you. He also said when you and Millie are ready, he thinks the two of you should join him, Beau and Bruno for a playdate at the park."

"That's so nice of him. I'm sure she'll like a chance to make friends."

"We should go sign off on the paperwork. I was so sure you'd be bringing her home that I already loaded a bunch of stuff into the van that the two of you will need to get started. There are some chew toys for her, a bed, a bag of the same food she's been eating, and a certificate for a free exam and the first round of her shots at the vet in town."

That was so thoughtful, but he'd already done so much. "I'm grateful, but I could've bought all of that."

"I know. I also did the same thing for Luca and

his dogs and a bunch of other people. I call them starter kits. They don't cost me all that much, and it makes me happy to help people get off to a good start with their new family member."

There was no use in arguing with him. "In that case, Millie and I both thank you for your thoughtfulness."

He stood and held out his hand to tug her back up to her feet. "I also borrowed a crate from the shelter for Millie to ride home in. There's no way to know how comfortable she is riding in a vehicle, and it's better to be safe than sorry."

Juni clipped the leash on to Millie's collar. "Sounds like you thought of everything."

"I've had a lot of experience. You'll figure it all out. Don't forget, Luca stands ready to help anytime you need it. Me, too, for that matter."

That last part had her reaching for his hand, needing that small connection. But rather than get all caught up in mushy thoughts, she decided to tease him a bit. "Remember that when I call you for advice in the middle of the night."

He laughed. "Call away, just don't be surprised if I'm a bit grouchy."

"How is that different from how you usually are?"

Ryder put his hand over his heart and staggered back two steps. "Well, that hurts. I'll have you know most people like me. In case you're wondering, I learned everything I know about being charming from Titus."

She snickered. "I'm not sure he's the best role model. He's got that whole grumpy biker vibe going on."

"Well, that's mean." He winked at her as they walked back into the shelter. "But you're not wrong. To give the man credit, he's lightened up a lot since he and Moira figured things out."

Trisha, the director of the shelter, was waiting for them at the counter. "So, Juni, I heard from a good source that Millie is going home with you today."

"She is." Juni grinned. "I don't know about her, but I'm really excited about the prospect."

"I'm happy for you both. She's a really nice dog. I also wanted to thank you for helping Ryder with the booth today. Between the two different events, we've succeeded in placing a lot of our current residents."

She handed Juni her business card. "I'm sure Ryder can answer any questions that might arise after you get Millie home, but don't hesitate to call us if he's not available."

Juni tucked the card in her pocket. "Thank you."

After Trisha went back to her office, Ryder led the way into another room. "Let's get this harness on Millie and then we can head out."

Ten minutes later they pulled out of the shelter's parking lot. When Millie whimpered, Juni panicked. "Is she all right? Should we pull over and check on her?"

"She's probably nervous because she isn't sure what's going on. Talking to her might help reassure her."

"What should I talk about?"

He chuckled softly. "About anything. She'll take comfort from simply hearing your voice, especially if you sound calm and reassuring."

Ryder's suggestion worked. As soon as she started talking, the whimpers stopped. "We'll be home in about ten minutes, Millie. When we get there, we'll walk around the property so you can start getting to know your new home. Afterward, we'll head inside and get settled in."

"Where are you going to put her bed?"

The question puzzled her. "Is there somewhere special that you'd recommend?"

"That depends on where you want her to sleep at night. For example, Luca's dogs sleep in their beds in the living room but on his bed at night. It's better to start off how you plan to continue. She might have her own opinion on the subject, but remember you're the boss."

By that point, they were pulling into her driveway. "I'll wait until you let Millie out of the crate before I unload everything else. I know you plan to let her explore outside for a few minutes, which is a good idea. While you do that, I'll carry everything else inside for you."

"I'd appreciate that."

She couldn't help but notice that Ryder was back to acting a bit twitchy. Life would be so much easier if he would just come out and say whatever was on his mind. Not that she had room to talk. It wasn't as if she'd confessed her growing feelings for him.

Millie joined them on the ground, and Ryder stopped to give her a thorough scratching before stepping back. "Be a good girl, Millie, and take care of Juni for me."

What an odd thing for him to say. "Ryder?"

He shoved his hands in his hip pockets and stared up at the sky. "I know this isn't the best time for this discussion, but then there's never really a good time."

"What discussion?"

Rather than wait for him to answer, she hazarded a guess. "Is this about Logan? I already told you that the two of us don't have any plans to see each other again."

"I know you did, but I have no right to make that kind of demand on you. That wasn't part of our agreement. Besides, Logan isn't the problem. I am."

Millie tugged on her leash, wanting to go exploring. Rather than hold her back, Juni let the dog set the pace and hoped the Ryder would eventually get to the point. "You're not a problem, Ryder. We're friends. That hasn't changed."

"That's not true, Juni. Our relationship has changed in ways I never expected. Looking back, we entered our agreement on the spur of the moment without thinking things through. Neither one of us was looking to get involved beyond the cover stories we provided for each other. The more we're together, the more the lines get blurred, and that's a problem."

"Why?"

"You'll be moving on soon, and I'm still figuring out my life here in Dunbar. We might enjoy each other's company, but neither of us would be happy with a long-distance relationship. A clean break now before either of us gets hurt would be the smart thing to do."

That wasn't true. Because even if he could simply walk away unscathed, that wasn't the case for her. Not when each word he'd just said cut like a knife. It was even worse than when Phillip chose Erin over her. "So to be clear— we can't even be friends? Is that what you're saying?"

"Our relationship was never intended to be long-term. Your cousin has her wedding coordinator, so that problem has been solved. You did your stint as my plus-one and finished the art-work for the festival. I'll transfer the payment for that to you when I get home. The bottom line is that we've each held up our end of the bargain."

When he fell behind, she turned around to see what he was doing. It looked as if he were struggling to find the right words. When he did, she wished she'd kept walking. "Avoiding each other completely might not be possible in a town like Dunbar, but we shouldn't hang out together anymore."

She still needed to hear him say it. "So you don't even want to be friends."

He shrugged. "Like I said, we should give each other some breathing room. I've finally got my life back together here in Dunbar while you're only beginning to explore the possibili-ties of where your dreams will take you. Those two things aren't compatible."

Juni blinked like crazy, hoping to ward off the burn of tears. He was definitely right about the lines blurring. Thank goodness she hadn't ad-mitted how she felt about him, much less asked him to extend her lease. She'd have to start look-ing for another rental in the area, but not in Dun-bar. There was no way she could keep living so close to Ryder. She'd miss the other people she'd met, but a clean break would be necessary for both of them. "Fine. Thanks again for your help with Millie and everything else."

When he took a step toward her, she backed away. "Just leave Millie's things on the porch. I'll bring them in when we're done exploring. I think I'll take her down to the river for a few minutes."

Then she walked away, wishing he would say or do something—anything—to stop her.

But he didn't.

CHAPTER NINETEEN

JUNI DEBATED LONG and hard about whether she should attend the book club meeting on Tuesday night. She had a legitimate excuse to skip it if that's what she decided to do because Millie was still adjusting to her new home. She hadn't been very happy the first time Juni had left her alone to make a quick trip into town to buy groceries and pick up the mail. She worried that it was too soon to leave the dog alone for an entire evening. Since Millie was a stray, there was no way to know what her life had been like before she ended up at the shelter. The bottom line was that it might take time for Millie to trust that Juni would always return to her.

But as much as Juni loved her new roommate, she couldn't stay locked up in the A-frame for the next few months with no human contact. After the little bombshell Ryder had unleashed on Saturday, she could really use an evening out with…well, if not exactly friends, then at least acquaintances whose company she enjoyed.

It didn't hurt that both Shelby and Moira had made it sound as if the wine flowed freely as the group discussed the book they'd all read. Everyone also brought a small contribution in the way of refreshments. It could be sweet or savory, store-bought or homemade. Juni had made her aunt's recipe for zucchini bread, one of her personal favorites.

That had solved the problem of what she should bring, but still left the question of what to do about Millie unanswered. The most obvious solution would be to ask Ryder to check on her, but she hesitated to do that when he'd been all too clear about the two of them taking a break from each other. On the other hand, he'd also said she could call if she needed help with Millie. If he was going to be home, surely he wouldn't mind checking on her a couple of times. It wasn't as if he would have to spend any time in Juni's company.

She'd gone back and forth on the issue so many times at this point, she was getting disgusted with her indecisive self. More than once she'd picked up her phone only to set it right back down. "Stop dithering, Juni Voss. If you don't ask him soon, it will be too late to go to the meeting at all."

Finally, she sent him a text. I hate to bother

you, but you said I could reach out if it was about Millie.

A few seconds later, her phone rang. "Is she all right?"

She hadn't meant to worry him and hastened to explain the situation. "She's fine. The problem is that when I adopted her, I forgot I had promised to spend this evening with Shelby's book club. I'm worried about leaving Millie home alone for too long. When I got back from the store yesterday, she was frantic. It was as if she'd thought I was never coming back."

It was a relief that he didn't hesitate. "Do you want me to bring her over to my place or do you think she'd be happier if I spent the evening over there? Either's okay with me. I'm off tonight."

"If you really don't mind, over here would probably be best. I have to leave at six-thirty. I should be home around ten, but I can come back earlier if you need me to."

"That will work. I don't turn into a pumpkin until midnight."

"Thanks, Ryder. I know this is asking a lot. I'm probably suffering from new parent syndrome and worrying more than I should."

"It's fine, Juni. I'll bring a book to read and let Millie curl up beside me on the couch. Well, unless you're one of those pet parents who don't allow the four-legged members of the family on the furniture."

That made her laugh. "She's sitting next to me with her head in my lap even as we speak."

"I knew she was a smart girl."

"Thanks again for doing this, and there's a piece of Titus's fresh peach pie in the fridge with your name on it."

"So you bought that to reward me for helping out?"

Should she tell him the truth? Figuring he'd find it funny, she went ahead and confessed. "Actually, it was more of a bribe if you waffled on whether you wanted a babysitting job tonight."

His laughter rang out loud and clear. "You know me too well. I would have fallen for it in a heartbeat. I'll see you then."

THERE WERE ALREADY a couple of other cars in the driveway when Juni arrived at Shelby's place, only a short distance from the center of town as the crow flies. It was located at the edge of a small clearing surrounded by a dense thicket of huge cedars and Douglas firs, which afforded Shelby and Cade a lot of privacy. She bet they loved living there.

Shelby must have been watching for new arrivals, because the door opened before Juni stepped onto the porch. Shelby offered her a warm smile. "I'm glad you could make it."

"Me, too. I love your place. I bet you spend a lot of time out here on the porch in the evening."

"We do. We especially enjoy our neighbors stopping by on a regular basis."

Then she pointed toward the edge of the woods. "If you look closely, you can just see them."

A few seconds later, a small group of deer stepped out of the trees. They took a long look around before dipping their heads down to start grazing. "They're beautiful. I'm surprised they don't act scared at all."

"They've been visiting ever since Cade first moved in. I'm pretty sure they think it's really their home, but they're willing to put up with us sharing it. They don't scare all that easily, even when Titus shows up with Ned. You know how big and tough-looking that dog is, and the deer don't even bother to look up if he wanders over to visit them."

Shelby turned back toward the door. "Speaking of dogs, I hear you adopted one. I think Titus said it was a Lab mix."

Juni did what new parents did everywhere. She whipped out her phone and brought up a picture to share. "Our best guess is that Millie is mostly yellow Lab with some other kind of hunting dog thrown in for good measure. She was found as a stray up near the interstate and brought to the shelter. When no one came looking for her, she was put up for adoption. The vet said she's about a year old."

"She's lovely. I'll look forward to meeting her."

They'd been about to go inside when an older model car pulled into the driveway. Five more women piled out in short order. Juni recognized Ilse and Bea, but the other three were strangers to her. Shelby called out, "Just come in, ladies. I have to start the coffee and put the kettle on to boil, so we'll do introductions later."

Juni followed her into the kitchen. "Is there anything I can do to help?"

"You can open those two bottles of wine. We usually start with both a white and a red. Once in a while someone will show up with a six-pack just for variety's sake."

Then she dropped her voice. "We found out early on that the discussion gets more lively if a little alcohol is involved, so we take turns being the designated driver. We also offer decaf coffee and tea. No one wants to go home too wired to sleep. Something ridiculous about needing to be able to function in the morning."

That seemed like sound thinking to Juni. "I'll probably stick with coffee. I have to walk Millie and then finish up a few details on a sketch I started this afternoon, so I'll need a clear head."

Juni decided to hang out in the kitchen and help Shelby organize the refreshments. After opening the wine, she put a different flavor of tea in three teapots before adding the hot water. As the two of them worked, Shelby asked, "Was Millie okay with you leaving her home tonight?"

"Actually, Ryder is watching her for me. I think she'll be fine spending more time by herself once she gets used to living with me and settles into a routine."

"That's nice of him." Shelby gave her an innocent look from across the counter. "We can't help but notice how quickly the two of you hit it off since you moved here."

Okay, that wasn't something Juni wanted to talk about. She aimed for sounding calm and collected but wasn't sure how successful she was. "He has been a good neighbor."

Shelby was busy arranging a variety of cheeses and meats on a tray along with several different kinds of crackers. She looked up again, frowning just a bit. "Has been? As in past tense? Is there trouble in paradise? Because the vibe between the two of you that night at Shay's place felt like a lot more than being neighborly."

That was the trouble. Juni had begun to think that way, too. "No, we're still just friends."

Sort of verging on not really.

Shelby mulled that over as she arranged the last type of cheese to her liking. "So what happened?"

"Nothing bad." Almost against her will, Juni found herself adding, "Neither of us is looking for anything long-term, but it was easy to forget that sometimes. We agreed to take a break from spending so much time together. So, friends and neighbors, nothing more."

The sympathy in the other woman's eyes was almost Juni's undoing. "I'm guessing there is more to it than that, like maybe he's running scared. However, this probably isn't the time or place to press for details."

"There's really nothing more I can say."

Sure there was, and they both knew it. Otherwise, why was there a steady stream of tears flowing down Juni's cheeks? Shelby gave her a napkin to dry her face and then came around the end of the counter to stand next to her. Wrapping her arm around Juni's shoulders, she said, "If there's anything I can do, call me. We could meet for coffee or something if it would help."

Before Juni could find the right words to tell Shelby how much her offer meant to her, Moira came into the room. "Hey, what's the holdup on the wine and refreshments? I came straight from work and I'm—"

She stopped talking as soon as she got a good look at Juni. "Okay, what's Ryder done now?"

Her spot-on assessment of the situation startled a laugh out of Juni. "What makes you think it was him?"

Moira sighed and shook her head. "Unless you've been seeing someone else, who else would it have been? Besides I've been there, looked like that. If you don't believe me, ask Carli. She was there to help pick up the pieces."

Carli had followed her into the kitchen and immediately confirmed Moira's story. "That I was. In turn, she was there for me when my ex-husband announced he wanted a divorce because he needed to marry his new wife before their baby was born."

Juni wasn't sure what to say about her brutal revelation. "I'm so sorry that happened to you."

Carli waved it off. "There's no denying I was devastated at the time, but I'm over it. In fact, I count myself lucky to be rid of him. Now I have Shay and Luca, and life is so much better. I'm not saying everything went smoothly for us at the beginning, but we got through it together. That means everything to me."

Shelby shared her own romance troubles. "And don't forget that Cade put me in jail, because we were on opposite sides of a major crisis here in town. We also got past it."

Bea appeared in the doorway. "Hey, ladies, we really need to get started."

Shelby picked up the tray she'd put together. "Sorry, Bea. We got to talking and lost track of time. We're coming."

Moira and Carli grabbed the wine and two of the teapots, leaving the third one for Juni. Moira gave her a commiserating look. "The bathroom is right down the hall. Take a minute to gather yourself and catch your breath. We'll save you a seat."

Shelby was already back for another load. She glanced around as if to make sure the four of them were alone. "I say we three take Juni to Shay's tomorrow evening for a girls' night out. In fact, we should also ask Rikki if she can join us."

Boy, that sounded like fun, but Juni had Millie to think about. Turning to Moira and Carli, she explained, "In case you don't know, I adopted a rescue dog over the weekend. I really shouldn't be gone two nights in a row."

In the way that lifelong friends had, Carli and Moira gave each other the kind of look that communicated a lot of information without either having to speak. When Moira nodded, Carli took charge of the situation. "Change of plans. We'll meet at Juni's cabin for a movie night. I'll pick up dinner for everybody from the bar. Moira can get the usual munchies, and I'm sure Rikki will bring dessert if she can come. Shelby, we'll need wine…well, unless you think beer goes better with pub grub."

Shelby wrinkled her nose. "I'd prefer wine, but there's no reason we can't offer a selection of drinks. Moira, what do you think?"

"Either is fine with me."

Carli pointed at Juni next as she continued handing out assignments. "We'll leave it up to you to pick the movie. Rom-coms are always fun, but you might not be in the mood for one of those. I would ask that it not be a horror movie or anything that's over-the-top violent and bloody."

"I'll see what I can come up with. What time will you be coming over?"

"Say around five-thirty or six. How does that sound?"

Her mood vastly improved, Juni grinned. "Honestly, that sounds perfect."

THE REST OF the evening was everything Juni had hoped it would be. Not everyone had loved the book they'd read, but that was okay. It had made for a lively discussion. As the meeting came to a close, they chose the next month's selection for discussion, and then everyone pitched in to clean up.

Juni was now on her way home, tired but in

a much better frame of mind. Better yet, she had something fun to look forward to tomorrow evening. Once she walked Millie and finished her sketch, she'd spend some time figuring out what movie would best fit her current mood. It was so thoughtful of Shelby, Carli and Moira to welcome her into their mutual support group. While she didn't know the details of the rough patches they'd experienced before finding their happily-ever-afters, it was clear that they had come through with their spirits and hearts intact.

Maybe someday Juni would find what they had with the men in their lives. She hoped so. Maybe she could give online dating a try. Even if she ever ended up moving back home, there had to be some eligible men who lived within a reasonable driving distance of Crestville.

Back when they first met, Ryder had pointed out that one reason he hadn't dated anyone since he and Jasmine broke up was the limited number of single women in town. Then there was the fact that it was impossible to avoid running into people in a small town. Getting involved with someone locally could prove awkward if the relationship went south. She and Ryder were the perfect example of that.

She turned into her driveway and parked. Not that she was trying to impress anyone, but she checked her appearance in the rearview mirror and touched up her lipstick before heading for the front porch. Her heart warmed when a spate of happy-sounding barking on the other side of the door welcomed her home. Millie's pretty face appeared in the window next to the door, her tongue out and her eyes bright with excitement.

The door swung open, and Millie charged out to greet Juni in person, who knelt on one knee and gathered the ecstatic dog into her arms. "I'm home, Millie. I take it you missed me."

She continued to murmur soft nonsense to her furry roommate to calm her down. Rising back up to her feet, she asked, "Can we go inside now?"

Millie led the way and headed over to where Ryder stood watching them. The dog circled around him and woofed a couple of times as if saying, "Look who I found!"

He patted her on the head. "Yes, I see her, Millie. I told you she'd be back."

That sounded worrisome. "Was she all right while I was gone?"

"Yeah, she did okay. Every so often she'd go sniff at the door and whine. Then she'd come back to flop on the couch next to me." He shook his finger at Millie. "She's also mastered the art of guilting me into giving her a treat every time she looked a little sad. If I didn't know better, I'd say she's been taking lessons from Titus's dog, Ned."

Juni dropped her hand back down to her side. She'd been about to reach for a treat for no other reason than Millie had given her a hopeful look. "Sneaky dog—now I'm onto your wily ways."

She looked at Ryder. "Thanks again for watching her for me. I really appreciate it." To give herself something else to focus on besides the man in front of her, she picked up Millie's leash and clipped it on to her harness. "Now I need to take her for a short walk and then try to get some work done."

Ryder nodded to acknowledge her dismissal. As they both started for the door, he asked, "How was your meeting?"

"I had a great time. We picked a cozy mystery for next month. I guess I'll have to buy a copy online since I don't have a library card. I didn't see much use in getting one when I'm only going to be here for such a short time."

Although more and more, the thought of leaving Dunbar had her feeling all kinds of sad. The people she'd met since moving there had been so welcoming, and she already thought of many of them as friends. She could easily envision a future full of book club meetings, girls' nights out and Bea's bacon-maple bars. Unlike back in her hometown, no one here saw her as fragile, as if she were still the lost little girl she'd been after the loss of her parents.

Millie picked that minute to lurch forward and drag Juni out the door. The unexpected action served to end Juni's depressing train of thought. She laughed even though she nearly hit the ground thanks to the dog's determined efforts to get outside as fast as possible. Ryder had jumped forward to grab Juni's arm and prevent her from falling. As soon as she was steady on her feet, he released his hold and took a quick step back. She missed his touch even if she understood maintaining some distance was best for both of them.

Instead, she focused her attention on making Millie sit, a reminder of who was in charge of this little outing. When the dog was settled at her feet, Juni risked looking at Ryder. "Sorry about that. I guess she really needs to get some fresh air."

"No problem. Do you want me to come with you?"

"No, we'll be fine. We're not going far. I thought we'd cruise up and down the driveway and then circle the clearing before going back inside."

Besides, she wasn't about to ask him to stay longer when he'd made it clear that he wanted to limit the time he spent in her company.

"Thanks again, Ryder. I'll try not to bother you anymore."

He stared at her, his eyebrows riding low as he watched her. It was impossible to read his mood, but he didn't look happy. For a second, she thought he wanted to say something, but then he shook his head and walked away without looking back.

Her vision turned blurry again as her eyes filled with tears just as they had in Shelby's kitchen. Frustrated, she swiped them away with her sleeve. Enough of this feeling sorry for herself. It was her own fault that she'd let herself get too attached to Ryder. She should've known better, especially considering it was clear from the outset their romantic relationship was both temporary and fake.

Too bad the heartbreak was all too real.

Juni let Millie guide her steps as they explored one side of the driveway on the way down and the other on the way back. After that, they followed the edge of the tree line that encircled the clearing. Millie kept up a steady pace, stopping occasionally to sniff whenever something drew her attention.

As she gathered her thoughts, Juni found herself needing to talk to someone. At least Millie could be trusted to keep Juni's confidences to herself. "I meant to tell you that we're going to have company tomorrow evening. You'll like the four women who are coming to hang out with us.

It's what's called a girls' night out, so no men allowed. Don't get me wrong—there's not a problem with the majority of the male population. For sure, all four of my friends are happily married to really great guys. They decided I needed cheering up, so we're going to consume a bunch of food and wine while we watch a movie."

Millie stopped to look up at her. Maybe Juni was imagining things, but she was pretty sure Millie wanted to know why Juni was feeling a bit sad. After all, she had Millie in her life now. Who else did she need? Not Ryder Davis, that was for sure.

She decided Millie deserved to hear the truth. "Your babysitter tonight has decided he was spending too much time with me. I'm not sure what made him decide that, but I wasn't about to argue if that's how he felt. Don't worry, though. He was perfectly happy to hang out with you, so he's still your friend even if he's not mine."

Millie came close enough to give Juni's hand a quick lick, showing her some doggy love. With that simple gesture, Juni's mood immediately improved. She gave the leash a tug. "Okay, girl, we should get moving. I have work to do, and you have some more treat mooching to do."

As if understanding exactly what that meant, Millie cut directly across the clearing toward the porch. Once they were inside, Juni turned off the outside lights and locked the door. Time to get to work.

But not until after she tossed Millie a treat.

CHAPTER TWENTY

TWO DAYS LATER, Ryder seriously wished he'd said no when his mother called last night. It was too late now, since she was due to pick him up soon. He had the strangest feeling that he was going to regret accepting this particular invitation. According to his mother, she had some shopping to do in a nearby town famous for both its alpine architecture and its eclectic mix of shops. The deal was that they'd spend a couple of hours browsing the gift shops and then have lunch together.

This expedition wasn't exactly what he'd had in mind when he'd suggested that they spend some time together. That said, he was willing to meet her halfway if she wanted to work on repairing their relationship.

Titus had called earlier to say his truck was in the repair shop and to see if he could borrow Ryder's van for a few hours. He needed to pick up more pet food donations and then deliver them to the shelter, so Ryder had offered to drop the van off at the café. Since his mother had never visited him in Dunbar, he then texted her the address of Bea's shop and that he'd be waiting out front for her to pick him up.

He'd deliberately arrived early at the bakery, so he could duck inside and get a cup of coffee to go. He'd missed breakfast, so he added one of the maple bars to his order. It would have been polite to also get one for his mother, but he suspected she would give it a hard pass. She rarely ate sweets even at one of her dinner parties. With his makeshift meal in hand, he went back outside and sat on a nearby bench to enjoy the sun. A few seconds later, a motion off to his left caught his eye. Someone was headed his way. As soon as he realized who it was, he sat up straighter and gave the approaching pair his full attention.

Unfortunately, only one of them seemed happy to see him. Millie immediately tried to crawl up onto his lap, but her owner was having none of that. "Down, girl. You'll make Ryder spill his coffee."

Then she eyed the half-eaten pastry in his hand. "Is that what I think it is?"

He shot her a smug grin. "It is."

She immediately shoved Millie's leash at him. "I'll be right back."

The dog whined softly as she stood in front of the door, watching her owner disappear inside. Ryder reached out to scratch her back. "It's okay, girl. I bet she brings you a snack, too. Bea keeps a jar of doggy treats on the counter for just such occasions."

Sure enough, when Juni emerged a few minutes later, she held a treat in her hand and firmly said, "Sit, Millie."

The dog was only too happy to comply, earning herself the treat along with a heap of praise from her owner. Ryder loved seeing how well they were getting along. "I knew she was a smart girl."

"She is, isn't she?"

On impulse, Ryder scooted closer to the other end of the bench. "Have a seat while you eat your pastry."

He hated that she hesitated, but then he was well aware he was giving her mixed signals. "I won't be here long. My mom is picking me up any minute now. She called last night to invite me to lunch."

No sooner had he spoken the words than his mother pulled up at the curb right in front of them. There was only one problem—she wasn't alone. He watched in stunned silence as Jasmine smiled at him. She climbed out of the passenger door and moved to the back seat, leaving the front door open for him. His mother gave him a hopeful look. He wasn't sure what to make of that, but right now he was too furious to ask questions.

It was hard not to laugh, though, when Millie took an instant dislike to Jazz and started sounding the alarm at the top of her lungs as soon as she stepped out of the car. Juni's face went ashen and then flushed red as she stared at the two women and then at him. "Enjoy your lunch with your mother and your fiancée or your ex or whatever you're calling her these days."

Then she stalked off, leaving him staring at her back. In her hurry to get away, she'd left her coffee and maple bar sitting on the bench. He considered picking them up and running after her, but he had a suspicion that he'd end up wearing the coffee. Instead he remained on the bench, glancing first at the woman in the back seat of his mother's car and then back at Juni as she quickly disappeared around the corner.

That's all it took for him to realize that one was his future, the other his past, and he'd managed to hurt both of them. It was time to stop spinning his wheels and take action. First up, he'd deal with the two women in the car and then do what he could to mend fences with Juni.

The truth was he loved her, and she deserved to know that.

With that in mind, he tossed his coffee in the trash and then got into the car, slamming the door hard enough to rattle the windows. Rather than say anything right away, he waited until they'd gone a short distance down the road before finally speaking. "Care to explain what's going on here, Mother?"

She watched him out of the corner of her eye for several seconds before finally responding. "Jasmine happened to drop off some papers for your father to sign when I was about to leave to pick you up. I told her I couldn't stay and chat because I was going to Leavenworth to do some shopping. She's off today and thought it would be a fun outing. When she asked if she could come, I told her that you would also be joining me."

"And you couldn't just have told her no?"

"I could have, but I thought it was time for the two of you to clear the air. As I have already explained, there will still be occasions when you will cross paths. It isn't fair for any of us to have to walk on eggshells whenever that happens."

She made a point of looking at their surroundings. "You have to know this is not the life we wanted for you. There is so much more you could be doing."

He was so tired of this. "Even if it's the life that I want?"

His mother didn't have anything to say to that, but then he hadn't really expected her to understand. He twisted around to glare at the woman in the back seat. "As for you, why decide to tag along even when you know things are over between us?"

"Because like your mother said, it's time to clear the air. You've had your say. Now it's my turn. I'm tired of pretending everything is okay when we see each other." Her gaze shifted to the side as if she was unable to look him in the eye. "Everything was so much easier when your life was on track and we were happy. Waiting for you to get your head back in the game has grown quite tiresome."

He briefly glanced at his mother before responding. "First, I've already told my mother that the solution to the problem is simple. If she wants to invite you to dinner—fine. Just don't expect me to show up, too. I also told her that I'd be glad to meet her or both her and my father for dinner or lunch whenever they had the time. That's what today was supposed to be, not some ill-advised intervention. At some point you both need to accept that I'm already living the life that makes me happy. Even if that changes someday, I'm not looking to repeat the mistakes of my past."

Jazz flinched. "This isn't an intervention."

"What else would you call it?"

"A chance to tell you how I feel." She finally

looked at him directly. "I meant what I said to your little friend. I prefer to think of our engagement as being on hold, not over."

That did it. "Could you possibly be more condescending? Her name is Juni, which you well know. You can leave her out of this discussion. She's not the reason we broke up."

Jasmine's tenuous hold on her own temper slipped. "Maybe not, but she is the reason you won't give us another chance."

That remark scored a direct hit. Deciding this discussion was going nowhere fast, he pointed toward an intersection just ahead. "Mom, turn right at the next corner."

She gave him a puzzled look. "That isn't the road to Leavenworth."

"No, it's the road to my place. You can drop me off there."

"But what about lunch?"

He hated the note of hurt in her voice. "I'm sorry, Mom, but I can't do this."

He had nothing else to say other than to give her directions to his cabin. Since neither of his parents had ever shown any interest in visiting him, they'd never been there. He kept hoping that eventually they'd realize that his living in Dunbar wasn't a temporary aberration that would simply go away if they ignored it long enough.

When they finally pulled into his driveway,

his mother parked the car and got out after asking Jasmine to wait in the car. Without offering any explanation about what was going on, she walked to the far side of his small front yard before turning around to face his home. He joined her, trying to figure out what she was thinking. After studying the A-frame for the longest time, she did a slow three-sixty turn to study the surrounding forest.

Finally, she looked at him with a stunned expression on her face. "Ryder, I didn't expect anything quite so…"

He tried to see his home through the filter of her taste. "Primitive? Rustic?"

"Don't be a nitwit." She grinned and rolled her eyes. "Actually, I was going to say it was stunning. I can see why you find living here so appealing. Calling it a cabin doesn't do the place justice. If it were mine, I'd call it a chalet."

Then she laughed. "I'm not exactly sure what a chalet actually looks like, but it sounds fancier than a cabin."

"This probably isn't the right time for the grand tour, but we can do that the next time you visit."

"I'm betting your father will want to come back with his easel and paints when I tell him how beautiful it is here."

"Anytime. There's a small river at the other

end of that path over there. He'd like painting that area, too."

"I'll tell him."

By that point, his anger had faded, leaving him tired and frustrated not just with the whole situation but himself as well. "Mom, I'm truly sorry about Jasmine. I know I hurt her, but you have to admit there's no way you can picture her living here, or that she'd be happy telling her coworkers and friends that her husband is a volunteer fireman and animal shelter volunteer. I'm not the same man she knew. I hope she can finally accept that and move on. She'll be happier in the long run."

"You're right, of course. I'll talk to her. For the longest time, she seemed to accept the situation. I also know she's dated other men since the two of you broke up. My guess is that it finally hit her that your relationship was really over when she saw you with Juni."

Then she leaned into his side, her head against his shoulder. "Again, she's not the only one who struggles to understand the choices you've made. Walking away from everything you worked so hard to build causes us great concern as well."

"I know, Mom. I even understand why, but I'm happy here. I have good friends, ones who like me for me, not because of my money. There might come a time when I decide to do something different, something more, but for now I keep busy doing things I enjoy."

He pointed toward his house. "You should've seen this place and the one next door when I bought them. They were a mess. I loved fixing them up. In fact, I've done the same thing with several other properties in the area."

That surprised her. "You did all the work yourself?"

"Not all of it. I hire professionals to handle things like the electrical and plumbing. I also paid a retired contractor to work with me to make sure I didn't get in over my head."

"I'm impressed."

He gave her a soft nudge. "As well you should be."

"One more question, and then I'd better go."

"Ask away."

"Is Jasmine right in thinking you have some serious feelings about Juni?"

That was something he should talk to Juni about first, but he wasn't going to lie to his mother. Not when they were finally starting to understand each other again. "Yeah, although without going into detail, I admit I have managed to mess up big-time with her, too."

"What are you going to do about it?"

"According to a friend of mine, when all else fails—grovel."

That had her laughing again. "Sounds like good advice to me."

She gave him a quick hug. "I should get going. I'll convince Jasmine to do some therapeutic shopping and then have lunch."

"Tell her… I'm sorry. I know it's not enough, and it won't change anything. I'm the one who changed the rules. Seems I have a habit of doing that to the women in my life, but I never meant to hurt her this badly."

"I'm not saying moving on will be easy for her, but it's time she did. Jasmine is a strong woman, and she'll find her footing eventually. For now, your father and I will refrain from inviting both of you to the same functions. I can't promise you won't eventually run into each other again, but I'll do my part."

He kissed her on the cheek. "I'd appreciate that."

Looping his arm through hers, he led her back toward her car. "I feel like you're taking one for the team by going shopping and to lunch with Jasmine."

"Nonsense. I've come to consider her a friend in her own right, not just because of your previous relationship with her."

His mother stopped short of getting into the car. "Let me know how it goes with Juni or if there's anything we can do to help."

"I will."

He waved as she backed down the driveway. Before going inside, he took a minute to enjoy the peaceful silence of the surrounding woods. He still felt bad about Jasmine but at least his relationship with his parents appeared to be on an upswing.

That left Juni.

He needed a plan going forward, but right now his head was too messed up to think straight. One way or another, he had to figure things out. Spending time walking the dogs at the shelter always helped him clear his head. Crossing his fingers that would prove true this time, he called Titus and asked if he could bring the van back to Ryder's house when he was done with it.

CHAPTER TWENTY-ONE

ONCE AGAIN JUNI regretted taking her cousin's call. Normally, she would have let it go to voicemail since it was in the middle of her workday. She'd worked so hard training her family to save up nonemergency family business for their regular weekend calls. But seeing Ryder going to lunch with his mother and Jasmine yesterday had hit Juni hard. Right now, any distraction was welcome.

It didn't help that she'd woken up with a headache and feeling sorry for herself. Looking back, she'd probably had a little too much wine last night. Okay, that wasn't true. She'd had a lot too much considering she rarely had more than one glass of wine on any given occasion. No regrets, though. She and her new friends had had a wonderful time. They'd gorged themselves on Shay's burgers, onion rings and fries. They followed that with the cherry cheesecake Rikki had made for the occasion as they watched the rom-com Juni had chosen.

She'd loved that in between everything else her new friends had offered both sympathy and advice about dealing with the men in their lives. At the end of the night, those same guys had shown up to drive their rather tipsy wives home. After waving goodbye, Juni had walked Millie one more time before stumbling upstairs to bed. Despite how tired she was, sleep was a long time in coming. Instead, she'd stared up at the ceiling for what felt like hours as she mulled over the stories shared by the others.

The common thread had been that at some point each woman had made the hard decision not to give up on the possibility of a happily-ever-after with the man she loved. Her last thought before sleep claimed her was to wonder if she'd reached that same inflection point in her relationship with Ryder. She needed to find the strength to lay it on the line and tell him that she needed more than simple friendship from him, that she wanted it all. That would leave the ball firmly in his court, but at least she would have tried.

Before she could decide if there was anything else she could do, Erin hollered into the phone. "Hey, lady, are you even listening to me?"

Juni cringed and immediately apologized. "Sorry, Erin. I might have missed that last part.

Well, actually all of it. I have a lot on my mind right now."

Erin sighed. "Look, I know I'm not supposed to call like this, so I'll keep it short. The thing is that one of the other bridesmaids is going to be out of the country for the next week. I swear trying to get the bunch of you together at one time is like herding kittens. All I need from you is a firm date when you can be here to go shopping for dresses together. Two weeks from next Saturday will work for everyone else, but I don't want to set it up for then if you can't be here. It wouldn't be the same without you."

Juni could use some time with her family right now. "As long as my neighbor can keep my dog overnight, I can be there."

"That's great." There was a brief silence. "Wait—did you say you have a dog?"

Juni turned her phone so Erin could see Millie, who was currently sleeping next to her on the couch. "Erin, meet Millie. She's a Lab mix and a real sweetie. I got her this past weekend."

"She beautiful, but does Mom know?"

"Not yet." Juni sighed. "I haven't figured out how to break the news, but I will."

"Good luck with that. You know how she feels about having animals in the house. What if she won't let you have her in the mother-in-law apartment?"

Might as well admit her decision about that, too. "Yeah, that's the other thing. That won't be a problem. I plan to get my own place."

By that point, her cousin's eyes were huge. "Wow, remind me not to be around when you tell her."

Juni managed a small laugh, but it might not have sounded quite right because Erin leaned in closer to the screen. "Hey, are you feeling all right? Your eyes are all red like you're having an allergic reaction to something."

Sniffling, Juni tried to offer Erin a reassuring smile. "I'm fine."

But she really wasn't. Erin was sometimes a little self-centered, but she was also pretty obser-vant. "You're not fine. In fact, you've been cry-ing. What happened?"

By that point, Juni gave up all pretense of hid-ing how upset she was. "You know the guy who hung up on you?"

Erin immediately frowned. "Oh, yeah. I defi-nitely remember him, but Mom told me that you insisted that he's a nice guy. What's he done now?"

"It's complicated. Let's just say that I thought we were friends. Turns out I was wrong."

"What happened? Did he say something to upset you?"

Yeah, but Juni didn't want to talk about it. "Listen, it's no big deal. I'll be okay."

"Do you want to come back home? Because Mom and I can be there in a few hours with empty boxes and packing tape."

Erin's intentions were good, but Juni needed to deal with this herself.

"I appreciate the offer, but I'm fine. Really. Besides, I still have professional commitments that I need to finish up here."

Erin didn't look convinced, but at least she changed the subject. "Back to why I called. For sure it's okay if I set up the shopping expedition for two weeks from Saturday?"

"Yes, it's okay. Thanks for calling."

"We'll be seeing you soon."

As she ended the call, it struck Juni that Erin's last words might have sounded more like a promise than a simple goodbye. Surely not. Should she call her back and ask for clarification? No, she was overreacting, thanks to the fact she was exhausted, headachy and hurting. Rather than dwell on it, she decided that the best course of action was a long nap.

As soon as she stretched out on the couch, Millie joined her, wedging herself between Juni and the back of the couch. Smiling at how much better she felt with her furry friend snuggled in next to her, Juni covered them both with a blanket and drifted off to sleep.

RYDER WAS GOING to wear a hole in the carpet if he didn't quit pacing back and forth, but he couldn't seem to help himself. He'd always thought better on the move, but right now his brain was stuck in neutral.

He couldn't get the image out of his head of the pain in Juni's eyes as she'd watched him get in the car with his mother and Jasmine. He needed to make amends, but he wasn't sure if she'd even let him get close enough to explain that he'd been blindsided, too. Would it be cowardly if he outlined everything in a text?

He answered his own unspoken question. "Yeah, it would."

Flowers might work.

No, that would be too impersonal.

Before he could come up with another option, someone pounded on his front door. Maybe Juni had decided to confront him. If so, he'd listen to every word she said and then shift into grovel mode.

But as it turned out, it wasn't Juni. Not even close.

Titus already had his fist raised, ready to pound on the door again. Considering how angry the man looked, Ryder wouldn't have been surprised if Titus took a swing at him.

"What are you doing here?"

"To make sure you are aware of how badly you screwed up. I'll be only too glad to explain the situation if you haven't already figured it out for yourself."

"Believe me, I'm aware. The question is how you found out about it."

Titus gave him a disgusted look. "How do you think? My wife shared all of the sordid details. I'm pretty sure she was hoping I'd bruise you up some. I still might, but at least I'm willing to hear your side of the story first."

Ryder really didn't like anyone getting all up in his business, but he knew Titus well enough to realize that he wouldn't leave until he got everything off his chest. Might as well offer him some refreshments.

He pointed toward the chairs on the deck. "Have a seat, and I'll be right back. If I have to listen to a lecture, I want to sit down. I also want a cold one."

Titus dutifully headed toward the closest chair. "Get me one, too."

When Ryder got back, Titus took a long draw on his drink but didn't say a word. He finally gave Ryder a questioning look. "When I brought your van back yesterday, you didn't mention anything about what had happened. Seems I should've known that you already had a fian-cée. How am I supposed to do damage control with Moira and Juni's other friends when I don't know what's going on?"

"For what it's worth, Jasmine is my ex. Juni knows that. They've met before." He paused to ease his dry throat with a drink. "Anyway, how did they find out? None of them were around when my mother and Jasmine picked me up yes-terday."

"Near as I can tell, it all started when they found out that things had gone south between you and Juni at their book club meeting. Evi-dently that called for an emergency girls' night out yesterday—a show of support and to give Juni a chance to vent if she needed to."

Ryder closed his eyes and groaned. "Who all attended? I need names, so I know who I have to avoid for a while."

"The usual suspects—Moira, Shelby, Carli and Rikki. After listening to Moira's take on the situation, you're lucky they didn't head this way last night armed with pitchforks and torches."

Titus's rough laughter had Ryder wishing he'd brought out more beer. He was going to need it. "If I tell you what really happened, will you ask the ladies to at least give me a chance to make things right with Juni? I'm not good at this kind of stuff, but I'm determined to try."

"Why haven't you already talked to her?"

"Because I don't know what to say or how to make her believe me."

"The truth would be a good place to start. Have you tried telling her that you got scared because you finally realized that you're in love with her? After that, you should explain you're not going anywhere until she admits she feels the same way."

Ryder rubbed his chest, trying to soothe the pain he'd been living with ever since Juni had stormed away from him in town yesterday. "How can I tell her I love her when I've barely admitted that much to myself? I did think about sending her flowers."

Titus gave that idea all the respect it deserved—which was none at all. "Tell me, would you be spinning your wheels like this if you didn't care so much about her?"

Titus had never told Ryder what had happened ten years ago between him and Moira, but it had to have been bad. "Is this what it was like for you? Knowing you screwed up and hurt the one person you shouldn't have?"

His friend grimaced. "You let Juni see you leave with your ex-fiancée after telling her that you needed your space. Trust me, what I did was far worse. Moira was a rookie cop when we met, but I couldn't tell her I was one, too. I was working undercover to bring down a drug cartel. When things fell apart, I got arrested along with our target, and she saw me being led away in cuffs. They did that to try to protect my cover. It failed miserably, because some of the target's business associates found me."

By that point, Titus was rubbing his knee as if it hurt. "It took multiple surgeries to put me back together. Rather than let Moira know what really happened, I walked away from her to make sure she didn't become a target, too. It took me ten years to get my head on straight and my life back together. I count myself lucky that Moira forgave me when I finally got up the courage to tell her the truth."

Titus went silent, maybe to let Ryder digest that much before continuing. "Juni doesn't need flowers, Ryder. She needs to know what's going on in that thick skull of yours. Women are often better with this emotional stuff than we are, but they aren't mind readers. If you want to figure out what to say, practice with me. Start at the beginning."

Ryder did as he suggested, explaining about his family, his fiancée and his short career. "Turns out both my ex and my parents have been waiting all this time for me to rejoin the rat race. That's probably not surprising considering Jasmine works for a high-end law firm, and my folks are both tenured college professors."

"That's a lot to live up to."

"Yeah, it is. Anyway, yesterday was supposed to be a chance for me to spend some quality time with my mom. When Jasmine invited herself along, Mom decided it might be a chance for the two of us to make peace. Regardless of her good intentions, I was furious and had them drop me off back at home."

He stopped to gesture toward his house and yard. "If you can believe it, that was the first time either of my parents saw this place. I'm guessing they thought I was living in a shack or something, because Mom was pretty stunned when she saw it. We talked briefly and came to an understanding. She also knows Juni is important to me. And I think Jasmine finally accepts that things are over between us."

"So when are you going to tell all of that to Juni?"

Feeling better and definitely more focused, Ryder stood up. "Right now."

"Good idea." Titus drained his beer and set it down on the deck before getting up. "But you might want to shower, shave and put on some clean clothes. You're not going to impress the lady by showing up looking as if you slept in the woods last night."

Ryder rubbed the stubble on his jaw. "Good thinking. Thanks for stopping by."

"Let me know how it goes. Worse comes to worst, we'll schedule a boys' night out at Shay's."

Ryder was already on his way inside. He stopped to look back at his friend. "If things don't go well, I'll need it."

MILLIE LIFTED HER head and woofed as she scrambled over Juni to head for the front door.

Juni pushed herself up to sit on the edge of the couch and tried to clear the fog from her brain. She blinked sleepily at the clock, trying to convince herself that it wasn't really four in the afternoon. When she'd hung up after talking to Erin, it had only been ten o'clock. Had she really slept the day away? It was a sign she had been both physically tired and emotionally exhausted.

The clock on her phone only confirmed the time. Meanwhile, Millie was sitting by the door, staring at it intently. No doubt the poor girl needed to make a trip outside. "Okay, Millie. Let me get your leash."

It wasn't until she started to open the door that she heard voices coming from the front of the house. Ones she unfortunately recognized. Closing her eyes and praying for patience, she opened the door. Sure enough, Erin and Aunt

Ruby were standing on her porch with an arm-load of boxes and packing tape.

She shot a dark look at her cousin. "I told you I was fine. I also told you I'm not ready to come home. I still have work to finish here."

Aunt Ruby wasn't having it. "You can work from our house. You've done it before. I can't stand the thought of you over here all by your-self, especially since that awful man has been treating you badly."

"Ryder isn't awful, Aunt Ruby. If he was, I wouldn't have liked him so much. We just wanted different things. Regardless, I'm fine."

Ruby shook her head. "You don't look fine. You look like you've been run over by a steam-roller. Now, are you going to let us in or what? We need to get to work."

No, they didn't, and it was past time to put her foot down. Crossing her arms over her chest, she gave each of her visitors a stern look. "I won't let you in unless you accept the fact that I am not going anywhere. I signed a lease, and I'm stay-ing right here until it runs out."

At that moment, Millie finally managed to wriggle her way past Juni to greet their guests. Erin grinned and immediately held out her hand to let the dog sniff her fingers before petting her. "Juni, she's even prettier in person. I can see why you wanted to adopt this little sweetie."

Aunt Ruby looked at her daughter and then at Juni, her alarm all too clear. "What is she talking about?"

"I decided to adopt a dog. Aunt Ruby, meet Millie."

Millie moved from Erin to Ruby with a happy doggy smile on her face. Finally, Ruby relented and awkwardly patted Millie on her head. "What are you going to do with her when your lease runs out?"

Might as well lay it all out there. "That's easy. My plan is to get my own apartment, one that allows pets."

Her aunt's shock at that announcement was obvious. "But why? You've always lived with us."

Erin surprised Juni by running interference. "Mom, she's an adult. It's okay if she wants to have a place of her own."

Before her aunt could do more than sputter, Juni opened the door wider. "Look, you two have had a long drive. Come on inside. After I take Millie out for a minute, I'll make coffee. While it brews, I'll go get cleaned up. It won't take long."

Ruby made shooing motions with her hands. "You take care of Millie and yourself. I'll handle the coffee."

Juni gave her a quick hug. "Good idea. If you're hungry, there are sandwich makings in the fridge as well as some cheesecake if you'd rather have something sweet."

Leaving them to it, Juni took Millie out for a quick trip around the yard and then raced upstairs to make herself more presentable. She made it back to the kitchen in record time, because the coffeemaker beeped it was done just as she walked into the room. Aunt Ruby and Erin had made good use of their time, too. They'd set the table and made sandwiches along with a tossed salad. They'd also divided up the last of the cheesecake.

She poured the coffee and joined them at the table. "Thanks for doing all of this."

The three of them dug right into the make-shift meal. Juni was grateful for the chance to figure out how much she was willing to share about her life in Dunbar. It probably wasn't the best time to mention Sabrina's suggestion that Juni should seriously think about extending her stay in the area.

Aunt Ruby took a bite of the cheesecake and all but moaned. "This is absolutely delicious. Where did you get it?"

"Four friends came over last night to watch a movie with me. One of them baked it for the occasion. Another one brought burgers with all the fixings for dinner."

Her aunt arched an eyebrow. "I'm guessing

they also brought the wine and beer I saw in the fridge."

"They did."

"Does this sort of thing happen very often?"

Before Juni could answer, there was a knock at the front door that set off another round of barking from Millie. Erin looked puzzled. "Were you expecting company today?"

Already heading for the door, Juni called back, "No, I really wasn't."

Her aunt sniffed. "I think it's rude for people to show up without calling first."

Even Erin laughed at that. "Then I guess we're rude, Mom."

"We're family. That's different."

Meanwhile, Juni realized that she hadn't heard a car in the driveway. That seriously narrowed the possibilities as to who might be standing on her front porch. Both hoping she was wrong and that she wasn't, she cracked open the door to peek out. Sure enough, it was Ryder. He was currently glaring at the stack of moving boxes and packing tape that her aunt and cousin had left sitting by her front door. Speaking low, she glanced over her shoulder and then back at him. "Ryder, this isn't a good time."

He widened his stance as if signaling he wasn't going anywhere. At least he took his cue from her and spoke quietly. "Sorry, but I really need to explain a few things and apologize for yester-day. Then we need to talk…you know, about us."

He pointed toward the stack of boxes. "Pref-erably before you put those to use."

She slipped out onto the porch and closed the door behind her. "I'm willing to listen to why you want to rehash everything, but I meant what I said. This isn't a good time. My aunt and cousin are here."

He frowned at that. "You never mentioned that they were coming for a visit."

She prayed for patience. "I thought we were staying out of each other's lives right now. If that's the case, you can't really expect me to keep you in the loop on everything that happens."

Before he could respond, the door flew open behind her, and her aunt joined them on the porch. "Assuming you're the man who hung up on my daughter and made my niece cry, I think you should leave. We have packing to do."

That did it. Juni planted herself directly be-tween Ryder and her avenging angel. "Aunt Ruby, I've already made it clear I'm not going anywhere. I know you mean well, but it's not your decision whether I should listen to what he has to say."

Ryder stepped around Juni to confront her aunt directly. "Ma'am, you have every reason to be angry with me, but this is between me and Juni. She and I need to talk."

"He's right, Aunt Ruby. Why don't you and Erin relax while he and I take Millie for her afternoon walk?"

Her aunt frowned, her concern over the situation plain to see. "Are you sure?"

"Yeah, I am."

She reluctantly left her aunt alone with Ryder while she ducked inside to put on shoes and grab Millie's leash. While she couldn't make out what they were saying, at least there was no yelling going on. Right now, she'd take that as a win. Meanwhile, Erin glanced out the window by the door. "He's a handsome one, I'll give you that much. I'm also guessing he's seen the error of his ways. I hope so, because it's obvious he means a lot to you. Forgive him if you can, but make him work for it."

Then she gave Juni a quick hug before opening the door to coax her mother to come back inside. Juni immediately slipped out the door and grabbed Ryder's hand. Holding Millie's leash with her other one, she tugged them both along in her wake as she said, "Let's head down to the river."

"Good idea."

He looked relieved to be putting some distance between them and her aunt. When they reached the river, they let Millie set the pace as they wandered downstream from the trail. A short time later, Ryder finally started talking. "Yesterday was supposed to be a lunch date with Mom. I swear I had no idea Jasmine would tag along. That was never part of the plan, and I refused to go with them. In the short time we were together in the car, I made it clear to both of them that I have no interest in resuming any part of my old life. And while I'm sorry that I hurt Jasmine in the process, it was the right thing to do for both our sakes."

"How did she take the news?"

"Not well, but my mom seems to think maybe now Jazz can start moving forward with her own life."

Juni found herself feeling unexpected sympathy for the other woman. "I'm sorry if I overreacted, and I hope she finds someone who will make her happy."

"Me, too."

He wrapped his arm around her shoulders as they walked, holding her close to his side. "Enough about them. I'm really here to talk about us."

It might be smarter to shrug off his arm and put some distance between them. Right now, she needed that small connection and hoped he did as well. When he didn't keep talking, she asked, "What about us?"

He turned to face her. "Weirdly enough, I seem to be the last person in town to realize that I've developed some incredibly strong feelings for you. Somehow you managed to set up house-keeping in my heart without me even noticing. Maybe because everything is so easy with you, mainly because you get me in ways my folks never have. Being around you has also reminded me how much I loved the creative portion of my old life. I'd like to find a way to bring that back, but that's a problem for another day. Right now, the bottom line is that while I've enjoyed my time here in Dunbar, it's no longer enough to satisfy me if you're not part of my life, too."

He tugged her into his arms, pulling her in close as he stared down into her eyes. "Do you think you can forgive me for hurting you? Maybe even give me another chance? I'll do whatever it takes, even if it means packing up and following you back to your hometown."

She settled her head against his chest, finding peace in his arms. "That won't be necessary. I'm not going anywhere. I'm happy living here in Dunbar and would love to make it my home. I've met so many wonderful people, and I love watching the sun rise over the mountains."

She hesitated, feeling shaky as if she were standing out on a limb just as Ryder had been the first time she'd seen him. Taking a deep breath, she whispered, "But the real reason Dunbar feels like home is because it's where you are."

He gently cupped her cheek and angled her face upward. "I love you, Juni Voss. So very, very much. You don't have to answer right now, but I hope you'll eventually agree to marry me."

Then he kissed her. So softly, so carefully, and so full of promise. It felt like coming home.

Feeling a little breathless, she whispered, "I love you, too. Would it be okay if I accept your proposal now? It would be nice to be able to tell Aunt Ruby in person that she gets to plan another wedding."

"Only if I can call Titus right afterward and tell him that he'd better get that tux I promised him altered soon. He'll need it because I'm going to ask him to be my best man."

"It's a deal."

He kissed her again. "Let's go break the good news to your aunt and cousin. If all goes well, we'll take them to the café for a celebratory dinner."

"And if it doesn't go well?"

"Then the two of us will sneak off to Shay's to regroup and plan our next move."

"Perfect."

* * * * *

*Be sure to look for the next book in
The Heroes Of Dunbar Mountain series
by Alexis Morgan, available soon wherever
Harlequin Heartwarming books are sold!*

Harlequin® Reader Service

Enjoyed your book?

Try the perfect subscription for Romance readers and get more great books like this delivered right to your door.

See why over 10+ million readers have tried Harlequin Reader Service.

Start with a Free Welcome Collection with free books and a gift—valued over $20.

Choose any series in print or ebook. See website for details and order today:

TryReaderService.com/subscriptions